Bump. Set. Spike! Author  book for girls in competi and on the court? Lorali .... an-swer as she strives for success in sports and in friendships. Will she be able to reach Gwen, a setter who offers up spite with every pass? This wonderful blend of Christian principles and volleyball suspense makes for a satisfying and exciting read.

—MARIANNE HERING, co-creator and bestselling author
Adventures in Odyssey Imagination Station book series

A high school volleyball player with a desire to win a scholarship struggles to deal with her own personal loss, social frustrations, and the challenges of competition. Inside the Ten-foot Line is a clean story that offers deeper themes to ponder. Former Wheaton College volleyball player Lori Scott uses a touch of humor and an element of faith to realistically portray the hopes and dreams of many student athletes.

—JOHN SHONDELL, former setter at Ball State University,
founder of The Academy Boilers Juniors volleyball club,
Associate Head Coach at Purdue University, former Varsity
Head Coach at New Castle High School, coach at Muncie-Burris and Delta High Schools, North Central Conference
Coach of the Year in 1996, 1997, 2000, and 2001 and Class 4A
Coach of the Year 2001.

INSIDE THE TEN-FOOT LINE

LORI Z. SCOTT

End Game Press books may be purchased in bulk at special discounts for sales promotion, corporate gifts, ministry, fund-raising, or educational purposes. Special editions can also be created to specifications. For details, contact Special Sales Dept., End Game Press, P.O. Box 206, Nesbit, MS 38651 or info@end-gamepress.com.

Visit our website at www.endgamepress.com.

Library of Congress Control Number: 2022932704
ISBN: 978-1-63797-041-6
eBook ISBN: 978-1-63797-040-9

Published in association with Cyle Young of the Cyle Young Literary Elite, LLC.

Cover by Dan Pitts Design
Interior by Typewriter Creative Co.

Printed in the United States of America
10 9 8 7 6 5 4 3 2 1

To Michael and Meghan. I'll always be on your team.

CONTENTS

VOLLEYBALL TERMINOLOGY

Ace – a serve that an opposing team cannot return.

Approach – an offensive player's movement toward the net prior to a spike.

Attack – a spike.

Attacker – the person performing an attack, also known as the spiker or hitter.

Attack Line – also known as the ten-foot line. A painted line on the court that is ten feet from the net. It separates the front row players from the back row players.

Backcourt – the area of the court behind the attack line.

Back set – a two-handed overhead set pushed backwards behind the setter.

Back row attack – an offensive spike done by a player

jumping from behind the ten-foot line before hitting the ball. Crossing the line prior to the attack jump is illegal.

Block – when front row players jump at the net with raised arms to prevent the ball from passing over into their side of the court.

Bump – slang for forearm passing.

Dig – slang for passing a hard-spiked ball.

Dink – also known as a tip. Tapping the ball over the net to an unguarded area of the court. Players must use knuckles or an open hand to direct the ball. It is often used on tight sets but can also be employed strategically.

Dive – when a player lands on the floor in an attempt to dig the ball with their arms.

Deuce – when two teams are tied on 24-points, deuce is played until one team establishes a two-point lead for a win.

Five-One offense – an offensive plan that designates five hitters and one setter. While rotating through the front row, the setter can also attack and block the ball.

Forearm pass – when a ball hits a fleshy platform made by holding wrists together and arms straight and extended in front of the body in an underhand position.

Free ball – sometimes called a chance ball. A ball returned over the net with a forearm pass instead of an attack. Usually the result of a broken play.

Hit – when an offensive player attacks the ball with the intention of landing it on the opponent's side of the court for a point. Also called a spike or an attack.

Hitter – the player executing a hit. Also known as the spiker or the attacker.

Jump set – a set requiring a leap into the air by the setter prior to contacting the ball.

Kill – a spike that results in an immediate point or side out.

Libero – a defensive specialist with special rules of play, designated with a jersey of a different color. This player never plays in the front row and can substitute for any player without counting against a team's allotted number of substitutions.

Outside hitter – a left-front or right-front attacker.

Overhand pass – also known as a set. A ball that is passed with both hands open and fingers held just above the forehead.

Pancake – a one-handed defensive move where the player dives to the floor and fully extends their arm under the ball. The ball bounces off the back of the hand.

Pass – see Forearm Pass.

Pepper – a two-player warmup drill where the ball is passed back and forth.

Quick set – a short set delivered as the hitter leaps to attack. This set requires precise timing between the setter and hitter.

Roll – a forearm pass where the defensive player extends an arm, passes the ball, lands on the floor, and rolls over the shoulder or back after passing the ball. Usually employed on hard-to-reach balls.

Rotation – the clockwise movement of players through

designated positions around the court. Each player advances to the next spot following a side out.

Serve – an action executed behind the end line where one player sends the ball over the net to begin a volley.

Server – the player located in the first position on the court who serves the ball.

Set – an overhand pass in which a ball is positioned for a player to spike it into the opponent's court.

Setter – the player who contacts the second of three allowed touches of the ball before sending it over the net. A setter places the ball for hitters to spike and usually runs the offense.

Shank – slang for a passing error that results in an ace or broken play.

Side out – a change in possession of who controls the serve. The team gains control of the ball and rotates a position on the court.

Six-two – an offensive plan that uses two setters opposite one another in the rotation. The setter in the back row runs the offense, while the setter in the front row is a hitter. When the front row setter rotates into the back, the roles switch.

Spike – see hit.

Strong side hitter – a right-handed hitter striking from the left-front position or a left-handed hitter striking from the right-front position.

Turning in – the act of an outside blocker positioning their hands toward the court so that a blocked ball is deflected into the court.

Volleyball – a sport involving two teams of six players separated by a net. Scoring occurs when one team grounds the ball on the opposing side of the net.

CHAPTER ONE

LOSER

Shrill cheers burst around me. I crouched, my breath ragged. The muscles in my legs tensed, ready to spring.

The spiker poised to attack.

I'd studied her moves. Deadly, but predictable. One step, two steps, a fluid approach. And on a tight set, she would shy away from the net and push the ball lightly over with an open-handed—

"DINK!" I screamed, straining skyward. One inch. One inch more...but the volleyball skimmed over my fingertips.

I'm not sure which dropped faster, the ball or my stomach.

Our setter, Gwen, hesitated. Then she dove forward, hand smacking the ground. The ball bounced to the floor in front of her, untouched. Groans and shouts erupted from the crowd.

Match over.

Brows cinched, Gwen picked herself off the gym floor. "You missed the block, Lorali."

She spat my name like a curse.

Heat rose in my cheeks. Catching my breath, I watched her storm off.

What was her problem anyway? My job was blocking hard strikes. Dinks belonged to the defense. But I knew better than to trade words with someone with a spear for a tongue. Mom taught me, "A gentle answer turns away wrath, but hard words stir up anger."

Did *no answer* count as gentle?

I dropped my hands to my sides. My legs ached to sit, but Gwen dominated the bench, yanking on her sweats. Her lips flattened, as if she sensed something foul in the air. Pausing, she lifted her gaze and caught me staring at her. *Loser,* she mouthed.

Don't respond. I ducked my head. As if answering would change anything.

"Hey, Gwen!" a boy called out.

A group of them hovered behind her, all boundless energy and testosterone like hairy ping pong balls in a blender. "Party at Zeke's tonight. Wanna come? I'll drive you."

Standing, Gwen shouldered her duffle bag. "Sorry, can't. School rules. I gotta ride the bus home with the team." Two quick steps cozied her up next to the guy. "But maybe I'll stop by when we get back."

Audrey, a teammate, rushed to flank her. Leaning over, Gwen whispered something to her, and the two laughed.

Shooting a dark look in my direction, Audrey smirked.

I pretended not to notice their private conversation as they walked away. But I could guess who the topic of discussion was. Me.

Last year, as a junior, Audrey sat on the bench. She expected to start this year. Then I moved into the district and started instead of her. When Coach announced the lineup during practice, the look on Audrey's face could have sliced leather. From then on, she was quick to point out my mistakes.

Trying to turn myself invisible, I wandered to the bench and lowered myself onto it. *I don't mean for any harm. I just want to play volleyball like everyone else on the court.*

Our libero, Emily, plopped down next to me and slid her kneepads down. Gray dusted the cotton pads, proof of her effort. After all, as defensive specialists, liberos spent a lot of time on the floor digging up spikes. Clean kneepads would have been an insult to her game. Drawing a sharp breath, she shoved up the right-hand sleeve of her uniquely colored uniform. She poked an angry red spot on her elbow.

"Another battle scar?" I winced. "That looks painful."

"Yup." Emily grinned. "I got a matching one on my hip too. Want to see it?"

I shook my head, which only made her grin even wider.

Typical Emily. She captured your attention like a puppy tangled in bubble wrap—cute, crazy, and loud. Unlike Gwen, Emily didn't wear makeup when she played. Well, she did one time, but it ended up wiped down her shirt in grisly black-and-red streaks. After I pointed out her scary new stains, she hunched like a monster and scrabbled after loose balls screeching *mine!* The next practice, Coach brought her a full pack of facial wipes.

"Yeesh, stop looking so intense. I was only teasing. I know

you don't like seeing blood." Emily craned her neck until it popped. "Besides, the match is over. Now we can eat. And that's the important thing here. Food."

I passed Emily a water bottle. She firehosed it into her mouth. A good portion dribbled onto her chin. Grunting, she wiped it away with the back of her hand.

An unsettled weight in my chest kept me from laughing. "We were so close."

"We'll get them next time." Emily smacked her lips.

"Yeah." I sighed. "Next time."

Michelle, a junior and our best substitute, reached out. "I'll take that if you're done with it."

"Thanks." Emily handed her the water bottle.

"No worries." With practiced precision, Michelle dabbed moisture off the bottom edge of the bottle before tucking it into the six-slotted holder. After straightening the load, her gaze wandered, as if searching for another stray container to add to the collection. "I mean, except for another loss. I guess we should worry about that."

"Wrong." Emily bobbed her head. "We should worry about food. Because I'm hungry enough to eat the ball cart right now."

A smile brightened Michelle's face. She set down the carrier, squared it, then pulled a brown bag out of her sweatsuit pocket. "Would you settle for M&Ms?"

"Settle?" Emily snatched it. *"You're a goddess."*

While Emily tore open the bag, Coach called out directions. As usual, her voice grated in a hoarse rasp, probably from too much sideline yelling. "Good effort, girls. Pack up, we're headed home in five. Practice tomorrow, seventh period."

As we left the building, Emily bounded along beside me. "It's a relief to get out of that place. I miss our court."

My mouth dropped open. "Are you kidding? Did you see that huge weight room we passed on the way in? Mirrored walls? Thick mats? Polished dumbbells? And the gym had vaulted ceilings, home team bleachers with chair backs, a state-of-the-art sound speaker, and multiple courts. That facility could have its own zip code in paradise."

Emily wrinkled her nose. "It's like every other oversized gym in our district. Big schools, big budgets, big bling. Big deal. Their gyms have no *personality.* Ours does."

"Personality? You mean foundation issues."

"Whatever." Emily popped a candy into her mouth. "I know every inch of our gym. I love the creak of the hardwood floors. The smell of our rustic locker room."

"Rustic or rusty?" I raised a brow. "Or maybe you're the source of the odor."

Lifting her arm, Emily sniffed the pit. "Nope. I smell much worse. At least I earned my scent."

I stifled a laugh.

"The best part is the old relic painted on the wall." Emily swept her arm out as if introducing the mural. "All hail the class of the 1965 Williamson Wildcats."

"It's probably a historical landmark, along with our uniforms," I said. "Those are at least thirty years older than Coach."

"Don't pretend you don't like our gym." Emily planted her fists on her hips. "You spend more time in it than the cockroaches."

"There is a difference between loving the facility and loving the sport. I'd play in a gravel pit if I had to. I wish we had better resources."

Emily crumpled her empty bag. "That's not why we have a losing streak."

My eyes shifted toward Gwen and Audrey, charging ahead of our group. "I know."

Our transportation sat in the parking lot like a rotted banana. Its doors squeaked open as we approached.

"Hello, bus." Emily patted the battered hood. Her hand came back dirty, and she wiped it on her pant leg. "She's a classic."

I snorted. "So is a horse and carriage. But at least she's reliable."

The ride home was quiet. Everyone buried their heads in their phones, texting, flipping through videos, and taking selfies. I silenced mine and studied the storefronts with their neon signs popping in and out of view as we rumbled past.

Aunt Tina invaded my thoughts.

Both my mom and Aunt Tina loved volleyball, but it was my aunt who'd played outside hitter in college while my mom hit the books. When I joined the sixth-grade school team, Aunt Tina suggested that Mom enroll me in club ball—elite leagues that played competitively during the off-season.

Mom hadn't responded well. "I've got two words for that. *Cost* and *Commitment.*" After an uncomfortable pause, she'd added, "Make that three words. *No.*"

I didn't think much of the exchange. Back then, the sport was new to me, a refreshing challenge. I didn't understand the depth of passion the game could inspire.

Midway through that school year, volleyball fever caught me. After promising my mom that I'd keep up with my homework, she finally agreed to let Aunt Tina work with me.

I spent hours in the backyard with my sport hero. I begged her to teach me the crowd-pleaser, the glorious spike, but she insisted I master other skills first. We focused on passing techniques, especially moving my feet the ball. She taught me

20

an overhand serve, starting with a consistent toss and solid hand contact. Each small success spurred another. I couldn't get enough. Like a toddler learning to walk, even a tiny step forward thrilled me.

I practiced on my own too, wanting to impress her with my improvement. Over and over, I bumped the ball against the garage door or served balls up the slope of the driveway and let gravity bring them back for another try.

I also convinced my mom to let me workout with a club team that summer. Aunt Tina cheered me on the whole way. When her schedule allowed it, my mom came to the court too. She wasn't as vocal as Tina from the sidelines, but she always showed up decked out in enough bling to open her own accessory shop.

My seventh-grade year was the first time Aunt Tina arrived at my games with a camera in hand. "If we record everything, you'll have plenty of footage you can submit to college re-cruiters," she claimed. And just like that, my game grew a bigger purpose.

After each match, Aunt Tina and I would grab a big bowl of popcorn and a bottle of water—she insisted on healthy eat-ing for athletes—and curl up on the couch in her apartment. As we watched the replay, she'd analyze it, pointing out ways to improve. "Maybe you'll be the second one in the family to win a volleyball scholarship," she'd say.

More than anything, she wanted me to succeed at the sport.

Embracing that goal was the only meaningful thing left I could offer her.

Even though Mom refused to record games anymore, Aunt Tina's habit of breaking down each play still plagued me. Even now, during the bus ride home, the urge to analyze overpowered my fatigue. Soon, the passing storefronts faded, replaced by mental replays. *Sometimes when I blocked, the ball ricocheted out of bounds. I need to turn my hands inward. How many times has Coach reminded me of that? If I jumped four more inches, I could block better.*

What if our middle hitter, Brianna, hadn't missed her serve in the second game? Missed serves killed momentum.

Pain shot up my arm. I glanced down at my fisted hands. My fingernails, what little I had left, had pressed into the palms of my hands, leaving dark imprints.

Releasing the tension, I sighed. What was I doing? Was I even half as good as my aunt was at my age? If my insignificant team kept losing to those attention-seeking powerhouses, would I ever be noticed by a Division One coach?

I shook my head, tucking those doubts away. Aunt Tina had said that I if I believed, I could achieve. So I would believe and focus on ways to improve.

A sudden idea made me sit straight up. Tonight, when we ran out of substitutes in the third set, Gwen had to rotate through the front row as a hitter and I had to stay in as a receiver in the back row. I was fine playing defense, but the other team capitalized on the height difference between Gwen's 5'6" and their taller 6'2" blocker.

How could we avoid the situation?

The only way to do that would be for me to play all the way around—not as a hitter, but as a setter. With me in that position, we would only need one of our two setters, saving us an additional substitution every three rotations on the court. A plan like that would keep Audrey hitting in the front row in a tight match instead of the shorter player, Gwen.

But again, it would mean me replacing one of our setters. How would Gwen react to that? Scary thought.

With a few clicks on my phone, I searched the internet. "Wow," I whispered.

Emily crowded me. "What is it? A picture of a cheese puff shaped like a cross? For the record, holy or not, I'd still eat that thing."

"It's just some interesting information." I scrolled to a table on the website. "Did you know the average height of a Division One setter is 5'10"? And college coaches prefer lefties."

"How tall are you again?" Emily asked.

"5'10". And I'm a lefty."

Frowning, Emily cocked her head. "Too bad you're not a setter."

My mind raced. "Yeah." I took a screenshot. "Too bad."

CHAPTER TWO

DEBATE

When we arrived back at school, the moon's feeble light cast our lonely parking lot in shadows.

A few steps off the bus, I spotted my mom climbing out of our car. She waved, and I headed her direction. She met me halfway there and fell in step with me.

"Good, you survived the bus ride." Mom frowned. "That yellow death trap is dated."

"But she's reliable," I said, repeating the comment I gave Emily.

Across the lot, Emily screamed, "Bye, Lorali!"

I cupped my hand to my mouth. "See you on the court tomorrow!"

"Not if I wear my camouflage practice shirt and hide in my locker," Emily yelled back.

Grinning, I snagged the keys from Mom. I needed forty-four more hours of driving practice with an adult since I only owned a learner's permit.

After fastening her seatbelt, Mom talked game. "Another loss. Sorry, honey. And poor Gwen. The team had her chasing down bad passes the whole time."

"Gwen isn't our only setter." I clicked my own belt in place. "Did you forget about Caroline?" The senior came in for me in the back row.

Without missing a beat, Mom made a dismissive gesture. "Caroline always struggles, so that's nothing new. Did you notice the speed of their offense? And no holes in that defense. Your coach should address that."

"Coach can push all she wants," I said. "But unless our team listens better and works harder, it won't make a difference."

"It might." Mom rubbed the back of her neck. She probably got whiplash tracking our game volleys. "It also might help if those line judges paid better attention. That was *not* a foot fault on Brianna's serve in the third set."

No argument there. Sometimes we had official line judges. When we didn't, each team contributed two JV players to call lines. Most of them spent more time gazing off into space. A hubcap would do a better job.

"The strong outside hitter lacked confidence," Mom said. "Block her once, and she dinked the ball."

"But it worked, didn't it?" I turned the key in the ignition. Mom shrugged. "Yes."

Reviewing a mental checklist, I turned on the headlights, then shifted into reverse to back out of the parking space.

Before I moved, Mom touched a hand to my wrist. "Don't forget to check the rear-view mirror. 'Student-ran-over-teammate' does not look good on a high school transcript."

Obediently, my eyes flicked to the mirror, then over to the tight line of Mom's lips. She stiffened when I backed out. But after a moment, she relaxed into the seat. "Did you have fun?"

Her game day mindset had returned.

"Yeah. To quote Aunt Tina, 'If playing the game is fun, then losing means nothing. But if playing the game isn't fun, winning means nothing.'"

I took her words to heart. Except we hadn't done a whole lot of winning this season.

Grimacing, Mom shifted in her seat and turned her head toward the window. "You played like her tonight." Her voice cracked. "She would have been proud."

I swallowed. "Thanks."

As the quiet between us stretched, I pulled a hand off the wheel and rested it on Mom's knee. She lifted it back to the two o'clock position and patted my fingertips.

"Best be safe," she murmured.

"Can you put some music on?" I asked, eager to change the conversation.

"Classic or contemporary pop?"

"Classic."

"You got it." Mom plugged a car jack into my phone. Humming, she scrolled through my playlists.

Soon, Kelly Clarkson's voice crooning "Breakaway" filled the car. As if in response, rain kissed the glass. I turned on the wipers, letting the hypnotic rhythm direct my thoughts. *I should set. I should set. I should set.*

Distracted, I hit a puddle, throwing up a spray of water. The car bounced hard enough to jar my teeth.

"Woah!" Mom slapped her hands on the dashboard. "Avoid puddles. You don't know what's underneath or how deep they are. And drop your speed. Rain makes for slippery roads. If you go too fast, the car might hydroplane."

I eased off the pedal. "Remind me again, what is hydroplaning? I might have dozed off a little in Driver's Ed class."

"It's when water gets under the tire, making it lose traction with the road."

My stomach clenched. "So, I'd basically be flying over the asphalt?"

"Yep. With no control." Pain lined her words.

"Got it." I tapped the brakes. The car shuddered, and I chanced a peek at Mom. Her wide eyes and stiff posture seemed overdone since I wasn't going that fast. Was I?

A quick breath steadied me. I didn't want to focus on anything but my new plan for volleyball. And driving. But mostly volleyball. "I think we'd win more games if I were a setter."

The stillness that followed my announcement proved I'd caught Mom off guard. Or perhaps she'd fallen under the spell of her memories of Aunt Tina.

"Well?" I prodded. "What do you think?"

"You're the team's ace hitter. Why would you want to switch?"

"Not switch." I jutted my chin. "I can do both."

I explained my save-the-subs thought process.

"I suppose there is a logic to that," she said.

Which was a non-answer. *Was the idea that horrible?*

Pressing my lips together, I forced my attention back to the road. Mist cloaked the pavement, fogging the front window.

I could barely spot the painted dividing marks. "Wait! I can't see. What do I do?"

"Put on the defroster." Mom's voice held an edge.

Defroster? What? Like a microwave oven? Or something actually on the car's control panel? I snapped a button that blasted cold air in my face. I fumbled with another switch, and the headlights flicked off. I swerved, and Mom squawked.

As I righted the wheels and the lights, she turned a knob to my far right. "Stay calm. I got it."

Air poured out of the vents, warmer this time. Seconds later, the haze retreated, pulling the road back into view. I flashed Mom a grateful smile.

The wipers swept back and forth three more times before she spoke again.

"This seems sudden."

"I know, I freaked out a little when I couldn't see." I laughed. "My windshield looked like a mirror after a hot shower."

"I meant you. Setting." She said it with the same enthusiasm as a disgruntled mail clerk. Which could mean trouble for my dreams.

I chose my words carefully. "You know I've wanted to play Division One volleyball for a while."

"Ever since your aunt planted that foolish idea in your brain. But you're smart enough to be a lawyer, like me."

I tightened my grip on the wheel. "You know I like courts, not courtrooms."

Mom lifted her chin.

"I'm sorry." I gritted my teeth. "But please hear me out."

"I already listened." She shrugged. "You think playing all around will save the team subs and keep Gwen out of the front row in a tight match."

"Yes, and—" I took a breath. "No Division One school

will give me more than a glance as an average-sized hitter. But I fit the profile of a Division One setter."

"Ah." Mom lifted a finger. "And that's why you want to switch roles. Because less emphasis is placed on a setter's height."

The flatness of her tone held all the warmth of a toad.

We'd been down that road before.

"I want to play. More than anything else in the whole world." For Mom's sake, I tried to keep the desperation out of my voice.

"Excuse me, but you're talking about a big adjustment." Mom turned the music off. She let the silence grow before continuing. "I don't want to discourage you, but you'll have a lot of catching up to do to become a successful setter."

"I'm a fast learner."

"It's not that simple, and you know it." She snapped her seatbelt. "Setting is a complex skill."

The light ahead turned yellow. I lurched to a stop, making both of us jerk forward.

Mom pulled a sharp breath. "Like I said, a lot of catching up."

"That doesn't make me want it any less."

The steel in my voice must have caught her attention. "I don't think you understand how much work learning a new role will take. Besides, even if you're good, getting noticed by the right people at a top school takes a huge effort."

"Like what?"

"The same steps Aunt Tina took, only I'll update it for you by about twenty years."

"So, you've looked into it?" I asked, suddenly more eager.

"I hear things in the stands." Raising an eyebrow, Mom counted off on her fingers. "First, you pour every waking moment into practicing. Then you record video highlights. Then you put together a reel and post it online with your stats. Then you email schools with letters of interest. For extra exposure, you attend multiple camps run by college coaches. Then you ignore normal, everyday life experiences and obsess over your profile status for days on end."

My throat thickened. "Did Aunt Tina do that? Obsess?"

"Yes!" Mom snapped. Then she sighed. "Sometimes. She loved the game."

"But..." I paused, almost afraid to make my point. "But she got recruited."

"She did." Mom braced her hands on the console. "Look, why not join a college recreational team instead? It's a great way to meet people and scratch that itch to play. They participate in a lot of local tournaments. But it would be less pressure, less of a commitment. You'd still have time to study and hang out with friends."

I shook my head. "I don't think that would be enough volleyball for me."

"I've heard that before," Mom mumbled. She ran her fingers through her hair. "Listen, most setters start training young. You didn't. You lack experience."

"But my skill as a hitter gives me an advantage," I said. "I can read players and anticipate their attack."

Mom crossed her arms. "Good point. But right now, you're the lead hitter on your team. If you set, who's going to put the ball away?"

"Still me." I turned down the heater, thinking. "Why would that change?"

"So idealistic." She spoke to the ceiling of the car. "And how's your jump set?"

I bit my lip.

"Then you'll need lessons." Her voice rose. "And you must keep your grades up too. How much sleep are you willing to sacrifice?"

Was it possible to function without sleep? "If I finished my assignments at school, I could squeeze in extra lessons without losing sleep."

"Says the girl who's heading home for the first time all day at 10:03 P.M."

When she mentioned the time, every ache in my body flared up. I smothered a yawn, not willing to show my fatigue. "I know it won't be easy. But how many athletes are successful because they're prepared to work hard? Aunt Tina used to say it takes effort to reach any worthy goal. She said if you have the passion it takes to get up every day, push yourself to exhaustion, and then do it all over again, you'll succeed."

"All that effort comes with a cost. You'll sacrifice time with your friends. Your family. Me. And all the other things you love."

I rolled to a stop. "I love volleyball."

An odd hissing sound came through Mom's teeth. "I'm not convinced pursuing setting is worth the tradeoff of time and energy. Right now, you should be enjoying life, exploring other hobbies."

Longing flashed through my veins, threatened to consume me. "Volleyball *isn't* a hobby. Volleyball is life." *I just want to play.*

"Yes. Of course. A true mentee of Tina." Mom rubbed her eyes. "Here's my suggestion. Sleep on it. Pray about it. Then decide. I love you, and I'll support whatever course you choose. But remember, whatever you do, it is the Lord Christ we serve. That's a volleyball joke."

"Ha. Thanks, Mom." I licked my lips, relieved, at least, that she was open to the idea.

The rain picked up after that, drowning out everything else. Forced to kick the wipers into high gear, I leaned forward for better visibility.

Good thing I learned that defogging trick. I almost missed my turn for home.

CHAPTER THREE

PRESSURE

The next morning, hope filled me like the fizz in a Coke. Still intrigued by the possibilities offered by switching roles, I planned on catching Coach Remi before practice to talk about it. Usually, she left the door to her office wide open in an inviting way. Even if she sat in her outdated vinyl desk chair going over the latest stats, she'd set the paperwork aside to chat.

Instead of strolling right in, I found her office door shut tight. Strange, but nothing a solid knocking on the panel couldn't fix. But before I could rap on the worn surface, a male voice boomed from the other side.

"It's unprofessional the way you play favorites." The guy's tone grated harsh as a feral dog.

Hesitating, I glanced over my shoulder. No one else was around. After tucking a stray strand of hair behind my ear, I leaned in to listen. The mystery man couldn't see me, but not being able to view him either made my skin prickle the way it used to when I played hide-and-seek as a kid. The door muffled the words, but the conversation still bled through.

"Even when your precious starters miss serves or shank balls, you leave them on the court. Meanwhile my daughter sits on the bench, waiting for things to go terribly wrong before you *finally* put her in. As a hitter, as a serve receiver, who knows? The starters can't handle the situation, but you expect her to perform flawlessly the moment she subs in. Because unlike them, if she makes one little mistake, one *tiny little* mistake, you yank her right back out."

"A lot of factors go into planning a lineup." Strained patience coated Coach's voice. "A player's skill. Instinct. Work ethic—"

"Which your players should all possess *if* you coach them correctly," the man snapped. "Why don't you sub more often?"

"I have a limited number of substitutions per game," Coach said. "I must use those strategically."

The man cursed. For, like, ten seconds.

Wincing, I stepped back. It's one thing hearing those words slapped around the school hallways. Somehow, they sounded nastier coming out the mouth of an adult.

Without pausing for breath, he lashed out again. "As a senior, my daughter deserves more playing time, not to serve as some random fixer-upper in your grand 'lose-every-game-because-I-suck-as-a-coach' plan."

I cringed. Oooh, he did not just say that! I could imagine Coach's eyes bulging and her hands balling into fists.

"At this school, we do not operate on a seniority system," Coach said. "Each player earns their spot on the court."

A slam sounded, like a fist striking a desk. "She would already own that spot if your bias wasn't so appalling. No wonder Judy's ready to quit."

Ahh. So, the voice belonged to Judy's dad. Mom once commented about his bleacher behavior. Apparently, he blasted whichever player made the latest mistake and preached how much better Judy could have done. Anyone within earshot got pummeled with his tongue. Which, in our small gym, was everyone.

I wished Judy's dad could see her in practice. Judy cut corners when she could. She skipped sprints when Coach wasn't looking. Cheated on her push-up count to finish faster. Barely went through the motions during warmups.

"I understand your frustration," Coach said.

"I don't think you do." A new voice exploded.

Heart pounding, I jumped back, barely restraining a squeal. This person sounded close to the door.

"Both our girls should start. They're seniors. They've paid their dues. Those sophomores have time enough left to play."

Sophomores? My throat went dry. He could only mean me. And Emily. Swallowing hard, I took another furtive look around to make sure I was alone, then hugged my body to the door.

The man's voice grated on. "I don't know what you're seeing on the court. From where I sit, Audrey matches or surpasses Lorali's skill level. So, what kind of sweet-talking did her lawyer mama do to cloud your judgment?"

I scoffed, then immediately covered my mouth.

"As I already stated multiple times, being a senior doesn't guarantee more playing time." Coach's tone sharpened.

"You're losing anyway, so what difference does it make? Why not start a *senior* who has been *loyal* to you for four years now, who has spent time on the bench waiting for her turn, over a less experienced sophomore?"

What? I ground my teeth. Just because I was two years younger didn't mean I lacked experience.

"Some combinations work better than others. I put the team on the floor that best capitalizes on those strengths and weaknesses," Coach said. "I can't switch out players like batteries on a clock."

"You *can* switch. It's easy." An ugly, condescending tone oozed out. "Keep the same players, just alter the lineup order. Instead of starting Lorali, put Audrey in the right front spot and let Lorali come in off the bench for Gwen. Then you could give my daughter the respect she deserves. All other things being equal, it's the right thing to do."

So the other voice belonged to Audrey's dad. Great.

"All other things aren't equal. Lorali has better stats than Audrey." Coach's words came out clipped.

"Lorali only has better stats because she starts." His voice hardened. "More time on the court means more touches on the ball, which leads to more impressive numbers."

I chewed my fingernail, focusing on the tip to prevent myself from overthinking. On the surface, his argument made sense. But I knew it wasn't only the stats that Coach took into account. *Lorali,* she'd told me privately, *when I see how you push yourself, your passion, the way you adjust during a game, it reminds me of myself at your age. I need that kind of fire to rub off on our team. They've gotten lazy.*

The man continued. "On paper, Audrey only *seems* to

lag behind Lorali because she has Caroline setting her. And Caroline is the weaker setter. She won't backset unless the pass is perfect. Audrey can go through her whole rotation and never touch the ball. When Audrey and Gwen pair up, you'll see a different story."

"Trust me, I've tried the girls in many different combinations," Coach said. "The current lineup is the best one. Lorali's blocking can shut down their strongest attackers. And Audrey hits better against the second line of defenders."

"Lies," he snarled.

"I'm sorry you feel that way, Mr. Morrison."

"Coach." His voice went dangerously quiet. "I'm president of the booster club. I rub elbows with a lot of important people at this school."

"And I very much appreciate all you've—"

"Imagine what rumors about your preferential treatment of players might do to your reputation." Mr. Morrison talked right over Coach. "Imagine the backlash on social media."

About five seconds of acidic silence followed that subtle threat. That bully! I wanted to protect Coach. My hands curled into fists. What right did he have to—

A chair scraped against the floor. Was someone standing? Holding my breath, I tensed.

"I cannot control how you conduct your affairs, but in *my* gym, I expect each player to give a hundred percent effort. To support their teammates and play cohesively no matter where I place them." Iron coated Coach's voice, and I couldn't help but feel proud of her. "If I demanded anything less, I would not only be doing a disservice to your child, but to every other athlete on this team. And I will remind you again, as I did at the beginning of our conversation, that my policy is for players to come to me *themselves* if they have questions or complaints about how I coach. This is a crucial life skill for these kids to learn. It helps them mature into adults who can think independently and solve issues for themselves in a civil manner."

She emphasized the words *civil manner.*

The chime ending the school day sounded, making me jump. A hollow slap followed. Had Coach thrown down her clipboard? "The team will be arriving soon, and I won't expose them to unnecessary pressure. We're through here."

A guttural agreement. Movement toward the door.

Heart pounding, I scrambled to the locker room. Its familiar musty smell calmed me. Releasing a breath, I wiped my hands on my sweatpants to keep them from shaking.

A slam stopped my heart. It was only Emily throwing open the door, making her daily grand entrance into the locker room. She plopped her backpack on the bench, then fished around in her locker. Not surprisingly, she pulled out a fresh bag of M&Ms and a not-so-fresh pair of bright yellow knee-high socks.

I wrinkled my nose. "Yuck. Aren't those from yesterday?"

After tossing the socks on the dirty floor, Emily tore open the bag. "So? They're my favorite."

"I can loan you a clean pair."

Raising an eyebrow, she popped a yellow candy-coated chocolate into her mouth. "I was referring to the M&Ms."

I laughed. It seemed Emily craved food with as much addicting passion as I craved Division One volleyball.

Division One. My stomach sank. I'd watched enough game reels to know I'd never get there if something didn't change. Because where I stood now, I was not tall enough. Not noticeable enough. Not indispensable enough.

Not enough. Period.

Unless something changed.

Unless *I* changed.

I rubbed the stub of my thumbnail against my leg, a flicker of determination growing in my heart. Setting opened a whole new pathway. Except after overhearing that heated debate over starting positions, now didn't seem like the right time to pursue a new role.

"Do you want a bag of M&Ms too?" Emily hovered at my shoulder and shook a snack bag in my face. "I have more."

Focusing on my locker combination, I shook my head. "No."

"Refusing sweets?" Emily scrunched the wrapper. "What's up?"

Should I tell her about the near parental mutiny I'd overheard? Or would telling her cause more problems on the court between the players?

I decided to keep things to myself. "No, I'm just tired." I stretched my mouth in an exaggerated yawn. My jaw popped in a satisfying way. "I had trouble sleeping when we got home. It was a tough game last night."

"True." A puff of air escaped her lips, and she jutted her chin toward the gym. "That means it's going to be a tough practice today."

If only she knew about Coach's current mood. "That's okay. My aunt used to say that a true competitor digs deeper when they're down because they aren't content to stay there. They don't just make the best of what they have. They make their best better."

Holding up a green candy, Emily examined it. "Right. And the better best you have, the better best you can make your best better be. Wait, did that make sense?"

Her answer solidified my resolve. "More than you know."

INSIDE THE TEN-FOOT LINE

With new determination, I located my wrinkled practice jersey and pulled it over my head. Tonight, I would work harder than ever to prove I belonged on the court. Smart. Tough. Relentless. Confident. A leader, like Coach. Like Aunt Tina. That's what I had to bring to the table today.

For that, I'd need energy. "I changed my mind. Still got that bag of candy?"

Emily held up the crumpled package. Empty. "Sorry, too slow. But—"

Winking, she opened her other hand. "Lucky for you, good things come in threes."

CHAPTER FOUR

CAMPFIRE MOMENT

During warmups, Emily took full advantage of my distracted state of mind, taking hard swings at the ball. I still deflected her projectiles, but, like my thoughts, they spun off target.

Our libero didn't seem to mind. No matter how impossible my mishaps looked to touch, Emily kept flinging her body forward and popping up the ball. She operated with the ferocity of a rabid Chihuahua. With definite growling too. And maybe a few barks.

We continued moving back and forth until my jersey clung to my back and sweat streaked down my neck. Each bump, each wrist flick, each quick sidestep drew out the toxins in my system. Muscle memory took over. By the time Coach whistled to circle us up, even my body had worked out its stiffness, leaving my muscles loose and ready for action.

As we corralled around her, I wondered if Coach would treat Audrey or Judy differently because of the recent verbal bout with their parents. Or would she continue to operate as if nothing happened? I studied Coach's face for reactions, but other than a tightening of the skin around her eyes, I didn't notice any changes.

Audrey, however, hung back into the surrounding players, shifting from foot to foot. She didn't make eye contact with Coach and laughed a little too loud, almost as if trying to act innocent. And Judy? Let's just say she wasn't coated in sweat.

Once everyone settled, Coach gave us the rundown on the latest game. "I saw a lot of improvements in our offense last night." Coach Remi nodded toward Brianna. "Middle hitters, you stepped up your game. And Lorali, you were like a firing squad in action. Fourteen kills."

Pleased with her praise, I grinned. But the euphoric feeling didn't last. Gwen elbowed Audrey and then puffed her lips in a fake pout. Audrey glared at me.

Swallowing, I reminded myself that even if I met adversity, God had brought me to this school for a reason. Perhaps so I could take the role of setter.

"So, well done, front line," Coach continued. "We need that kind of consistent, well-executed offense to score. But we need a consistent, well-executed *defense* to win. The other team can't get a point if the ball doesn't touch the floor on our side of the net."

Emily elbowed me. "Yes! Job security," she whispered.

"That last play of the game keeps cycling through my mind." Coach ground out the words. "Time after time, we got burned by those easy little dinks!"

Without turning my head, I glanced sidelong at Gwen. Her lips flattened and her nostrils flared. Maybe she was poised to blame me again. Swallowing hard, I tuned Coach back in.

Coach gestured as if fielding an invisible ball. "We've got to move our feet. Anticipate. We've got to eliminate what some coaches call 'campfire moments.'"

"Why?" Emily asked. "I'm always up for a plateful of hot-dogs and s'mores."

"No." Coach quirked an eyebrow. "That's an actual camp-fire. In volleyball, *campfire moment* is a phrase that means the ball drops untouched to the floor in the center of several defenders."

"I was kidding. I know what a campfire moment is." Emily's words spilled out like marbles. "The players circle around the spot where the ball lands, making it look like everyone's standing around the campfire roasting marshmal-lows. Except there are no marshmallows which makes the whole situation sad."

Coach snapped her fingers and pointed at Emily. "Bingo."

"That's a dog." Emily pointed back. "Or, wait. Did you bring marshmallows? For an object lesson?" Her eyes wid-ened. "Because that would be totally awesome. Tell me you've got marshmallows hidden in your pockets."

Coach's lips curled into a wry grin. "Sorry, kid."

Michelle cleared her throat and shot a glance Gwen's way. "How many campfire moments did we have last night?"

"Too many."

Gwen glared at Michelle. A quietly hissed, "Like you

could do better, benchwarmer," pricked my ears. Michelle's face reddened, and she looked down at her feet.

The gym quieted enough to hear the air conditioner wheezing overhead. Eyebrows drawn low, Coach tucked her arms behind her back and started pacing.

The familiar move made my stomach tighten. Aunt Tina used to create that kind of silent appraisal whenever I struggled with my passing. A war machine analyzing my weaknesses. A captain calling for my strengths.

Finally, Emily raised her hand. "But the last play of the game wasn't really a campfire moment because Gwen hit the floor, right? She executed a perfect belly-flop smack. And, by the way, Gwen, yay for bruises. Fashion statement. Am I right? But anyway, that makes it more like a picnic. Except picnics are more chaotic than campfires, especially if it's a family reunion and your thirty-six-old yodeling cousin from the back hills shows up with her two pet hogs on a leash. Not that I have personal experience with that. My point is, marshmallows are welcome at both picnics and campfires. And also here. In the gym. Now."

Hiding a smile behind my hands, I waited for Coach's reaction.

She grunted. "No more pet hogs or food interruptions, Emily."

Our libero slouched. "Yes, ma'am."

"Back to business. Defending against a hard spike is mainly about positioning." Squatting, Coach extended her arms to demonstrate. "Find your assigned spot on the court, and the ball comes to you almost like a magnet."

Emily pumped her hand in the air. "Now you're talking."

Holding up a finger, Coach paused. "And I'm still talking."

Emily's teeth clicked when she closed her mouth.

After letting her eyes sweep over us again, Coach resumed pacing. "But you can't defend against a dink waiting for it to come to you. That's why it's important to stay on your toes. You must be ready to go after the ball."

Emily growled under her breath. "Like a hunter after prey."

I poked her on the shoulder and shushed her. I love her, but sometimes being around that girl is like teaming up with a hyper-active octopus.

"A good offensive player will place the ball in a spot where coverage overlaps." Coach lifted a volleyball with her finger-tips. After giving it a slight push, she caught it with her other hand. "As the ball drops in the open space, the defensive play-ers are all thinking, *Is that ball mine?* That split-second hesi-tation often means the ball hits the floor. Untouched." Coach let the ball dribble out of her hand. It bounced a few times.

Michelle scooped it into her lap. "How do we avoid that?"

Coach reached out her arm, and Michelle handed the ball back to her. "The first step is commitment. You need to devel-op the mindset that you will never, *ever* give up on a play. You will touch the ball with some part of your body."

"But that final play of the game last night." Gwen's scowl deepened. "That dink. Whose ball was it?"

Frowning, I turned my head her way. I swear, if her eyebrows got any lower on her face, she'd have sideburns. Catching my gaze, she made an L shape with her fingers and mouthed *loser*.

Coach shrugged. "The easy answer is, whoever can get there first."

A triumphant smile crept across Gwen's face.

Acid churned in my stomach.

But Coach wasn't done. "The more specific answer to your question is that the person who fields the ball is the one directly behind the block. On the left side, it's one of your defensive specialists. On the right side, it's the setter."

The blood drained from Gwen's face. Glowering, she crossed her arms. "But it's better if the setter doesn't have to play the first ball, right?" she asked, her voice tight.

Nodding, Coach said, "True. But sometimes it can't be helped. When that happens, we need the person in the best position to take the second ball—the right-side hitter. Or our libero."

"Me?" Emily's jaw hit the floor. I'm not kidding. She was perched in an awkward position anyway, and she toppled.

Gwen scoffed. "So, Lorali or Emily would set?" Audrey's back stiffened. "I'm right-side too."

Frowning, I tucked my hands under my armpits.

"Yep. Lorali. Emily. Or—" Coach raised a brow. "Audrey. Maybe Audrey too. And that's what we'll work on today."

Wait. My heart raced. I would work on setting today? Without asking permission? Thank you, Lord!

Coach introduced a new drill where back row players picked up the dink and then front row hitters made the set. It involved a lot of diving on the floor. The way Emily's eyes lit up as Coach explained how it worked, you'd think the girl enjoyed collecting bruises. She actually clapped her hands when Coach warned that sometimes she would hit the ball instead of dinking, to keep players from creeping out of position.

Once we understood the directions, Coach grabbed the ball cart. "Front row, back row lines. Now."

As usual, Emily sprinted to claim the first spot with me close behind.

Judy sneaked off for a bathroom break. A really long one.

Whenever my turn came, time seemed suspended. I drank in the pressure, the motion, the gritty sweat. I flowed from one spot to another, a swirl of cream in coffee pumping flavor into the day.

During our water break, Coach pulled me aside. "Lorali, you surprised me in a good way. I didn't know you could set so well."

I drew in a breath. Maybe I could plant a seed in the coach's head about me being a full-time setter. Even though Gwen stood within earshot, I wanted the job so badly I had to speak up. "I enjoyed the challenge." The words tumbled out faster than I could think them. "In fact, I'd like to work more on my setting skills. Maybe I could be a backup setter. Especially since statistics show that having a left-handed setter is a huge advantage."

When Coach cocked her head, I held my breath. Was she considering it? Or was she hesitating? I needed someone to support me.

I yanked Emily to my side. Although completely absorbed by a granola bar in her fist, she let me handle her.

"Emily and I will work together." I squeezed Emily's shoulder. "We could stay after practice for fifteen more minutes running the same types of exercises you do with the setters. Then you'll have a reliable backup plan when the setters take the first ball. And who knows, maybe I could even take over setting for a game, to let them rest, you know?"

Over by the bench, Gwen slammed her water bottle down. My stomach tightened, but Coach only raised an eyebrow. "Interesting idea. Why not? If you don't mind the extra work."

Knowing Emily embraced anything involving sweat, I wasn't surprised when she crumpled up her empty wrapper and saluted. "I'm in."

Coach grinned. "Okay. We'll start tomorrow."

"Woo-hoo!" Emily did a little happy dance. Then she

pushed my shoulder. "You owe me a bag of marshmallows for helping you out."

"Still thinking about campfires?" I laughed. "I'll bring some."

Across the court, Gwen and Audrey shared a meaningful look, filling me with sudden doubt. Had I made a mistake by asking? No, if things remained the same, our team would never win, I'd never get noticed, and I could kiss my college volleyball dreams goodbye.

I squared my shoulders. If I wanted to play Division One volleyball, this was a course I had to follow. And with the same determination as Aunt Tina. The question was, would Gwen make room for me, or would she undermine my efforts?

Who am I kidding? It's Gwen.

Which meant I was in for a rough ride.

CHAPTER FIVE

NEW KID

After practice, Emily and I showered fast. Like every Wednesday, after a long day at school, a brutal practice, and a quick nod to homework (not the sleeping kind of nod), our day still wasn't over. Tonight, our church held youth group.

I checked my phone. "Hurry. Ten minutes until Mom picks us up."

"Me? It's you I'm worried about," Emily said. "I'm the fastest one on the team."

Michelle stopped by my side. "I know you're in a rush, but

don't forget these." She picked up my socks and held them out. "If you leave them on the floor, they'll get moldy."

Laughing, I snagged them from her. "Michelle, my hero. Our team would dissolve into a pile of dust bunnies, empty food wrappers, and lost ponytail holders without you. Thanks for cleaning up after me."

Michelle picked a fuzz off her sleeve. "Old habits. I asked Coach if I could install towel hooks near the showers. She said it wasn't in the budget. Still, I might sneak in some of those portable metal racks. Do you think Coach will notice?"

"Coach doesn't miss anything," Emily said. "Except the opportunity to use marshmallows for object lessons."

I gasped, then choked back a laugh. "Emily!"

She slapped a lopsided grin on her face. "Kidding! I don't hold that culinarian oversight against her."

Michelle saluted. "It will be my mission to bring you some angelic puffs tomorrow."

"Psst. I like the miniature rainbow-colored ones best," Emily whispered.

Shivering, I pulled on a fuzzy blue sweatshirt. When my head popped out the neckline, I spotted Gwen pulling her phone out of her locker.

I swallowed. *Teammates. We are teammates.* Something had to change so that word didn't sound like a death sentence.

"Gwen! You're still here." I smoothed down my shirt. "Do you...uh...I mean, do...do—"

Her fingers snapped together like a puppet. "Duh, duh, duh." Gwen's lips twisted. "Spit it out or shut up."

I bit back the urge to scream. *Teammates. Right.* "Do you need a ride?"

"My uncle's picking me up. As if you care."

Pushing forward, Emily inserted her face between us. "I

care. Hey, is that a fruit snack peeking out of your pocket? Are you going to eat it?"

Gwen pressed her lips into a thin line. "Good girl. Like a dog, you've sniffed it out." Crumpling the snack between her fingers, she held it out. "Help yourself."

As Emily snatched her prize, Gwen's phone buzzed. She glanced at it, then lifted her bag.

"Bye, Gwen," Emily said, already popping gummy nuggets into her mouth.

Gwen grunted and left without a backward glance.

A rare frown marred Emily's face, as out of place as an onion on a plate of cupcakes. "I feel sorry for her," she whispered. "Coach pushed her hard today."

"Coach pushed all of us." I massaged my left shoulder, then shook out the muscles and switched to my right. "That's her job. That's how we get better. You're jealous because someone else earned as many spectacular bruises as you did. Including me."

I showed her my elbow.

That brought Emily's smile back. "We're bruise buddies!"

Makeup bag in hand, I headed to the restroom. The sinks were crusty, the faucet heads squeaked, and the narrow countertops held permanent stains, but at least the mirrors worked.

Bending closer, I dabbed on fresh mascara. My phone vibrated, disturbing the dust around it. I checked the screen, then ducked my head toward Emily. "My mom is outside waiting. Are you ready to go?"

"Almost!" Emily shoved wrinkled clothes into her gym bag. In her rush, she knocked over her water bottle. The metal sides clanged as the container hit the floor, and water exploded from it. Emily squealed as liquid confetti drenched the front of her shirt. "Shoot!" Emily cried. "I forgot to tighten the lid."

In a flash, Michelle turned the bottle upright. "I have an extra t-shirt you can borrow." She snagged it out of her locker and handed it to Emily. "Where are you going anyway?"

"Youth group." Emily's voice came out muffled as she tugged the shirt over her head. "Come with us some time. It's fun!"

"Maybe." Michelle drew the word out like a question.

Emily pointed at Michelle. "Maybe isn't a no. We'll talk later."

My phone buzzed again. "Hurry up, Emily!"

We hustled out the gym doors. Mom's Toyota sat by the curb, motor running. In the back seat, she had left me a strawberry smoothie, an egg sandwich, and grapes. Emily had an order of chicken nuggets, fries, and a chocolate milkshake. We ate dinner on the run.

I remember the first time Emily brought me to youth group. We played a relay game called "Bubble Gum Blow Out." Each player ran across the room, shoved a huge blob of bubble gum in their mouths, chewed, blew a bubble, and then stuck the gum onto a sheet of paper hanging on the wall. The catch? Once you had the gum in your mouth, you couldn't use your hands.

We laughed *so hard!* Plus, in addition to gum, I blew up social media that night. Imagine—a slow motion sequence of gum popping, dropping, or flopping out of half a dozen mouths. (Oh, the slobber!) Or, my favorite, a clip of Emily's rhythmic chewing paired with the classic band Yello's song "Oh Yeah" and a filter that changed her face into a horse. The longer the night went on, the higher the number of views my video got.

After the race, the speaker talked about how Christ will always "stick" with us in any situation. The story engrossed me so much, I didn't think about volleyball the whole time. His message reminded me that no matter what challenges I faced, I have a God who cares about me on my side. From that day on, I promised to make room in my busy week for youth group.

In my heart, I sealed the deal a week later after reading an article that said laughter relieves stress, and reduced stress levels lead to increased athletic performance. So it was a win-win situation.

Tonight, Emily and I followed a handful of teens crowding through the doorway and up the stairs. We met in a room called "the Loft," probably because it was located on the top floor. The area had the cozy, but distinctive, vibe of a treehouse furnished with leftover garage sale material. The large open space fielded two pool tables, a ping pong table, a row of nearly obsolete computers, a seventy-two-inch television, a snack area, and a handful of couches—some more worn than others, none of them matching.

At the top of the stairs, Emily abandoned me for the snack bar and rifled through the available food. She lifted an empty pizza box with such a forlorn expression, I could almost taste her disappointment.

Joel, one of our friends from fifth period, offered her the slice off his paper plate, and a wide-eyed Emily accepted it. Joel sidled closer to her, chatting awkwardly, like a wannabe zookeeper flirting with a hamster on a wheel. Emily nodded, eyes blissful, cheeks rounded with food. You'd never guess she just inhaled a number eight meal deal.

Not hungry myself, I idled near the pool tables until Hank, our youth director, clapped his hands. It was his signal to find a seat on the couches or carpet to start our meeting. I saved Emily a cushion. After extracting herself from Joel, she hurdled her way over.

Hank cleared his throat. "Before we get started, we have a new friend with us tonight. Taylor, please introduce yourself."

Across the room, a tall boy stood. He had dark hair that curled at the bottom to frame his face. Under that mop, warm brown eyes with long black lashes peeked out. His tan skin suggested he may be of Hispanic descent. A scruff of hair grew on his chin, giving him a mature bearing. He wore faded jeans and a red t-shirt with a cross on it. He looked lean, but a hint of muscle showed through his shirt. An athlete.

Hands tucked into his pockets, he glanced around the room. When his eyes passed me, my pulse dropped in a weird way. Suddenly I wished I'd spent more time brushing my hair after practice.

I expected him to shuffle and mumble, like most shy newbies. Instead, his face dimpled into a confident smile.

"Like Hank said, my name is Taylor—"

Someone clapped, and he paused to bow.

"And I moved here from Indiana. Go Colts! I'm a junior at Jefferson High School—"

"Boo!" I teased, hiding my disappointment that he attended a different school.

"Go Williamson Wildcats," Emily hooted, pumping her fist.

"Go Huskies," another student cried from the other side of the room.

"Whoa! Whoa!" As if breaking up a fight, Taylor held out his hands. His face took on a serious look, but his eyes twinkled. "I've got nothing against cats. Or dogs. Especially hot dogs."

Emily hooted again. "A man after my own heart!"

The crowd twittered, except Joel. His face went pale.

Taylor nodded, acknowledging her outburst. "But I'm a Mustang. Which means I can horse around with everyone, whether you're a Husky or Wildcat."

We all laughed. But it was a nice kind of laugh.

Taylor waved us off. "Okay, what else? I like gaming, science fiction books, football, animals, like wildcats…" He bobbed his head at me, and I blushed. "…and Jesus. But not necessarily in that order."

Hank extended his arm for a handshake. "Well, we're glad you joined us tonight, Taylor. We hope you'll come back next week too. And your introduction is a great segue into our Bible lesson this week because the character we've been studying is just like you—a new face in a new place. Tonight, we're going to continue our discussion about Joseph. Do you know anything about him, Taylor?"

Having a roomful of heads turn his way didn't seem to bother Taylor. He spoke with an easy familiarity. "I know his dad gave him a multicolored coat, and he had ten older brothers who didn't like that kind of favoritism. So they threw him into a pit and told Dad he was dead. They even shredded Joe's coat and hurled blood on it to trick everyone."

"Nice. Stop there." Hank held up a hand. "That's right where we're picking up today. As a review, Joseph started out on top of the world. This overconfident kid had dreams. And those dreams showed his brothers and even his own father bowing down to him. Can you imagine how irritating it would be to have your little brother brag about how important he was?"

In response, a ripple of nods and whispering swept through the group.

Emily spoke up. "My ten-year-old cousin is cute, but if she tries to braid my hair or paint makeup on me one more time because 'she's the expert,' I think I'll scream. Do you know she used red lipstick on my nose once?"

Without missing a beat, Taylor quipped, "That's funny. You strike me as a brown-noser kind of girl."

When the crowd groaned, Taylor shrugged, brown eyes glittering. "Just kidding. I couldn't resist."

I lifted an eyebrow. *Irresistibly cute and a fun sense of humor. Gotta appreciate that.*

Holding up a finger, Hank interrupted. "Back to our story from Genesis. Last week, we found Joseph at the bottom of a pit. His brothers sold him into slavery but told Jacob, his father, that he was dead. That's how Joseph landed in Egypt. But his story didn't end there. Let me tell the next part with emojis. It goes something like this."

With a flourish, Hank pulled out his phone and pressed a button. A moment later, phones around the room buzzed. I dug mine out of my back pocket. Hank had sent us an upside-down face, a brave face, a kissing face, a surprised face, a mad face, and a sad face.

"Translation." Hank pointed to each emoji in order as he talked. "When Joseph got to Egypt, his whole world was turned upside-down. He went from being the favorite son to a slave for an important official named Potiphar. Because Joseph remained brave and hard-working, Potiphar put him in charge of his whole household. Unfortunately, Potiphar's wife made a move on Joseph. A surprised Joseph ran away. And she didn't like that. So she lied and accused Joseph of sexual misconduct. Potiphar threw Joseph in jail."

"He got framed." Emily gripped my knee. Painfully gripped. "Totally unfair."

Hank shrugged. "Life isn't always fair. We question why God allows something to happen because we only see a little bit of the picture. But here's the cool thing. God not only sees the whole picture, He's the one that painted it in the first place. So even though the situation seemed horrible and, yes, Emily, unfair for Joseph, God used that hard time to teach Joseph about patience, humility, and, most of all, about how to trust God not just with the little things, but with the big things too. That was important because God had something greater in mind for Joseph than simply taking care of one Egyptian official's household, and He needed Joseph to be prepared to handle it. You see, Joseph had dreams, but God's dreams for him were even bigger."

As Hank dug into the details, my attention shifted. Someone far more interesting than my youth group director sat a few feet away.

What color were Taylor's eyes again? I tried to look at Taylor without looking like I was looking at him.

He shifted position.

A jolt of electricity shot through my veins. Pulse racing, I focused on an inspirational quote poster hanging on the wall behind him. Anyone who noticed me leaning into Emily and lifting my chin might think I was attempting to read the words.

Everyone except Emily. She pushed me back. "Quit crowding."

A few people turned their heads my way, including Taylor. My face heated, and I slouched back into the couch. Busted!

"This week, I encourage you to consider how Joseph conducted himself in the face of uncertainty," Hank said "How did he respond to disappointment or obstacles? To ridicule and humiliation? Do you see any lessons we can draw from what happened? Find a buddy and talk about it."

Automatically, I turned to Emily, but my eyes stayed on Taylor. From his place, he glanced around. Sucking in a quick breath, I ducked so he wouldn't catch me staring at him. Again.

To my relief, Joel tapped him on the shoulder and drew his attention.

Meanwhile, Emily jabbered away, all business. "Good for Joseph, running out of the house instead of getting mixed up with Potiphar's wife. I think that means we should run away from someone tempting us to do the wrong thing too. But that whole 'sell your brother into slavery' thing? That's messed up. And Joseph had all those big dreams too. Joseph be like—*what?*—and then he be like *dude!* And then when things went wrong, he be like—*what!*—and then he be like *dude?* Meanwhile, his brothers are all like—" She stuck her index and pinky finger up in a rock star pose. "What, dude? You know, with the whole attitude vibe going on."

Only half-listening, I nodded. That's all the encouragement Emily would need to keep chatting.

Across the room, Taylor's face lit up as he talked with Joel. What was he saying? Probably something insightful and funny.

Emily rambled on and on until Hank called us back together to summarize the lesson and launch us into game time.

Even while playing "The Floor is Lava," where everyone had to jump onto furniture within five seconds whenever the phrase was yelled, I had trouble staying on task. I strained to listen in on Taylor's conversations. When he stood nearby, I laughed too loud, talked too much, and felt compelled to take a bunch of selfies with Emily.

When Emily's mom picked us up afterward, I realized I had forgotten the lesson. All I remembered was Taylor's face.

And how my stomach churned when he left the meeting right before I did with a dark-haired beauty hooked on his arm. Someone I didn't recognize.

Probably his girlfriend.

CHAPTER SIX

PRIORITIES

After a restless night dreaming about college volleyball (and a certain boy who shall remain nameless), my alarm clock jerked me awake the way Emily might rip the meat off a drumstick. Bleary-eyed, I groped around to shut it off.

With the noise muted, the warmth of the bed and softness of the pillows called to me. But athletes must stay disciplined. Sighing, I flopped onto my stomach and reached under my bed. My hand brushed the volleyball my Aunt Tina gave me for Christmas one year. *For the future,* she had said. *So you can follow my footsteps. You've got the potential. Make me proud.*

I lifted the ball off the floor, oddly comforted by its leathery exterior. This round object was a tiny world full of promise. Who wouldn't want more of that?

Once I asked Aunt Tina why my mom didn't play volleyball in college too. She said, "You get the biggest payoff when you put your whole heart into something. Your mom never did. At least not into volleyball."

My stomach clenched as I crammed my emotions deeper inside, carefully tucking away any anxious thoughts to keep them from seeping out.

Settling back on the mattress, I uttered a quick prayer, like I do every day. Peace. For mom. And for me, to set an example in speech, faith, and love.

Then I added something extra. *Hello, God. It's Day One in however many days it takes to reach my goal. Please help me learn what I need to be successful. Amen.*

Drawing a cleansing breath, I opened my eyes.

Yesterday, I had searched online for simple setting drills I could do at home. After sorting through a dozen articles, I found one I liked.

Lying on my back, I lifted my hands. By angling them slightly, my thumbs and pointer fingers formed a triangle. Then I balanced the ball on top of my fingertips. With light pushes, I caught and released it, bouncing it popcorn-style. I counted fifty reps, then paused to rest my arms before starting again.

I completed fifteen sets before breakfast.

On the way to school, Mom rode shotgun while I took the wheel again. This time I remembered to check the rearview mirror before backing up and, more importantly, before she reminded me. But my brake-heavy lurch at the end of the driveway still drew a pained look of reproof from her.

"I got this," I said, pulling my shoulders back.

She traced a line on the window. "Good."

Even with the constant flow of traffic demanding my attention, volleyball clouded my brain. Would my morning efforts make a difference? Would I ever get good enough for a recruiter to notice me? Was Taylor dating that girl? *No, focus on volleyball.* They looked awfully friendly. Too friendly. *Stop thinking about Taylor.* Did she go to his school? *Who cares!* I wonder if he likes left-handed volleyball players. ARGH!

"Did you pack your kneepads?" Mom asked.

Her question clipped my wandering thoughts. I blinked. "Yes." Honestly, she could have asked if I packed an ostrich for lunch or if my favorite pizza topping was tree bark and I still would have answered yes—that's how distracted I was.

"And your homework?"

I tightened my grip on the wheel. "I should get to school early enough to finish it before class starts."

A quarter mile clicked past in silence.

"Good," Mom finally said.

When lunch time arrived, Emily and Michelle waited for me in the cafeteria. As usual, I toted reusable storage containers filled with "super foods"—strawberries, raw carrots, hard-boiled eggs, a protein bar, and kale chips. (Frankly, I don't care how healthy those kale chips claim to be. To me they taste like week-old grass scraped from the bottom of a lawnmower.)

Emily held a crumpled burger bag, a tall order of waffle fries, and a soft drink from the nearest fast-food restaurant. Michelle simply carried a good old-fashioned brown bag lunch.

We plopped down at the end of a long, wobbly cafeteria

table, probably a remnant from the World War II era. The yellowed laminate surface had *Frodo Lives* scratched into it.

While Emily tore into her burger, Michelle pulled a trial-sized bottle of hand sanitizer out of her pocket. After popping the lid, she squeezed a few drops into her hands. The strong scent of vanilla momentarily overwhelmed the stench of overcooked spinach souring the air.

I tapped the table in front of Emily. "You look ready to pop. What's up?"

Eyes bright, Emily blurted, "Michelle is coming to youth group with us next week!"

Nodding, Michelle tucked away her bottle. "Emily has been bugging me about it all morning. And you know her. If she wants something, she won't let it go."

"Way to go!" I lifted my hand for a high-five.

Emily slapped it. Hard.

"You'll like our group," I said, shaking away the pain.

"Emily told me all about the meetings." Michelle arranged a peanut butter sandwich on a napkin in front of her. "Especially the six-foot snack bar."

"Fix me up a heavenly plate." Students at a nearby table turned their heads at Emily's singsong voice. "Bagels. Donuts. Swiss cheese. Angel food cake. All holey things."

"Ignore her. The messages are the best." I leaned forward. "And a new boy showed up yesterday. Taylor. He's cute. I hope he'll be there next week too."

Michelle's eyes widened. Emily lifted her head, her mouth open.

The blood drained from my face when I realized what I said. "I mean, yeah." I shrugged. "I'm just curious. Because he's the new guy, you know? Like you, Michelle. New. To youth group. And he's a Mustang. I mean, that's his school mascot, a mustang. But he still likes cats. Wildcats. Like me. We're Wildcats. I'm a Wildcat."

"Lorali!" Emily punched my shoulder. "Do you have a crush on him?"

Mouth suddenly dry, I shook my head. "No. He just seemed interesting."

I was supposed to zero in on my volleyball goals, not get derailed by some guy.

But when Emily pretended to faint, I sputtered on. "Interesting but plain. Plainly interesting. Friendly. But not too flirty. Funny. I mean, he made me smile."

Emily slapped the table with both hands, loud enough to turn heads our way. "LORALI!"

I pulled my collar up in a feeble attempt to avoid her stare.

"Oh!" Michelle lifted a finger. "Okay, now I *really* want to go. No offense, Lorali, but you never talk about anything besides volleyball."

"Yes, I do!" Grasping for inspiration, I grabbed the nearest food item and held it up. "I talk about kale chips."

"Pfft." Emily rolled her eyes and snagged another mouthful of food.

Lowering my gaze, I took a calming breath and picked at my napkin. I mean, it's okay to like the guy. But how could I crush on someone I barely knew who already had a gorgeous girlfriend? I would be setting myself up for rejection. And if I had to endure teasing, at least I wanted it to be over someone whose affections I had a fighting chance to win. "You said he was cute." Michelle wiggled her eyebrows.

"Did I?"

Smirking, Emily needled me. "Oh, that's right! You did. And he is cute, I guess. If you like tall, dark, and handsome."

Me, I'm much pickier. If he doesn't know his way around a kitchen, I'm out."

Based on how much I wanted to crawl under a rock, I'm pretty sure my face turned five shades of red. "Can we talk about something else. Please?"

Emily laughed, adding another layer of heat to my skin. I love that girl, but she never did know when it was a good time to quit. Although I suppose that's part of what made her a good libero. Tenacity.

Luckily, Michelle changed the subject. "I heard you talking with Coach at practice." She leaned in, as if creating a private bubble. "I want to join your extra sessions."

Michelle must have misunderstood the look on my face because her words poured out faster. "I'm a junior, so it's now or never. Anything I can do to get better might help me earn a starting spot on next year's team. I know I can't get there without hard work, which I'm willing to do." She hesitated, then straightened her spine. "I don't want to end up like Judy. Bitter. Benched. I want to play."

I knew exactly what she meant. The competition intoxicated me. "Sure," I said.

Sighing, Michelle roughed a hand over her face. "Thank you. To be honest, I'm happy for every moment on the court even if it's only practice. If there's any opportunity to play more, I'm in. Besides..." She paused smoothing out the edge of her napkin. "I have something to prove to myself. And Gwen."

I wrinkled my nose. "What do you mean?"

As if seeking inspiration, Michelle looked at the ceiling. "I never told anyone, but when we started at Williamson, Gwen hated being on the Freshman team with the rest of us first years. She thought she should be on Junior Varsity. Every time someone made a mistake, she'd lash out. One time, she got so mad at me, she cornered me in the locker room and told me I was useless and should quit."

Emily's eyes grew round. "So, what did you do?"

"I told the Freshman coach, and she called us into her office." Michelle snorted. "Gwen apologized and said she was only kidding. You know how that goes. An adult slaps a verbal Band-Aid on a situation and assumes that fixes the problem. But Gwen didn't stop, she just got sneakier with her putdowns. And now, two years later, even though she *mostly* stopped, I still feel uncomfortable if Gwen's near me. Like somehow, I'm not good enough. I'm a disappointment to her."

My stomach tightened. Sadly, I understood that feeling too. "I'm sorry. Maybe one day we can connect as a team. In fact, I'll add that to my prayer list."

Michelle pursed her lips. The gesture gave her a determined look. "Team. I like the sound of that. We win as a team, and we lose as a team. That's why we've got to stick together."

∗ ∗ ∗

During practice that afternoon, Coach asked Emily and me to take over setting for our hitting lines for the last few minutes of warmups. Emily didn't seem to care how accurately she placed the ball, and the hitters struggled to make a play off her horrid sets. Then again, she had no aspirations to take over the setting position and, as libero, had to set from behind the ten-foot line anyway.

Meanwhile, I rolled up my sleeves, hoping for instant awesomeness.

It didn't happen. My sets went high and wide, which threw off everyone's timing.

To make matters worse, Gwen coiled on the sidelines, measuring my efforts with her eyes. Unless Coach stood directly nearby, she murmured things laced with venom, just loud enough for me to hear. Things like, "Perfect set if you're playing JV." Or "Did you snag that one on your broken fingernails?" Or "Not so easy, is it, Loser?" Or the real zinger, "Nobody can hit those bombs you're throwing."

Her intensity might have burned a hole through the net if Coach hadn't yelled at her from across the gym. "Stop standing around, Gwen. Take this opportunity to work on your defense."

Rolling her eyes, Gwen posted sentry behind the blockers to catch whatever dribbled over their hands.

Even though her barbs hardened my inner resolve, they still affected me. My body tensed under her relentless judgment, making it even more difficult to place the ball accurately.

Frustration must have bled onto my face because Coach stopped the drill. "Don't be so hard on yourself, Lorali. It takes repetition and awareness to find your groove, just like it did when you learned the other skills. You've got good instincts, but remember, you're not a setter."

Gwen smirked at me.

"Square your shoulders to the net." Coach modeled the stance. "Push more with your legs instead of your arms. That will help."

Jaws clenched, I nodded and made the adjustment. After a few more awkward tries, I started hitting my marks.

After warmups, Coach amped up the pace of practice. With a home game tomorrow against one of the leading teams in our conference, we needed the work.

Shifting back to my role of hitter lifted my spirit like coming home after a long holiday, but every time I rotated out, I studied Gwen's footwork and how she positioned her hands.

When Coach finally called it quits, my body ached like I had run a marathon with a chubby moose strapped to my back. Sweat coated my body, my quads hurt, and I'd already drained two water bottles.

Still, while the rest of the team left for the locker room, I sat on the floor by Emily and Michelle, waiting for our fifteen-minute bonus with Coach.

Emily lay spread-eagle on her back counting the water spots on the ceiling.

Propped beside her, Michelle yawned. "I'm beginning to wonder if it was a good idea to ask for extra practice after all."

Always the warrior, Emily laughed. "Bring it on."

Groaning, Michelle sat up. "You really enjoy pain, don't you?"

"It's my middle name." Emily flashed her toothy smile.

"Yeah? Well, my middle name is…" Michelle hesitated.

"Giggles?" Emily suggested. "Cucumber? Zonkers? Chlorox? Snorkel?"

Michelle shook her head. "I was going to say 'Aspire.'"

"Nah." Emily closed her eyes, the picture of contentment. "I like 'Snorkel' better."

We had little time to enjoy Emily's wisdom before Coach had us slapping our kneepads and getting back to work. Honestly, I was especially eager to start. During practice, I'd learned one thing—I still had a long way to go before Coach would let me set during a game.

At least it was a goal I could work toward. Not like catching Taylor's eye. With a beautiful girl already on his arm, I imagined that would take a miracle.

CHAPTER SEVEN

YOU AGAIN

Our gym is like the "Where's Waldo" of buildings. Visiting teams can only find the entrance because someone taped a sheet of paper on the outside door that says, "Gym." And, once located, there is little to see.

Inside, a drinking fountain that cranked out rust-flavored water separated two metal doors. Behind each sat a solitary toilet stool, both stocked with a single, half-empty roll of toilet paper. The gym floor came eight steps later. Two sets of bleachers, each with five total rows of seating, lined one wall. The concession stand—a wooden counter holding lukewarm cans of soda and stale candy—sat in a storage closet between them. A portable boom box piped music. The loudspeaker resembled two paper cups attached by a string. Our flip scoreboard with nylon numbers perched on a folding table between team benches. And a handful of bored-looking cheerleaders hugged the far wall, unable to do more than yell in the cramped space.

Compare our reality to the backdrop for tonight's match.

I entered a red-brick facility through glass-paned double doors. As I traveled down the hallway, my footsteps echoed off a crisp, white-tiled floor. Not a single sticky fingerprint marred the walls. I passed dust-free trophy cases lined with golden statues and medallions.

A concession stand loomed six paces in front of massive restrooms. The snack shop sported wide counters, decorative napkin holders, digital menu signs, and a carnival-sized popcorn machine shooting out tiny kernels of buttery bliss. The smell of hot dogs gently coddled on warm rollers saturated the air, each perfectly plumped. Rows of candy bloomed like flowers in every variety—yellow candy wrappers, lines of cherry licorice, and a rainbow of sugar-coated sweet-and sour sticks. Beyond that nestled granola bars, bananas, apples, oranges, pulled-pork sandwiches, nachos, and pizza. When Emily passed the stand, her jaw dropped to the floor.

And I hadn't even made it to courtside yet.

Sound hit me next, its volume rising with each second. The jabber of parents dressed in bejeweled shirts and filling half of the cushion-backed bleachers with their dazzle. The roar of students crowding the lower bleachers, climbing over each other like ants. The throb of fast-paced music blaring over the PA system. The screams of two cheerleading squads. The squeak of shoes on polished hardwood floors.

Meanwhile, guest bleachers on the opposite side of the three-court span swallowed our sparse fans with massive rows of industrialized metal teeth.

The smells, sounds, and sights of the gym swirled together in elite chaos, intent on intimidating all who entered.

But still, the vastness of it all wasn't what shocked me the most. Something else shook me up. During warmups, I chased down a loose ball, and a dark-haired beauty paused to kick it back to me.

I did a double take. That hair. Even pulled into a ponytail, there was no mistaking it as belonging to the girl who left church with Taylor on Wednesday.

At least that answered the question about whether he liked volleyball players. But if she was here, did that mean Taylor was here too?

Heart pounding, I scanned the crowd, looking for his mop of dark hair. Sure enough, he stood in the middle of a group of rowdy boys, the kind with muscles thicker than their brains. The teens wore matching Mustang shirts. The way they pushed and jostled each other, I suspected they'd out-scream the cheerleaders.

Lingering, I studied his girlfriend's controlled movements. Despite her height, maybe 5'9", she commanded attention. Their players pulsed around her presence, following her quick directions. She was everything I aspired to be but wasn't.

Yet.

"Quit standing around, you dork!" Gwen barked at me.

Catching my breath, I spun back to the sidelines before anyone else noticed my lapse in attention. I tried to ignore the heat building on my face, but only succeeded in moving the fire to my stomach.

I closed my eyes. I needed Aunt Tina's pre-game focus

routine. She always said, "Don't let anything stand between you and success. See it. Believe it. Achieve it."

With a calming breath, I schooled my emotions. Immersed myself in the tight, clean lines of the net. The flavor of the crowd's energy. The bead of sweat trailing down my back. The passion building in my gut to hammer the ball.

Better.

When the whistle blew, we lined up for the national anthem, sung by our opponents' regional champion choral group. After each player was introduced (that beauty who belonged to Taylor was named Teresa Lopez), the teams waved to the crowd.

We huddled around Coach. Over a burst of crowd noise, she gave us advice. "Their blockers are tall, so make them move, setters. Quick sets in the middle or shoot it low to the outside. Feed Lorali whenever you can. Move your feet on defense. It all starts with a good pass. On three!"

We slapped hand-on-top-of hand in the middle. "WILDCATS!"

Stepping onto the court, I attempted to mimic a look I'd seen on my aunt's face when she competed. Intense. Focused. Deadly. If matches could be won based on attitude alone, Aunt Tina would have dominated the field.

As the referee checked our lineup, Emily used her knee-pads to wipe dust off her shoes. Somehow that simple act made her look tough.

Gwen got us off on the right foot by acing the first serve. Instinct drove me to congratulate her, but her cold-shouldered glare kept me away. *Maybe she's really into the game.*

We went up 2–0 after capitalizing on another weak serve receive. In response, the other team shifted their rotation like a werewolf undergoing its change in appearance. This shielded their struggling player and brought their formidable middle hitter back to receive the serve. The change resulted in a quick side out, and an end to our one and only lead in the match.

In our one-sided battle, Teresa proved to be the most lethal weapon. She mixed up her sets, feeding her hitters in unpredictable ways. If the pass was tight to the net, she twisted her body mid-air to execute a nearly flawless jump set.

Occasionally she burned us by tapping the ball over on the second hit. And every time she made a good play, Taylor hopped up, pumping his fist or screaming, "Way to go, Terri!"

For her part, Terri never responded to the crowd. Instead, she maintained her cool execution of the offense, a queen among peasants.

I could see why Taylor liked her.

When the match ended, custom dictated we gather on the end line and thank the other team before leaving the court. Gwen stalked past me to find her spot, bumping against me on the way. Head hanging, I dutifully joined my team.

I consoled myself with small victories. As badly as we lost, we didn't run out of subs. Emily did her part too, flying across the court and swooping up stray balls like a crazed falcon after scraps.

As I shuffled to the bench to collect my bag, someone called my name.

"Lorali! Wait!"

Frowning, I turned toward the voice. Taylor pushed his way through the throng. He separated himself from the mass and planted himself in front of me, slightly out of breath. No wonder, given the size of the gym.

"You again." I tried to sound calm, but my voice cracked. "Taylor, right?"

"Yes! Taylor." He cocked his head. "You remembered me. From youth group."

His wide smile drew me in. In fact, much to my horror, I acted outright flirty. "Of course I remembered you. There aren't many Indianapolis Colts fans in these parts. Besides, you were the only new face in the room." I let my gaze travel the length of his frame. "I think what's more interesting is the fact you remembered me when there were at least thirty other kids there."

He didn't miss a beat. "But you were the only one to boo me."

"In a friendly way," I replied. "If I meant it, your ears would have melted off."

"The way you spiked the ball tonight, I believe it!"

His unexpected compliment choked off the clever response on my lips. Especially when he filled the sudden gap with even more compliments. "You were fast on the block too. Great game!"

"Thanks." I tugged my jersey. "Although I don't think you appreciate the fact that our team not only suffered a crushing defeat but did so while dressed in painfully ugly uniforms from the late 1960s."

"Old enough to be back in style," he quipped.

I grinned, despite myself. "Touché."

Holding up a hand, he leaned in. "No offense, but your school doesn't have the numbers like the other teams we've faced. How did you end up in our conference anyway?"

"My best guess?" I shrugged. "Maybe someone made a typo on the official school population census. They changed the six hundred to six thousand."

His cheeks dimpled. "Plausible."

Interesting word choice. Cute, funny...and smart.

Licking my lips, I glanced toward our bench. Michelle rounded up water bottles. The rest of my team collected gear. And that beautiful setter from the other team wasn't in sight.

Maybe they weren't dating.

Plausible.

Chest tight, I reconsidered the boy in front of me. "Why did you come to the game tonight? I thought football was your thing."

He cocked his head. "Now who's paying attention?"

For a moment, he caught me off-guard. I laughed. "I only had one new face to remember."

"True." He crossed his arms and shifted his feet in a wide stance. "Well, football *was* my thing. But after three wicked concussions last season, the athletic director forced me to stop playing. He cited some high school regulation. Now I'm stuck with sports that won't rattle my brain."

"Like volleyball?" I asked.

"Heck, no!" Shaking his head, he chuckled. "I've seen how hard y'all hit the floor. I mean non-contact sports like track or swimming. Or—" He tapped his chin. "Knitting."

His comment sparked a surprised snort from me. "I'm sure they'd ban knitting." I narrowed my eyes. "Those needles look dangerous."

With an innocent grin, Taylor raised an eyebrow. "Point well-taken."

Flushing, I nodded. I could get used to this kind of banter.

Then Teresa—or Terri as he'd called her—sneaked up behind Taylor and slipped her arm around his waist.

Taylor jumped. Then he turned, sweeping her up in the air before setting her back down. "Terri! Nice game."

All my good humor drained away.

Terri beamed, an obvious reaction to his praise. Cozying

up under his shoulder, the girl looked me up and down. "Associating with our enemies?"

Swallowing, I stiffened under her scrutiny.

Taylor kissed the top of her head. "Yup."

Yup? Just yup, and a kiss, like, no big deal?

I stepped back, a burning sensation forming in the back of my throat.

Lips downturned, Terri gestured at me. "And your friend is…?"

"Lorali." Taylor winked at me. "I met her at youth group."

A smile lit the girl's face. "I love that church." She held out her hand. Awkwardly, I took it. "I'm Terri. Nice to meet you."

Fighting a fluttery stomach, I searched for something to say. "I didn't see you in the Loft. Not until you left anyway."

She waved, a dismissive gesture. "I meet with the Freshmen group."

Despite my discomfort, I gawked at her. "No. Way. You start on Varsity as a freshman?" How had I missed that fact during team introductions?

Her lips flattened into a playful smirk. "Yes, I'm that good. But it's getting late, so if you don't mind…" She reached into the pocket of Taylor's coat and pulled out a set of car keys. Blinking innocently, she dangled them in front of Taylor's face. "I'm tired. Somebody needs to drive their favorite player home now."

"Yes, ma'am."

My temperature rose as Terri pulled Taylor toward the door.

Craning his head, he caught my eye and saluted. "You're my second favorite player, Wildcat. See you Wednesday!"

Which, in turn, only made my face blush hotter. *I'm not a player. He's a player, saying something like that in front of his girlfriend.*

"Huddle up, girls!" Coach yelled, pulling me from my embarrassment.

We gathered around her, dragging our feet. Except Emily, whose whole body still somehow crackled with energy.

"We are better than what I witnessed on the court tonight." Her words came out laced with frustration. "We're so close, so very close, to coming out on top."

Close? We got swept in three sets!

I lowered my eyes and picked at a hangnail on my finger. I would have bitten it off, but Taylor might still be watching me from the distance.

"I know you usually have the weekend off unless we have a tournament, but I want to run an extra practice on Saturday." She paused to adjust the bag on her shoulder. "How many of you are free tomorrow morning at ten? I'll bring donuts."

Emily's hand shot up like a shaken soda. "You had me at donuts."

Everyone else raised their hands too, except Caroline, our other setter. "My family is going out of town," she said.

Wincing, Coach rubbed the back of her neck. "Ah, that's too bad. But for all the rest of you, ten o'clock sharp. We're going to make some changes."

As we left the impressive gym, Gwen and Audrey bent their heads together, secluding themselves from the rest of us.

Judy stomped past me, her oversized backpack catching me on the shoulder. I regained my balance and gaped at her. And then, I noticed her clothes. While my shirt clung to me with uncomfortable dampness, she still looked fresh. She hadn't played one second.

That's why Judy's dad had confronted Coach! I searched the remaining crowd for him. Tight-lipped and red-faced, he still sulked in the bleachers. After the punishing loss we just suffered, I wondered if Coach was in for another earful from the man.

I sucked in a big breath. No matter. Coach handled him last time.

For a moment, I wondered what Taylor would be doing this weekend.

An image of Terri flashed in my mind.

On second thought, maybe I didn't want to know.

CHAPTER EIGHT

NEW PLAN

Before practice Saturday, I checked social media on my phone. Apparently, Gwen created a gif of me tripping and posted it on her account with the label "oops."

Dear Lord, please give me thick skin. Clearing the screen, I tucked my phone into my backpack. *I promised to pray for our team to connect. That includes Gwen.*

At least Coach brought the promised donuts. However, the sugar didn't chase away my yawns. On the weekend, waking any teen before noon required effort. It might actually be a federal offense too.

Still groggy, I scanned our team. Bleary eyes. Messy hair. But we all showed up to play. Except Caroline, of course. And—

My eyes widened. Where was Judy?

I craned my neck. She wasn't by the locker room either. If Judy arrived late, she'd probably have to run extra laps. And that wouldn't sit well with her dad. But what if Judy didn't arrive for practice today at all?

Coach clapped, shaking me out of my stupor. "Find a partner and warm up."

I snagged Emily. "Have you seen Judy?" I whispered.

"No. I was too busy eyeballing the leftover donuts to notice her missing. Maybe something came up."

Maybe, but not likely. Not after her dad's verbal assault on Coach. Time to share what I knew.

"I overheard her dad yelling at Coach." I glanced around. No one reacted to us, but I lowered my voice anyway. "He was mad about her lack of playing time."

Brianna jogged our way.

"Her dad yelled at Coach?" Emily said.

"Shh," I hissed. I fumbled with a ball until Brianna passed.

"No way!" Emily planted herself in front of me.

"It's true." I pulled her toward the ball cart. "But Coach didn't back down. Which made him scream even more."

Emily grabbed a ball. "What did he say?"

"More than he should." Not wanting to be overheard by the wrong ears, I leaned over to retie my shoelace. Like I hoped, Emily immediately crouched beside me.

"He claims Coach plays favorites and treats Judy unfairly," I said. "He thinks Judy is good enough to start ahead of me. But his complaints didn't seem to make a difference to Coach. Judy still sat on the bench last night."

Emily's forehead crinkled. "Poor Judy. Everyone wants to play. It must be frustrating."

Sighing, I nodded. Every fiber of my being understood the almost feverish pull of the court, the addicting thrill of a well-executed play, the insatiable craving to be a part of the action.

"Do you think she'll quit?" Emily asked.

"Girls, get moving," Coach yelled.

I turned sharp eyes on Emily. "I guess we'll find out Monday."

Ten minutes later, Coach whistled us together. With a ball hugging one hip and her eyes narrowed, she fit the image of a gun-slinging cowboy. "Today, we're focusing on offense. Since the setter is involved in almost every play, our offense is only as effective as the setter."

Gwen flashed me a smirky smile. "Got that right."

Shifting her attention to Gwen, Coach continued. "And setters are only as effective as the most basic component of volleyball—the passes. Remember, every good play starts..."

"...with a good pass." Our flat voices mimicked a Gregorian chant.

"A consistent pass made into a consistent set delivered to a consistent location with a consistent pace leads to consistent scoring." Coach paused, sweeping her eyes over us. "Did you notice how many times I mentioned the word *consistent?*"

"Five times, Coach." Emily raised her fingers. "Six if you consistently count the last one."

Coach tilted her head. "That was a rhetorical question, Emily, but thanks. Think of it this way. A good setter can make a good play out of a bad pass. But all the scrambling wears her down and leads to mistakes. But with a good pass, a good setter can rule the court. Her sets fuel the offense *without* exhausting herself."

Gwen pulled her lips into a tight line and nodded.

Raising my hand, I spoke up. "Are you saying that right now we possess the skills to do that, but we don't *consistently* execute them?"

"Yes." Coach challenged us with her eyes. "Consistent passing and setting develop with practice. And unless you work at it, last night's performance will repeat itself."

I cringed. If we kept shanking the ball, the powerhouse teams coming up would pound us into the floor.

Lifting the ball in her hands, Coach gritted her teeth. "When I'm through with you today, you will be better equipped to succeed under pressure. Lorali, you'll fill in for Caroline since she's not here. Gwen will need breaks."

Blinking, I nodded. Just like that, I had what I wanted. A shot at that setting position. All I had to do was perform as well as Caroline. Or Gwen. Or both.

But as practice progressed, I quickly learned the truth behind Coach's speech. Chasing down bad passes was exhausting.

With forty-five minutes left to go, Coach shifted gears. "You probably noticed most of the teams in our conference own a clear height advantage."

Our starting middle hitter, Brianna, grunted. At six-foot even, she ranked the tallest on our team. But as huge as she seemed to me (especially when she stood next to Emily!), hitters on better teams typically ran much taller.

Coach paced, making short work of the court. "Because of that, they shut us down with the block. And part of the problem lies in those off-target passes. They put our setters out of position and limit who they can set."

A pinched expression lined Brianna's face. "When Gwen moves away from the net, it's hard to even run a middle attack."

"Exactly. So, when the pass pulls the setter out of position, we're going to give our setters another option. I've got three words for you." Coach paused long enough to catch our attention. "Back row attack."

A chill ran down my spine. Anyone could do a legal backcourt spike as long as they started their attack behind the ten-foot line. Aunt Tina said it was one of her favorite moves, but our team had never used it before.

"That will definitely make us harder to block." Brianna furled her brows.

"I can hit the ball?" Emily's eyes took on a fevered glow. "I am a weapon."

"Your kneepads smell bad enough to be a weapon." I teased.

Rubbing her hands together, an evil grin snaked across Emily's face. "It's all part of my plan to take over the world one odor at a time."

"I shudder to imagine," Coach said, dismissing Emily's comment with a flick of her finger. "Line up!"

From behind the ten-foot line, we took turns attacking with varying degrees of success. Michelle ended up getting the ball over the net most consistently, but I had the most power behind mine.

At 12:30, an amazing, cheesy aroma drifted into the gym. A pizza deliveryman stood in our small entryway with a stack of boxes. My stomach growled in response, and I realized how long it had been since my last meal.

Emily squealed. "Surprise, Coach! My dad ordered pizza! Is practice over?"

"It is now." Coach laughed.

In a classic zombie apocalypse move, we swarmed the deliveryman, snatching away his burdens. At least no one took a bite out of him. The team lined up the boxes on the front row of bleachers.

Coach pulled out a key. "I think I can authorize a raid on the concession stand for drinks."

"And plates!" Michelle called out.

We settled down in a circle around the middle of the court. No one had their phones out. No one whispered in small groups. No one blamed someone else for their mistakes. Instead, we joked about crazy plays—most done by Emily—and where to get the best pedicures.

For the first time this season, we acted like we belonged together. Like ice cream and sprinkles. Peanut butter and jelly. Fuzzy socks and chocolate Kisses. Kale chips and, well, nothing.

During a lull in the conversation, I spoke up. "What if we did this more often?"

"Ate pizza?" Emily talked around a thick crust she was gnawing on. Talk about ravenous! The girl had four other crusts lined up on her plate compared to Gwen, who hadn't even finished her first slice.

"No." I waved to prevent Emily from launching into a monologue about her favorite toppings. "What if we got together outside of practice again? As a team. To build morale. Or bond. We could watch a movie. Or try an escape room."

Emily's eyes lit up. "Like the fun things we do at youth group!"

"Exactly." I turned my attention to Coach. "What do you think?"

Holding up a finger, Coach nodded. "Why not? Except my schedule is far too busy to coordinate it."

"I'll organize it," Michelle said. "But if we do this, everyone's gotta buy in. I don't want to put in a bunch of work and then have only three people show up."

"We'll make attendance mandatory." Coach brushed crumbs off her shirt. "All those in favor?"

A resounding *aye* echoed off the gym walls.

"Can we have a nickname too?" Emily asked.

Coach frowned. "What's wrong with Wildcats?"

"Nothing." Emily wrinkled her nose. "But the whole school is full of plain old Wildcats. We could be fancy ones."

"Okay." Coach stretched the word out. "Any suggestions?"

People shouted ideas. Lady Cats. Spiker Cats. Wild Things. Claws. Fast and Furry-us. Hit Kats. Bumpy Cats.

"Rally Cats!" Emily bellowed out over everyone. "Because we will not ever let a ball touch the floor. We'll scrap and fight to keep the rally going!"

The gym quieted as the suggestion sunk in. In volleyball terms, a rally was all the action that occurred between the serve and the point. The longer a team kept the ball in play, the longer the rally. Plus, *rally cats* was a nice word play on the phrase *alley cats*.

Michelle high-fived Emily. "Rally Cats. It's perfect."

A murmur of agreement put a broad smile on Emily's face.

Another idea gripped me. "How about for our first team bonding event we paint Rally Cat t-shirts. I mean, no offense Coach, but it's not like we have expensive warmup uniforms to wear."

I glanced at Gwen, gauging her reaction to my suggestion. Her body language—arms crossed, back stiff—said she hated it, but the spark in her eyes showed interest. That was good enough for me. Taking a big breath, I continued. "Everyone could bring a plain white t-shirt—"

"Long sleeve!" Brianna called out.

"Sure, long sleeve. And then—" I looked around. "Does anyone have paint?"

"I have acrylic paint. And brushes." Michelle choked back an awkward chuckle. "I used to do a lot of crafts, so I have tons of leftover supplies."

"Great." Coach checked her clipboard. "You can make them after practice on Monday. That way they'll be ready for our Tuesday game."

Holding an empty pizza box, Emily raised her hand. "Will there be food involved?"

Coach forehead creased. "I guess you can bring snacks to share. If you all promise to clean up after yourselves."

"You bet." Emily snapped her fingers. "And I have a week-old pair of unwashed socks in my locker for anyone who slacks off."

We all laughed. Except Gwen, who pinched her lips in a way that made me think she might not find Emily's socks amusing.

"All right then." Coach shooed us away. "Go clean up and enjoy the rest of your weekend."

As we took down the nets, I noticed a man in a worn leather jacket hovering in the shadows of the doorway. He looked maybe forty-five years old with a unshaven stubble on his face. Although he stood near enough for me to smell cigarettes and cheap cologne, his attitude erected a wall around him. His dark eyes lingered on Coach the way a spider tracks a delicate moth. Did he know her?

But Coach didn't give him a second glance.

"Who is that guy?" I whispered to Emily.

"Dunno," she said.

Before we could speculate any more, Gwen stormed across

the gym. The closer she got to the man, the slower her steps became. Even the clouds on her face faded to blank wisps. She stopped in front of him, shoulders hunched, and eyes glued to the floor. "Hello, Uncle John," she muttered.

I guess that foreboding-looking beast was her ride home today.

CHAPTER NINE

TEAM BONDING

y teammates only talked about it in hushed voices during water breaks, but the news traveled anyway. Judy had turned in her jersey before school Monday morning and quit the team.

Emily questioned the intel. "Why?"

"I told you. Judy wanted more playing time," I said.

"She had to realize that wasn't going to happen if she quit." Emily yanked my arm. "It had to be something else, like a giant mutant tarantula with hairy legs escaped from a government lab and devoured her purse and she had to trade her jersey to Coach because Coach knew the mad scientist who created the creature. It was the only way for Judy to get an opportunity to search the critter's droppings and locate her missing phone."

I freed myself from her grasp. "Emily, you scare me sometimes."

"I'm scary?" Emily's eyes bulged. "Judy's scary. She can't possibly love volleyball the same way we do if she quit. I'd do anything just to be in the gym, even if it only involved tossing balls or filling water bottles. In fact, the only thing that would keep me away from the court is Godzilla."

"Uh—" I stared at her. "Explain."

Emily made a huffing sound. "If Godzilla showed up, everyone would have to clear the courts, even if they loved volleyball. Because he would eat us all. King of the monsters, remember?"

Since Audrey had conveniently witnessed Judy in action—or in her deactivation—she served as the secret hub for information.

"It's true, Judy couldn't take it anymore." Her lips turned pouty. "The poor girl sat on the bench all last year waiting for her turn. And then Coach puts two sophomores ahead of her."

I cornered Emily during a water break. "Did you hear what Audrey's saying? Not just that Judy wanted more playing time. That it's our fault she didn't get it. We should defend ourselves."

"Okay. I'll need to borrow a sword from someone." Emily cracked her knuckles, undaunted as ever. "But I hate fighting. It gets bloody. Besides, I get it. Everyone wants to play."

"Here's the thing," I said. "We can't all be on the court at the same time."

"That doesn't matter." Emily frowned. "Whether you're on the court or not, we're still a team. Or at least we should be."

Emily's attitude gave me an odd sort of determination. She was right. Our shared struggles and victories, shared frustrations and dreams wove us together.

Losing a team member, even one who perceived their role as insignificant, was like a single thread pulled from a tapestry, leaving behind a tangled clump. After all, we were still a family of sorts. Without Judy, Caroline had to find a new warmup partner. Brianna seemed quieter than usual. And Audrey played with more defiance, as if letting us know she wouldn't suffer the same fate. Even though losing Judy broke our ranks, we were still together, one unit, with one goal. To win.

As the practice progressed, talk about Judy died out. The pressure of performing crowded all other thoughts.

After the last drill, Coach announced we could start our paint project. While Michelle fetched her supplies, we stuffed our gear into bags and gathered in the middle of the gym. When everyone was seated, Michelle held up a t-shirt. "I couldn't wait. I painted mine yesterday."

Turns out Michelle had an artistic flair. Her shirt featured a cat's clawed paw spiking a volleyball like a superhero bursting a fist through a building. Over the cat's head, Michelle had arched the words "Rally Cats" in bold letters.

Emily drew a sharp breath. "Ooooh! I love it. Gimme, gimme, gimme."

Laughing, Michelle turned her torso to block Emily's grabby hands. Her momentum pushed them into the ball cart.

"Girls!" Coach snapped.

After steadying herself, Michelle patted her hair back into

place. "Don't worry, Emily. I figured you'd like it, so I made a template for you to use with the same image on it."

Throwing the shirt over one shoulder, Michelle picked up her duffle bag and unzipped it. She pulled out a white piece of tagboard rolled into a scroll.

Emily planted her hands on her hips. "And how does that help me?"

Carefully, Michelle flattened the poster on the floor. "If you slip this between the front and back side of your shirt, the picture is dark enough to show through. You can trace it in permanent marker and then paint it."

"Genius! I'll grab my shirt." Emily pointed at the rest of us and glared. "And if anyone takes the template while I'm gone, you'll be visited by a pair of smelly socks I have stashed in my locker."

Michelle beamed. "Actually, I have two more templates if more people want to use my design."

Of course I did. I draw like a three-year-old using her feet to hold a broken crayon.

I wasn't alone either. Brianna and Gwen asked for the templates and promised to pass them on when they finished.

Before starting, Brianna held up a container. "I brought chocolate chip cookies. Should we paint or snack first?"

A squeal echoed from the locker room. "Food!" Emily sprinted back with a shirt wadded in her hands. "Food first. Definitely food!"

Before we knew it, our gym resembled a street carnival. Music blared from Brianna's phone which she'd hooked up to a portable speaker. Containers with cookies, strawberries, grapes, granola bars, chips—a mixture of healthy choices and junk—rested on the lowest bleacher seats. Laughing and chattering, we sat in a staggered circle in the upper seats. Even Coach joined us, piling treats on her plate.

Twenty minutes later, Michelle organized trash pickup while Coach laid down plastic garbage bags center court to protect the floor. It was time to paint.

I planted myself next to Michelle in case I had an artist emergency, like having to draw a circle. "I thought you were done with your shirt."

Michelle shook her head. "I'm adding a line of paw prints down my sleeves." She opened a jar of purple paint and dabbed a paintbrush into it. "That way when I pass the ball, the pattern will trail up my arm."

"Love it." I wiped my brush on a towel. "I'm going to copy your idea. How hard could that be?"

Then again, I'd be forced to paint ovals, and ovals were an awful lot like circles.

Settling nearby, Gwen ran an iron fist down the front of her shirt, pushing the crumples flat. "Caroline asked me to paint hers. We want our shirts to match exactly. I'm writing 'Setters' on one sleeve and 'Are Better' on the other."

"Better than what?" Light danced in Emily's eyes. "Dried glue? Stale gum? Toenails? Tofu-flavored ice cream? A dog with gas? Be specific, Gwen."

Gwen's back stiffened. "Setters are better at anything and everything."

Emily snorted. "We're a team. Try something like, 'I'll set you up.' It's shorter. And it has a little pop to it. Like me!"

Red-faced, Gwen clamped her mouth shut.

Even with the mild confrontation, we had a blast. Especially when Emily produced a helium balloon she some-how had stashed in her locker and inhaled a big mouthful from it. My stomach ached from laughing after she sang our school fight song in a high, squeaky voice.

Finally, Coach clapped to get our attention. "Time to clean up. But, girls, you seemed to have fun. Why not plan another team bonding event before you leave?"

After a chorus of *yeses,* several people shouted out suggestions. Movie. Potluck dinner. Phone scavenger hunt. Putt-Putt. Sleepover. Pool party. We certainly weren't hurting for ideas.

Holding up her hand, Coach stopped us. "You're giving me a headache. Just figure it out and let me know. I'm going to hole up in my office and catch up on some grading. It's been a long day."

Gwen's face darkened when Coach said that. Audrey leaned over and whispered something to her. Gwen shook her head. Audrey whispered again, more urgently, but Gwen cut her off with angry shush.

Puzzled about what they could be gossiping about now, I swept my eyes around the room. Other than the huge, sticky mess, nothing seemed amiss. Why would Coach leaving the gym sour Gwen's mood?

Curious, I kept an eye on Gwen while I gathered paint brushes. But she didn't give away any clues about the situation. Instead, jaw set, she worked in silence.

Emily rubbed a smudge of red paint off her cheek with the back of her hand. "My shirt is too wet to take home tonight."

I touched the front of my shirt. My finger came back with paint on the tip. "You're right. My mom will kill me if this gets on our car. I'll ask Coach if we can store them here."

Leaving behind a wad of paper towels, I headed for her office.

"Don't think that gets you out of cleaning up!" Emily

called after me. "In fact, I'll snack while I wait for you to help. There are still some cookies left."

Coach sat at her desk, frowning at her computer. I'd never thought about it before, but I guess grading papers can suck all the joy out of you.

I cleared my throat to let her know I was there. "We're almost done cleaning, but we've got a favor to ask."

Hesitating, I waited for Coach to respond.

She didn't.

Stepping closer, I tried again. "The shirts are still wet. Can you unlock the concession stand and let us lay them in there to dry overnight?"

Coach stirred but kept her eyes on the screen. "Sure."

I waited until awkwardness got the best of me. "So...can you unlock the door for us then?"

"What?" Coach blinked, as if surprised I was still there.

I gestured toward the concession stand. "We need the key to unlock it."

"Oh." After clicking the mouse, Coach tore her gaze away from the computer and stood. "Yeah, I got it," she said, reaching into her pocket

After we tucked away every shirt, Coach waved us together one last time. "Get rest tonight, girls. We have a big game tomorrow night. The bus leaves precisely nineteen minutes and thirty-seven seconds after the last bell." She winked. "So, don't be late. To save time, Lorali, can you collect the shirts since you arrive first?"

I nodded. "You bet."

On our way out of the gym, Coach pulled Gwen to the side. Seeing the dark scowl on Gwen's face, I dodged them. No doubt Coach was talking to her about my setting. What else would make Gwen grimace so much?

Outside, I spotted my mom in a line of cars idling by the curb. The creepy uncle who had picked Gwen up after the last practice sat in the car behind mine. A line of smoke snaked out the driver's side window. When it cleared, the man's hungry eyes followed me. I nearly leaped into the backseat to avoid his stare.

That afternoon, as I scrubbed off the day's sweat with lavender soap, my mind replayed practice. Emily laughing and eating and squealing and throwing her crazy self into the middle of everything. Michelle revealing her hidden talent. Brianna's funky dance moves. Gwen's unexpected smile. These invisible strings had bound our team together while we painted our shirts.

The only downer was the set of Gwen's jaw when we left.

I had a feeling that kind of look could only lead to trouble. But for who?

CHAPTER TEN

GONE

When I unlocked the door to the concession stand after school the next day, a blast of acrylic paint odor hit me. I pocketed the key Coach had given me, determined not to lose it while collecting our team shirts. Lifting the nearest one, I whistled. Its rough-edged lettering and splattered image made it ooze with gritty spunk.

"Now, that's what I'm talking about," I whispered, running my fingertips over the stiff surface. I could appreciate that kind of subtle intimidation tactic.

Each shirt highlighted our new nickname—Rally

Cats—but maintained its uniqueness. Emily used fingerprint smudges to add details. One splotch might have been ketchup, but it still worked with her design. Michelle's shirt held neat, symmetrical lines. Whimsical pink showered Brianna's shirt while black dominated Gwen's.

After making a hasty pile of half-folded shirts, I hefted the stash and headed for the locker room. If I laid them along the bench, people could grab them quickly. But first, I wanted to return Coach's key so I wouldn't lose it.

Unfortunately, her office door was shut. Voices drifted out, muffled and brusque. They probably belonged to another unhappy parent. No way I was walking in on that!

Instead, I laid out the shirts in semi-neat clumps. Except I dropped the last one when Gwen exploded into the locker room with the force of a landslide. Dark strands of hair covered her face as she stormed to her locker.

Strange. She came from the direction of Coach's office instead of the academic hallway. Was she the one I had heard? If so, maybe I could return the key now.

As I bent to pick up the shirt—Gwen's shirt—that had fallen on the floor, I spotted black mascara streaks trailing down Gwen's cheeks.

I stopped short. Gwen...crying? What kind of trouble had she stirred up? Who would she take her anger out on this time?

Unease prickled my skin. Something was bothering Gwen. And I was the only one around to see it.

Do to others as you would have them do to you.

Gwen might mock me or yell at me, but nothing would improve between us if one of us didn't budge. But what should I do?

Try to be a friend. Comfort her.

How?

Start with something safe.

Steeling myself, I pulled back my shoulders and held out her shirt. "Your practice jersey turned out nice. Scary and dope at the same time."

She slammed a fist against the metal lockers, rattling them. "Keep it, Loser," she snarled.

What? I lowered my arms. I didn't even know how to be a friend in the face of that kind of ferocity. Still, I had to try. "But...we're wearing them tonight."

Gwen whipped around, eyes wild. "I don't care!" Then she snatched her backpack out of her locker. Throttling it, she stalked out the door.

"Where are you going? We're leaving soon." I trailed after her, not willing to give up. "Are you okay?"

She slammed the door in my face, leaving me blinking in awkward confusion.

A throat cleared behind me, and I turned. Coach stood there, arms crossed and jaw set.

Her intensity made me curl myself in, minimizing my size. "What's going on?"

The anger drained from Coach's eyes. "I'm not allowed to discuss another student's academic progress with you."

Then she paused, as if studying my reaction.

When her words sunk in, I stiffened. She couldn't discuss it, but I could put two rather obvious clues together.

Gwen was on academic probation.

Straightening, Coach stood at her full height. "I need you to set tonight."

The enormity of her words slapped me. "Oh."

Coach patted my shoulder. "School ends soon, and I need

to rethink the lineup. Can you keep the team on task? They won't have much time."

Stomach churning, I nodded. "Only nineteen minutes and thirty-seven seconds."

A smile quirked the corner of Coach's mouth. "That's right."

Numbly, I held out the key. "I'm done with this."

Without another word, Coach took the key, turned on her heel, and left.

I dropped onto the locker room bench, right on top of the nearest t-shirt. Setting? Tonight? I studied my shaking hands. Was I ready? What if I bombed?

And what about Gwen?

Even though she harassed me, the same type of hollow loss crushed my chest as when Judy left. More, because Gwen didn't choose this course of action. She was angry—I witnessed that. But did she also feel despair? Heartache?

I shook my head. I couldn't think about Gwen now. Aunt Tina would set her emotions aside and focus on the game. I envisioned my aunt, a general on the court, barking out orders, directing her teammates. Yeesh, even my mom would have—

Sudden shame flamed into my cheeks. Mom wouldn't have fumbled with words like I did. *Your practice jersey turned out nice.* Lame! Mom would have found a way to encourage Gwen. To help. *We win as a team, and we lose as a team.*

Was it wrong to feel both concern and ambition?

The bell rang, and I flicked away the slender nail I'd chewed off.

Aunt Tina. Mom. Both were right. So I'd do both.

Like Aunt Tina, I'd seize the opportunity and pour one hundred percent effort on the court to reach my dreams.

And since Gwen's academics brought her down, I'd offer

to tutor her. Even if accepting my assistance made her hate me even more, this was one way I could help, like my mom would have done.

Emily bounced in, breaking my mental wrestling. Soon after, the rest of the team followed. A new camaraderie formed as everyone threw their outdated warmup shirts into a sloppy pile and slipped into their edgy new jerseys. Emily even pulled me aside to take a selfie. The ham.

Four minutes and nine seconds later, our bus left the school loaded with our whole freshmen and JV teams...but only ten out of twelve Varsity Rally Cats.

Speculation soared.

"Where is Gwen?"

"Did she miss the bus?"

"Gwen hasn't texted back yet. Is she in trouble?"

"Maybe she's sick."

"What are we going to do if she doesn't show up? She's our starting setter."

I couldn't bear to expose Gwen's trauma. Instead, I closed my eyes and prepared the way Aunt Tina had taught me—imagining myself executing perfect plays over and over.

When we arrived at our rival school, the gym swallowed us whole once again. Countless rows of seats stretched to the ceiling, twisting the sound of volleyballs, cheerleaders, and spectators in a dizzying tornado of motion.

By the time I threw my bag down, Gwen had finally answered Audrey's incessant texts, and Audrey had passed on the news to the rest of the team. She fielded their questions like a movie star addressing reporters. "Gwen can't play tonight. Something came up. No, she didn't say what, but I'm sure it was important. Probably a college interview or something. Or maybe she's at a party, ha-ha. She wishes you all good luck. Yeah, she knows we'll miss her. No way we win without her, but we'll try, right?"

During our hurried warmup, I set the entire time. Even though I wanted to take a few swings, it was more important for me to get comfortable with my latest role. Still, my body itched to slam down the ball. I liked establishing dominance with my spikes before the game even started.

Nervous energy coursed through me as the regular pre-game ritual played out. My body quivered during the national anthem, and a wave a queasiness swept through me. My gaze flicked to the Raider mascot painted on our opponent's center court. Even he seemed to leer back at me, as if doubting my ability to play.

Before we took the court, Coach called us over. "Girls, Gwen is out until further notice."

A few girls shifted, stealing glances at Audrey. She crumpled her nose and shook her head as if to say *don't worry.*

Coach tapped her pen against her leg. "Lucky for us, Lorali started training as a backup setter, so she'll fill in. Lorali, you'll stay in your starting spot. Caroline, you'll start in Gwen's position. Audrey, you'll rotate in front row like before, only for Caroline instead of Gwen. Everything else stays the same. I want to make as few changes as possible."

Audrey glowered. I knew what she was probably thinking. Even with Gwen out, she still wouldn't start. And instead of having Caroline for a setter, Audrey would be forced to hit off of my sets instead.

My throat dried as I considered what kind of spin her dad might give that. *Lorali never sets Audrey because she wants her to look bad.* Or something like that.

"Work together and talk, talk, talk!" Coach yelled over the

growing noise of the crowd. "No campfire moments! If the ball hits the floor, so does everyone else. Wildcats on three."

"No!" Emily cried. *"Rally* Cats on three!"

With an almost feral smile, Coach nodded. Players leaned in eyes wide yet determined. We piled our hands in the middle. "RALLY CATS!"

While the ref checked the lineup, I wiped the palms of my hands on my shirt. *You got this, Lorali.* Brianna high-fived me and Emily flashed a thumbs up.

My stomach dropped.

Our first game didn't go well. We lost 13–25 as our hitters struggled to adjust to my setting style. At least I got the balls in play. The referee only called one double hit on me when I attempted a jump set on a tight pass to the net.

I learned something too. Setters run around a lot during the game. As a hitter, I may or may not touch a ball on any given rally. But setters touched every second ball.

Coach pulled us together before the second game. "Caroline, if the pass is off, set it over short or set Michelle in the back row. Not every time, that's too predictable. Trust your instincts."

"What about when I'm setting?" I asked.

Coach tilted her head. "Set if you can. If it's tight, spike the second ball. The other team doesn't know what you're capable of on the net. They view you as a setter, not a hitter. Let's take advantage of that. Got that?"

I nodded.

"Hope this works." Coach shot a look toward their bench. Then she transferred her attention on us. "Rally Cats on three!"

We mixed our attacks enough to catch the other team flat-footed. Caroline earned a kill setting the ball over on the second touch. Michelle proved to be a respectable back row attacker. But the biggest surprise was me, pounding the second ball three separate times. The blockers weren't expecting it, so no one contested me. The sting the ball left on my hand empowered me.

We won the second set 25–22.

In the third set, the other team anticipated our plays and picked up many of the balls we scored on in the last set. Plus, I missed one of my serves and Michelle missed two. We lost 21–25.

This brought on the fourth set.

"Girls," Coach shouted, "you can win this!" Intensity flooded her words. "Focus on the basics and don't let anything hit the floor. Caroline, set Brianna more often to speed up the offense. Lorali, be alert on defense. As they tire, their hitters have been dinking more often."

With this advice in mind, we forged into the lead. We were up 10–2 before the Raiders started their comeback. They racked up strings of three or four points for every single point we scored.

Unfortunately, the long game went to a deuce. Since no one could win without a two-point lead, we continued to play until our team ran out of subs. That kept Caroline in the game rotating through the front row. On our third round of game point, she went up for a block. She missed, but the ball landed out of bounds, so we won the point.

"Yes!" I pumped my arm, a rush of adrenaline filling me.

"No!" Brianna cried, hands held to her mouth.

Caroline remained sprawled on the floor. Pain etched her face, and she grabbed her ankle.

Brianna wrung her fingers. "I'm sorry, Caroline."

I knelt beside our fallen setter. "What happened?"

"Caroline landed on my foot," Brianna said.

Caroline winced. "I think I twisted my ankle."

My stomach dropped. "Can you play?"

A tear escaped, and Caroline swiped it away. But the pinched look on her face said it all. No.

I rocked back on my heels. No Caroline. No Gwen. Our fourth-game win had brought us to the last set and its special rules. Instead of twenty-five points, winning by two, the first team to fifteen points would win. And I was the only remaining setter left on our team.

CHAPTER ELEVEN

THIS IS WHAT I WANTED

After helping Caroline hobble to the bench, I let the trainer take over.

The sounds and smells of the gym faded away. When I envisioned playing Division One volleyball, this is what I had in mind. A 5–1 offense revolving around an aggressive front-line attack and only one setter, me, who doubled as a hitter in the front row. A cheering crowd. A worthy opponent. The fate of the game in my hands. And here I was, put into that exact situation.

This was what I wanted.

So why did it feel like the world no longer made sense? Why did my hands shake so much?

Around me, time slowed. Drops of sweat hovered, suspended in the air. Bodies moved toward the bench as if trapped underwater. The court stretched out long beside me, then shrank back on itself.

A second later, Coach's raspy voice cut through my numbness, and the noise and chaos of the gym snapped back into place.

"Girls, we have to change tactics again. We run a 5–1 with Lorali."

My stomach fluttered. A 5–1 offense meant one setter running the offense at all times. I wouldn't have an opportunity to hit off a set, but at least when I was in the front row, our middle hitters could swing to the right side for an attack.

Emily twisted her shirt. "Coach! We've only practiced a 5–1 offense a few times."

A cloud descended on Coach's face. "Then you'll recall your role as libero doesn't change. Lorali, can you handle it?"

Chest hitching, I nodded.

"Good." Coach patted Audrey's shoulder. "You'll, take Lorali's spot in the front row. Congrats on your new starting position."

Eyes wide, Audrey stole a triumphant glance toward the bleachers where her parents sat. Using her hands, she signaled to them and mouthed, *I'm starting.*

Coach snapped her fingers, grabbing her attention again. "Audrey, you'll be in the whole game, filling in the defensive spot the setter usually takes in the back row. Remember, the second ball belongs to Lorali."

"What if she can't get there?" Audrey asked, chest puffed. "I'll take it, right?"

"If she can't get there, she'll call for help." Coach pointed. "Then you can bump pass to the hitters, like we practiced."

Audrey frowned. "*I* could set it."

"No," Coach said. "Just keep the ball in play." Coach directed her next comment to me. "Lorali, do your best. We won the toss, so you serve first. Make every point count. Now, let's win this!"

We took the floor, our steps slow. Brianna shifted and Audrey flipped her ponytail. I paced behind the serving line. Maybe our switched lineup would throw off the other team. Maybe we could win a bunch of rallies before they adjusted.

Fifteen points. No room for errors. If we could hold on, I might prove my worth as a setter.

It was a big *if.*

When the referees finished all the formalities, the line judge rolled me the ball. I cradled the leather between my fingers, feeling the unforgiving firmness of the sphere. It held no loyalties. On the first point, their outside hitter pounded the ball down the line. I threw my hands up. The ball ricocheted into the air. Everyone hesitated, waiting for Audrey to step up and take the second ball. Instead, she froze. Coach fumed as the ball dropped campfire style just shy of our own ten-foot line. The score, 0–1, felt like an insult.

After that, the game went back and forth. Coach called a time out when the score reached 12–12. The other team had the ball, and it was a weak rotation for us with Audrey receiving in middle back position. She had shanked the last two serves.

"Audrey, pull up to the net with Lorali and stay put. Leave

only two defenders in the back to receive the ball. Emily, can you pass the ball tight?"

Teeth gritted, Emily nodded. "Tight enough to kiss."

"Good. When the pass comes, Brianna, fly to the right side. Michelle, call for it outside. They'll expect the set to come to one of you. But Lorali, you put it down yourself."

I pressed my lips together. "Attack the second ball? Instead of setting it?"

"Might catch them off guard," Coach said. "Especially with the jump sets you've been using."

She was right. It might work.

"Got it." I cracked my knuckles.

We took the floor again. The serve came, dipping low. Emily dove, scooping the ball high and tight. Our two players went in motion, one screaming behind me, the other flanking the front. As if in slow motion, I leapt to mimic a jump set. Then, twisting my body, I spanked the ball over the net. It hit the floor in front of their libero with a satisfying smack.

With the lead now 13–12, Michelle stepped up to serve. She dropped it short, and the other team scrambled to pick it up, sending over a free ball. Once again, Emily passed the ball tight to the net. This time when I jumped, the blocker lunged with me, anticipating I might strike again. Instead, I tossed it to Brianna. Without blockers, she slammed the ball down. 14–12.

My heart pounded in my throat, threatening to choke me. So close. So close. So close.

If we could just finish it. "C'mon, Michelle!"

The stomping and whistling of the crowd carried away my words, so I flashed Michelle a thumbs up.

It didn't help. Michelle missed her serve. Side out, 14–13.

Licking my lips, I glanced at the server. She usually put

floaters across the net. Deceptive ones, hard to receive, because they presented themselves as long balls, then dropped inbounds near the backline.

Their blockers shifted, obstructing my view. They towered tall and tight on the other side of the net, no doubt trying to intimidate.

But we could still win on this one.

We had to. Otherwise, we'd go into another deuce, where one team had to lead by two points to end the game. I wasn't sure if we owned enough stamina to push our physical limits.

I shoved those negative thoughts aside. All I needed was a good pass.

A good pass? I scanned our team. Audrey was our weakest receiver. If it were me, I'd serve to her.

The referee whistled. The server bounced the ball once, twice. When the ball shot into action, so did I, anticipating where serve would travel, and that Audrey would shank it.

She did.

Setting wasn't an option. My only chance was to get the ball in the air and hope someone could smack it over.

Instinct took over. Throwing my body at the floor, I extended my arm, slapping the ground. Almost simultaneously, the ball connected with the back of my hand, propelling it upward.

In volleyball terms, we call that a "pancake."

In my terms, I call it "the biggest thrill this side of North America."

One step behind me, Emily flailed at the ball, smacking it the right direction. It dribbled over their middle blocker's outstretched hands.

The ball landed.

The whistle blew.

Game over? Game over!

Like a popgun, our bench cleared. Teammates rushed onto the court yelling and jumping on each other. Fists in the air, Coach shrieked her own hoarse holler. From my spot on the floor, I rolled over on my back and screamed.

Game over. Game over! And we won!

Emily reached out a hand and yanked me up. "Rally Cats!" she cried. "Rally Cats! Rally Cats!"

From the bleachers, our parents and fans stomped their feet and joined in. "Rally Cats! Rally Cats!"

The chant pierced every quiet spot that remained in the room.

And believe me, the home side was quiet. Their mighty team with their posh locker rooms, polished hardwood floors, and stylish uniforms had lost to a bunch of ragtag, unranked players.

Unable to contain my joy, I squealed. Then I spotted Caroline hunched in her seat, her foot propped up on an ice pack, and my adrenaline drained.

Two steps rushed me to her side. "Are you okay?" I asked, stomach churning.

She gave a crisp nod, but pain or maybe frustration lingered in her eyes. "I hope so. Because I do not want to spend another second off the court! Man, that was awesome."

She extended her arms and pulled me into a hug. Reaching out, I snagged Emily and Brianna, who caught the others until the whole team encircled Caroline.

"We did it!" Emily screamed.

"You did it," Caroline whispered to me as everyone laughed and hooted. "I'm proud of you."

Her words released a tension in my chest I didn't realize I held. I knew I wasn't the best setter in the world, but her sincere encouragement made my heart swell. Even though Caroline had suffered a personal loss, she was still happy. Is this what respect felt like? Whatever it was, it felt good.

Our bus ride home was the rowdiest we'd had all year. This time, instead of individual people texting, we did group selfie shots and videoed boomerang celebrations to post. Emily asked me to take a video of her clawing the air. She looked like a cat having a seizure.

Scoffing, Audrey stopped her. "Why don't you do something normal?"

"Like this?" Emily shot two fingers at the camera. *"Pow, pow!* Guns blazing. But they have to be squirt guns, not real guns, because that would be socially irresponsible otherwise. Or—" She snapped her fingers. "I could pretend I'm pointing like those flirty guys that wink at you and you want to flirt right back so you cock your fingers like that and click your tongue and say, 'Right back atcha!' and look like a total dork, but who cares because, check-it-out-girls, some cute guy just winked at you. Am I right?"

Stifling a laugh, I clapped a hand on Emily's shoulder. "Do you actually need to breathe *ever?* Like physically stop and fill your lungs once or twice before things spew out?"

With a wolfish grin, Emily nodded. "But sometimes when I start talking, one idea after another pops into my head so fast that my mouth can't keep up with my brain so it seems like a lot of talking but really, it's not, and besides that's a stupid question because if I don't take a breath, I might pass out, which would totally ruin the effect of any of awesome things I say because you'd have to resuscitate me."

Too bad I didn't get all that on camera.

As we rounded the bend toward our school, my spirit soared. Our frumpy-looking building welcomed victors this time. What could get better than that? Then I spotted a familiar dark car waiting in the parking lot. "Wait. Isn't that Gwen's uncle's car?"

Emily, who had launched another avalanche of talking, stopped mid-sentence. "Don't know, don't care. Got bigger things on my mind. Like pizza. Thin crust. Extra-large. Maybe with tacos and donuts sprinkled on top. Do they make pizza like that?"

Pressing my face against the window, I zeroed in on the car. Cigarette smoke snaked from a window. It had to be him.

My mouth went dry. Why was he here? Hadn't Gwen been sent home early? And if Gwen wasn't at home with him and she wasn't with us, where was she?

Quickly, I scanned the other cars. Darkness made it difficult, but when the bus rolled to a stop, I spotted an SUV on the side of the gym. A door opened, briefly illuminating Gwen as she scrambled out. A boy in a baseball cap sat in the driver's side. Probably someone she'd hang with today and ditch tomorrow.

Puzzled, I watched as Gwen pulled up her hoodie and slunk into the shadows. She paused there. What was she waiting for?

The hinged bus door squeaked open with the finality of a dying seal. The old beast rocked as my teammates gathered their belongings and clamored out. Soon, players crowded the area outside the vehicle.

I stayed behind by my window, staring at the place Gwen disappeared. After a moment, she detached herself from the dark wall and slipped into the group. Head ducked she picked her way toward her uncle.

Hot breath tickled my cheek, making me jerk back.

Emily leaned in with a look of intensity. "Do they make spaghetti pizza?"

Letting out a hiss of air, I pushed her away. "In your dreams."

When I turned back to the window, only the smudge of my fingerprints on the glass remained. Gwen was gone.

Chapter Twelve

EXTRA

Adrenaline from our win kept me wired through the night and into the next morning. But as the day progressed, aches and pains appeared in parts of my body I never knew existed. By lunchtime, fatigue smothered me like a massive pile of laundry.

When Emily noticed, she shoved soda and cookies at me. "Caffeine and sugar. The food of the gods."

With a groan, I buried my head.

"Poor kid." Emily stroked my hair. "Yesterday you didn't sub out. Playing the whole time isn't as easy as it looks, is it?"

"No," I whimpered.

"You'll get used to it. But you'll need more calories, or you'll run out of energy. As libero, I eat six times a day."

"You've always eaten six times a day," I muttered, sitting up. "Or more."

Grinning, Emily popped a cookie into her mouth. "An early indication of my libero destiny." The food garbled her words.

"In case I ever doubted it before, let me say this now." I lifted a finger for emphasis. "Setters and liberos work the hardest."

A crumb escaped from the corner of Emily's mouth, and she swiped it with the back of her hand. "Maybe. But the hitters get all the glory."

How could my bleary mind respond to that?

It didn't.

* * *

After school, Caroline arrived at practice with her leg in a cast. "Fractured toe, sprained ankle." She thumped the plaster. It sounded as hollow as the look on her face.

Coach made Caroline hand off balls during drills until she seemed to tire of standing and lowered herself onto the front row of the bleachers.

Playing without Caroline or Gwen forced me to do all the setting again. But the hitters adjusted without complaint. I guess the win had boosted their confidence in themselves. And in me.

At the end, Coach called us together. "Girls, I'm proud of how hard you played last night. You never gave up, even with several strikes against you. Our biggest advantage was our ability to scramble. It's hard to beat a team that keeps the ball in play. It all starts…" She waited.

"…with a pass," we chanted.

Coach continued. "Lorali, kudos on an amazing save—"

"Pancake!" Emily high-fived me. "Too bad we couldn't eat it!"

Coach shot Emily a stern look as if daring her to interrupt again. "Yes. But we got lucky. We still can't run that consistent offense I talked about if our setters must chase passes. We'll need to do better to beat Central on Friday. Now get some rest. See you tomorrow."

Since it was Wednesday, I cleaned up for youth group. Would Taylor be there tonight? And if so, would he remember me?

Just in case, I decided to add a touch of eyeshadow. And extra mascara. After all, Taylor might be dating Terri, but he *did* say I was his second favorite player.

While I applied makeup, Emily pulled out her phone. "I'm checking last night's stats while you two take forever."

"I'm almost ready." Michelle sat on the narrow bench in front of the lockers. "Tying my shoes now."

Emily scooted to make room for her. "You're not the problem," she said, thumbs scrolling over her screen. "Lorali's taking forever, polishing every eyelash. Or is polishing the right word? Maybe she's sharpening them? Or dusting them. Or fluffing them. Or, hey, wow. Brianna had twelve kills last night."

"How many did I have?" I paused, watching Emily's reflection in the mirror.

Michelle peeked over Emily's shoulder. "Seven. Not bad."

My stomach dropped. Typically, I led the team in kills. Fumbling, I capped the mascara. "Let's go."

Emily hefted her backpack. "Brace yourself, Michelle. Lorali's mom probably brought you something disgustingly healthy to eat, but I'll share my fries with you."

* * *

After hiking the stairs to the Loft, I searched the crowd for Taylor. With his energy and quick smile, I pegged him for an extrovert. A burst of laughter from a group of boys pinpointed his position.

Michelle stood close to me, fidgeting with her sleeves. "Now what?"

"We sit." I kept one eye on Taylor while I talked. "Hank clapped for our attention which means we're about to start."

"Hank is our youth pastor," Emily explained, herding Michelle toward a seat.

We plopped down on the nearest couch. Two more girls squeezed in on the end, and five boys settled down on the floor in front of us.

My heart flipped. One of those boys was Taylor. Coincidence? Plausible.

Hank raised his hand, capturing everyone's attention. "Sorry, give me a moment. I left something in the other room. I'll be right back."

After he hustled out, Michelle squirmed, her arms pulled tight to her side. "Maybe we should sit on the floor. I'm squished. Is it always this crowded?"

Emily nodded. "Yes. Because Hank is awesome. And because we've got at least three high schools coming here. And there's food. But I spend enough time on the gym floor. I deserve a cushion." She waved at the other girls on the couch.

"Hi, Jenna. Hi, Hannah. Move over, would ya? I need some room for my friends."

The girls and whoever sat in front of the couch groaned but adjusted their positions.

"Thanks," Michelle murmured. As if appreciating the extra space, she took a deep breath.

"See anyone you know?" I asked.

"I recognize some of them, but I don't know their names."

Taylor leaned back and interrupted our conversation. "Everyone will know your name in about five minutes. Be prepared to introduce yourself. I had to last week."

"What?" Michelle's face flushed. "Emily, you didn't warn me about that!"

"It slipped my mind." Emily's wolfish grin said otherwise. "Simply tell them all your darkest secrets and everyone will adore you."

"Yeah, right," Michelle muttered.

"Kidding!" Emily pulled a bag of M&Ms out of her pocket and tore it open. "I knew you'd react that way. What kind of a friend do you think I am?"

"Crazy," Michelle said.

"Nah, I got you. I told Hank I'd introduce you."

Michelle's body sagged into mine. "Thank you."

Turning, Taylor faced us. "Michelle. You play back row, right?"

Michelle's eyes widened. "Yes. And occasionally front row, especially with some of our team injuries. But I'm not very good. Not like Emily or Lorali."

"Hey!" Emily swatted her on the shoulder. "Give yourself credit. No one on the team is as good as me."

While Emily and Michelle traded figurative punches, I studied Taylor's face. His crooked smile lured me in like a warm house on a cold day. But if he had a girlfriend, why was he interjecting himself into our conversation? Maybe he was just a friendly human being, unaware of his devastating effect on innocents like me. Or maybe, like Emily, he lacked the ability to scale back his personality.

Still, how could I resist finding out more about him?

I cleared my throat to draw Taylor's attention. "I think it's interesting that you only watched us play once, but you seem to remember a lot about our team. Why is that?"

"I guess all those years of watching football highlight films trained my brain to analyze opponents. You should see my sister pry details out of me after a game. She's almost as bad as I am."

I frowned. Cocked my head. "Your...sister?"

Blowing a raspberry, Taylor nodded. "Terri. You met her, remember? My favorite player. The setter."

"T-T-Terri is your sister?" I stuttered.

Taylor arched a brow. "Yeah. Didn't you notice the matching dimples?"

Sister? The room spun. My pulse quickened. *Sister!*

"Well, your sister killed us." Emily wrinkled her nose. "She's really, really, really good."

"She should be." Lacing his fingers together, Taylor cracked his knuckles. "I taught her everything she knows."

The easy smiles between them. The teasing. Their relationship made sense now. *Sister.* And an athlete.

"Get this." I paused for dramatic effect. "She's only a freshman."

Emily's jaw dropped. "What? Dude!"

Before Taylor could respond, Hank returned to the room.

Taylor shifted, leaning back with his weight resting on my legs. I didn't quite know how to interpret that move. Either he already felt super comfortable around me, or he accidentally mistook me for a piece of furniture.

"Sorry for the delay, everyone." Hank's voice quieted the room. "Before we get started, we have a visitor tonight. Emily, can you introduce your friend?"

Emily popped up. "Sure! This is Michelle. She goes to my school and…she plays volleyball…and…she's very organized…and…"

"And we discovered she's an incredible artist," I called out.

Michelle's face turned bright red.

"Welcome, Michelle." Hank inclined his head. "Anything else you want to add?"

Seemingly tongue-tied, Michelle shook her head. "I hate you both," she hissed, but I sensed the smile behind her words.

Never one to waste a good opening, Hank dove right into the lesson. "Last week, we left Joseph in an Egyptian jail. He had been in charge of Potiphar's household. But God had bigger plans for Joseph, which meant his comfortable situation needed to change. A false charge led to his arrest and put him in the right place at the right time to meet two officials in Pharaoh's court—the chief cupbearer and the chief baker.

"Now, like our new friend Michelle, Joseph had a special talent. If you recall, he could interpret dreams. When these two servants joined him in prison, Joseph could have given them a prolix speech about his innocence."

Emily's hand shot up. "What does prolix mean?"

"Marked by an excess of words." Hank paused, letting one side of his lips curl up in a playful smile.

Wide-eyed, Emily whispered, "Snorkel is no longer my favorite word."

Michelle snorted.

"Anyway, Joseph could have fixated on his own injustice,"

Hank continued. "Instead, he noticed their broken spirits and used his unique skill to help them."

Hank's lesson went on to talk about compassion. And humility. And dreams.

I had one big, dreamy guy sitting in front of me who may or may not think of me as an ottoman. As hard as I tried to focus on Hank's lesson, the only thing I remembered was the fact that Terri was Taylor's sister, not his girlfriend.

When the meeting ended, Emily and Michelle raided the remaining food at the snack bar. I took that opportunity to corner Taylor.

"Your sister is an incredible setter." It seemed like a safe opening.

Stepping closer, Taylor turned the full power of his gaze on me. "Like her big brother, she's incredible at a lot of things. But yeah, the kid can set."

I fumbled for more to say. *Stick with what you know.* "I wish I had a third of her skill. Setting isn't as easy as it looks. I never realized how much running around you do. No one thanks you for that."

Taylor crossed his arms. It made his biceps stand out. "Hitters get all the glory."

"For sure!" I chuckled. Chuckled? Why was I chuckling? "Do you think Terri could give me some tips?"

"Wait, what?" Taylor frowned. "Why would you need setting tips? You're a right-side hitter, and a good one too."

"Caroline injured her ankle." I shuffled from foot to foot. "And Gwen is out too. So I'm filling in."

Taylor puffed out his cheeks. "Both setters gone? Oooh, that's got to hurt. Especially losing Gwen. Terri talked about her for, like, five hours after your game. She always evaluates the opposing setter if she thinks they're any good. What happened to her?"

Biting my lip, I considered my answer. "Grades."

Taylor shook his head. "Bad, I assume. I tutored some of my linebacker friends back in the day. Maybe you can do that for Gwen too."

"I actually planned to offer her help," I said. "We'll see what happens."

"Meanwhile, you're stuck setting."

I pulled myself up to my full height. "I actually enjoy it. In fact, I'd love getting tips from your sister."

"The only tips she's likely to give you would be telling you to watch a YouTube video. You're on the opposing team, remember? But I would be happy to help you."

I laughed. "You? An ex-football player?"

A steely challenge hardened his face. "Who do you think taught his little sister all those fancy moves you admire?"

"I thought you were joking about that!"

"Nope. What did you think I do with all my spare time? Knit?"

The tease in his voice made me smile.

"All right." I steepled my fingers. "I'm game. Pun intended. When do we start?"

He grinned. "I'm free this Saturday. Can you meet me on the sand court at Echo Park at ten?"

Not trusting my voice, I nodded.

"Great. Give me your cell phone number then. That way if something comes up, you can text me. Or I can text you."

He handed me his phone, and I typed in my contact information.

"Perfect. Almost done." Holding up his phone, he leaned

close. A warm, musky smell followed him. The hair on my neck rose.

"Smile," he breathed into my ear, then snapped a picture.

A few seconds later, my phone buzzed. An image of the two of us showed on screen. My lips opened in a small smile, but he had a broad grin and one thumb up, almost like he photo-bombed his own shot. *Cute.*

Clearing my throat, I tucked my phone away. "Saturday then. Is that the only time that works for you?"

"I'm too busy on the other days." He didn't elaborate, but he had a spark in his eyes that begged me to prod him.

"Doing what?" I asked.

Taylor quirked an eyebrow. "Knitting."

CHAPTER THIRTEEN

PRACTICE IS PERFECT

"It doesn't make sense." Gwen held her paper at arm's length, as if it had somehow attacked her.

"Pepperoni and peanut butter don't make sense either." Emily stuffed her face with just that combination. "But they work well together. Same with pineapple and maple syrup. Or dark chocolate grilled cheese. Hey, Lorali, can I try your kale chips?"

"Only if you plan on dying a slow, painful, but incredibly healthy death." I held out the unopened snack bag.

"Otherwise, you can donate them to our country's nuclear weapon stockpile."

Emily's nostrils flared. "Never mind. I'll check the vending machines instead."

As soon as Emily wandered off, Gwen dropped her pencil. She lowered her head and massaged her temples. "Good Lord, does that girl ever shut up?"

"No." I inclined my head. *Prolix!* "It's part of her charm. She makes me smile."

"Whatever." Gwen grabbed a plastic fork and stabbed it into at a mound of mashed potatoes. Like a disgruntled factory worker, she smeared the white goo around the platter. "Can I have my phone back?"

I lowered my brow. "When we're done."

"Not fair." Gwen glared at me.

"Hey, I put my phone away too." I shrugged. "No distractions for either of us that way. Now, review the steps I showed you and try it again."

Gwen picked up the assignment again, irritation etched on her face. "Why do we have to do this during lunch?"

"Because you agreed to let me tutor you, and this is the only time I have free. Besides"—I caught her eye. "We need you back on the team."

Shifting in her seat, Gwen scrunched her face in concentration.

"Try reading it out loud." I crossed my arms. "Sometimes that helps."

She frowned but picked up pencil. She used the eraser portion like a pointer. "If an electric motor makes three thousand revolutions per minute, how many degrees does it rotate in one second?"

"And what did you try?"

"I took three thousand and divided it by sixty seconds. That's fifty. But you said my answer wasn't right." Her lips curled into a pout, as if she suspected I had rejected her response for personal reasons instead of the fact it was outright wrong.

"That's the first step, not the final answer." I held up a finger. "Now think about how many degrees are in a circle."

Gwen's eyes glazed over.

Time to switch tactics. Get into her world. "On the volleyball court, when coach tells you to spin around, she asks you to do a what?"

"Turn a three-sixty." Gwen blinked. "Oh. There's three hundred and sixty degrees in a circle."

I nodded. "How can you use that to solve the problem?"

"I take the fifty and multiply it by three hundred sixty?" The question in her voice hung in the air, exposing her uncertainty. This time when she looked at me, it wasn't a challenge. She wanted confirmation.

A strange eagerness bubbled up in me. "Try it."

With a white knuckled grip, Gwen moved the pencil across her paper, then showed me her calculations. "Eighteen thousand."

I raised an eyebrow. "Well done."

Maybe I imagined it, but something resembling a smile slipped across Gwen's face.

Emily interrupted the moment, plopping down next to me. "Anyone want a bag of peanut M&Ms? I bought five of them. That's how awesome I am."

Michelle and I both held out our hands. As if dealing cards, Emily slapped a bag in each.

"There's one for you too." Emily pushed the candy toward Gwen.

She shook her head. "I just want to finish this stupid assignment. I'm not hungry."

"Not hungry?" Emily's eyes lit up, and she reached for Gwen's tray. "Can I have your corn dog then?"

Michelle swatted her hand away. "Emily!"

"What? That's a perfectly good corn dog, and she barely touched it!"

Rolling her eyes, Gwen pushed her plate across the table. "Help yourself. I had a big breakfast."

"Thanks, Gwen. Nobody leaves a corn dog untouched." Emily claimed her prize and took a massive bite.

"Any time," Gwen mumbled.

Near the end of lunch, a phone buzzed in my pocket. Mine or Gwen's? Not knowing made my fingers ache. It might be Taylor. He'd sent me two texts before school.

Eager to check, I tapped the table. "One left. Let's do it."

With a frown, Gwen read the next problem. "Solve for x in this equation—"

Another vibration. And another.

"Is that my phone?" Gwen asked. "Can I have it back now? Say yes."

I hesitated, tempted to give in. But this was the closest feeling to "team" I'd ever had with Gwen.

"Let's finish that problem together," I said instead.

✳ ✳ ✳

Coach poked her head into the locker room before practice and craned her neck to survey the area. "Lorali. Anyone else here yet?"

"No." I twisted my ponytail holder into place. "But Emily

will be here soon. And don't worry—you'll hear her coming. It will sound like the wildebeest stampede from *Lion King.*"

"That's our girl." Coach sat next to me on the bench. "Listen, I have a question for you. I checked on Gwen, and she told me you were helping her with math."

"She told you that?" I asked, lifting my eyebrows.

"Yes. I encouraged her to find a tutor, and I'm glad you took the job."

"Me too," I said, surprised I actually meant it.

"There are still two weeks left in this grading period," Coach continued. "If Gwen gets her grades back up, she can return to the court for the second half of the season. In the meantime, we face at least four games with both setters out. Can you handle that?"

On the job training. My pulse kicked into warp speed. "No problem."

With a sharp glance, Coach studied me. I pulled back my shoulders, trying to look more competent than I felt.

"Good." Coach nodded. "If you play like you did on Tuesday, I bet we finish the season with a winning record. But it's not an easy spot for you to be in, learning a new position. Anyway, don't lose heart, okay?"

"Thanks."

Coach patted my shoulder. "And don't worry. I provided Gwen with a workout schedule to keep herself strong. That way when she returns, she can step right into the rotation. And then we can get you back where you belong—hitting."

My stomach dropped. Coach didn't get it. I *wanted* to set for real. No matter how hard I smacked the ball, I still wasn't tall enough to succeed as a hitter in Division One.

And apparently not skilled enough to make it as a setter either. Otherwise, why yank me out once the cavalry returned?

Would I ever reach my dream?

I clenched my hands. Yes. I would. I'd have to try harder. Prove myself. "Coach, even when Gwen comes back, I would still like to—"

Holding up a hand, Coach cut me off. "Oh, sure, we always need a backup."

Her words fell like ashes on my heart.

The sound of pounding feet echoed in the hallway.

"Here comes our fierce libero, right on time." Coach stood to go. "Nice talk."

Emily burst into the locker room, shattering all hope of further conversation about setting. "Hi, Coach!" She flounced straight to the bathroom.

Pausing in the doorway, Coach pointed at me. "Oh, one more thing. Have the girls planned the next team bonding event?"

I shook my head. "Not yet."

"Good, I have an idea." Coach winked.

From the bathroom came a holler. "I have no idea what you're talking about, but if there's food involved, I'm in."

With an amused grin, Coach yelled back, "There's food involved!"

Emily's celebratory whooping assaulted my ears.

Coach turned to me. "Do you think the team would enjoy playing sand volleyball on Saturday morning around 10:30, and then have a picnic afterwards?"

Saturday? That's when I planned to meet Taylor!

Think fast! "We've been working hard. How about we just meet for the picnic at noon? A little extra sleep couldn't hurt."

"I heard *picnic* and *sleep,* two of my favorite things," Emily said, barging back into the room. "Whatever you've got planned, I'm in! Unless it involves kale. And then it's *kale no!*"

Coach blinked, as if shocked Emily would refuse anything involving food.

I knew better. "You tried my kale chips?"

"Well, yes." Emily fidgeted with the bottom of her shirt. "I accidentally picked up your kale chips because you purposely left them on the lunchroom table, and I figured, how bad can they be? *And* then I purposely opened them up and accidentally ate a handful and found out. Blech."

Coach narrowed her eyes. "Too much detail, Emily. But I like your suggestion, Lorali."

Emily squeaked. "Do you know the last time I went on a picnic? *Forever* ago. But you can't beat the menu. There's potato salad, baked beans, hot dogs, hamburgers, and those weird, wiggly gelatin things you pick up with your fingers—"

"Jell-o?" I said. "Yes, Jell-o. Thanks." Emily took a big breath. "And deviled eggs, strawberries, chips and dip, corn—" She paused mid-sentence and glanced at Coach. "Fair warning. I'm opening up my locker now."

"I'm leaving." Coach made a hasty exit.

Hand on the handle, Emily cocked her head at me.

"Don't worry," I pinched my nose. "I've lived through kale chips. I'll survive the foul stench of your locker."

✳ ✳ ✳

The rest of Thursday flew by like a sonic boom. During practice, my feet only stopped during water breaks. Otherwise, I chased down passes, worked on my jump sets, spotted attackers, and targeted my outside hitters until my fingers ached like overcooked sausages.

As tired as I was, Michelle, Emily, and I still stuck around after practice for more drills. After all, even though my setting had improved enormously over the past week, I still had years of catching up to do.

But those fifteen extra minutes of practice seemed to last for two years. I almost expected someone to hand me my high school diploma at the end.

And when it ended, Coach's corrections chased around my head over and over.

Cradle the ball on all your fingers. Catch and release. Soft touches. Square up. Distribute your weight evenly on the bottoms of your feet so you can quickly change direction. Use your legs. On that backset, push the ball in a J motion...

I don't remember going to bed Thursday night, but I must have because the next thing I knew, my alarm blared.

Hello, Friday. Game day. But I didn't want to move.

My aunt's voice drifted through my mind. *That wall you face is called self-doubt. It's telling you to give up, that you aren't strong enough to make it. You need to ignore its voice and tell yourself, "I can do this. I have more in me. Just one more time. One more time."*

I hit the snooze button and rolled over.

Then I groaned and pushed myself out of bed.

One more time.

CHAPTER FOURTEEN

WEATHERFORD

"College recruiters." Emily leaned close and pointed.

My eyes followed the length of her arm. On the far side of the bleachers sat an isolated man and another one a few rows above him. "They're easier to spot than rainbow sprinkles on vanilla ice cream."

I wrinkled my nose. "Are you sure?"

"Yup. Old-fashioned clipboards for note-taking. Baseball caps with a college logo on it. A matching college shirt. And a knowledgeable air."

Biting my nail, I studied them. "They look as serious as Supreme Court Justices and, honestly, a little bored."

"Nothing a treat from the concession stand can't fix." Emily sniffed. "We should order them Supreme Nachos. Think of the entertainment value, trying to get beef and cheese *and* a jalapeño in every bite."

As soon as she brought them to my attention—the recruiters, not the nachos—I couldn't focus completely on warmups, the anthem, or game introductions. I could almost feel their gaze following me, judging my every move. Even though I knew better. Skills could be taught. Height couldn't. No, the 6'5" middle hitter from Weatherford probably held their interest.

But just because they might have come to watch her didn't mean they wouldn't notice other players. After all, with a limited number of bodies on the court, it would be hard to overlook someone who made an outstanding play. And the gym, the crowd, the noise, the pressure, the game? This was where I shined.

If only my hands would stop shaking.

When we stepped onto the court, Audrey took full advantage of her new starting status. She waved to the crowd, then paused to point to at someone in the audience and give a secret nod. "Politician on a campaign" move for sure. At least her dad wouldn't have a reason to yell at Coach now.

But I understood her pregame excitement. Stepping next to her, I lifted a hand for a fist bump. "I'm counting on you to hold down the right side."

Beaming, she tapped my knuckles. Her reaction was a pleasant surprise.

The line judge rolled the ball to me, and I scooped it up on my way to the end line. Fatigue forgotten, I cupped it in my hands and waited for the serving whistle.

We lost the first set 15–25. Without Gwen, Audrey had to play back row too, and she struggled with her passing. Plus, Weatherford's height and speed left our defense looking tentative.

Yet despite the way we slouched on the bench sucking water bottles and wiping sweaty hands on our spandex, Coach's fire never wavered.

"Now that you got all those jitters out of you..." Coach paused to sweep her eyes around the huddle. "It's time to execute our game plan. We're the *Rally* Cats. So let's keep those rallies going. Show them your claws. Emily, if Lorali fields the first ball, do a back row set, like we practiced. Or Audrey, you could bump set the ball, but only as a last resort. Blockers take away the line shot and let Emily pick up the hard-cross court. Brianna, shut down that middle."

Wide-eyed, Brianna let out a hiss of air. "But she's *five inches taller* than me and—"

Coach's steely glare cut her off. "Then play six inches tougher."

Nostrils flaring, Brianne's swift nod showed her determination.

Leaning in, I rasped over the noise of the crowd. "This game, we make them pay for every point they earn."

"And we charge them double," Emily added with a growl.

Backs straightened. Chins lifted. Eyes narrowed.

While the ref checked our lineup, a splinter of a thought lodged in my brain. Taylor analyzed players. So did I. What if our opponents did too? Could I bait them, plant a pattern, make them anticipate a move, then turn it around on them?

Plausible.

True to our new nickname, we rallied in the second game. In the backcourt, Emily was a beast, and she carried her insatiable hunger with her everywhere. Each time a hitter attacked, she materialized, a solid brick of a monster, whipping out her limbs, forcing the spikes to ricochet in the air with an audible smack. Sweat greased her impossible moves. Unfazed by their continuous assault, she slapped the floor with defiance between plays, spurring us on.

Her digs also made my job easier. Since I didn't have to chase as many passes, I could run the offense more consistently. I spread out the sets between the players, sending backsets to Audrey even when it wasn't the most fluid choice because I hoped to catch a lazy blocker off-guard. When the 6'5" player threatened to dominate the net anyway, I relied on Emily or Michelle to run a back row attack.

And I introduced the bait. Me.

As often as possible, I purposely attacked instead of setting on the second touch when I rotated through the front row. The success and frequency of my move established a pattern I believed Miss 6'5" would be motivated to disrupt.

At game point, my plan worked. When Emily passed the ball tight, I approached the ball like I had before. Their middle leaped with me, anticipating a spike. But instead of pounding it, I dinked the ball right over her long fingertips.

Although I would have enjoyed a campfire moment on the other side of the net, I still got great satisfaction from the loud squeak of tennis shoes on the hardwood floor as three defenders dove for the ball and the pleasant *thump* of the wayward sphere landing.

We won the second set 25–23.

I think our victory shocked the socks off the entire gym. The other coach slammed her clipboard on the ground.

Going road-rage overboard, she screamed at the refs, the line judges, and anyone else who got within earshot. Her two assistant coaches scrambled to calm her down, grabbing at her arms before she threw something else. Shrugging them off, she turned on her players instead.

Our fans went nuts. Some used their phones to record the tirade. Others chanted and stomped, creating a roar loud enough to drown out the rants of the opposing coach. "Rally Cats! Rally Cats!" My heart pounded in rhythm to their cries.

In the midst of all the turmoil, Coach pulled us into a huddle. Cocking her head toward our still fuming opponents, she raised an eyebrow at us. A feral smile snaked across her face. "Anyone want to do that again?"

"YES!" we all screamed.

"Then I say—" Coach's voice took on a dangerous quiet. We trembled, sweet anticipation coursing through us, waiting for the words she whispered next.

"Do it."

Coach had us worked into a frenzy, but Weatherford's coach didn't do them any favors. During the next game, her frequent outbursts seemed to undermine her team's confidence. They played at an almost panicked pace, snapping at each other and cringing whenever the ball dropped. We took set three 25–21.

By the time set four started, their coach's rage had turned inward. One glance showed her jaw clenching tighter and tighter and her face turning redder and redder, until it looked like someone had shoved her lips into a vise and screwed it tight.

Unfortunately for us, teams like Weatherford don't stay down for long. Sooner or later, they regain their composure. Our surge of energy waned, and we lost the fourth set 25–18.

When we took the floor for the final set, my legs shook with exhaustion. All the extra practice and loss of sleep left little energy reserves in my body.

Sucking in air, I glanced at the recruiters. No longer lounging, they perched on the edge of their seats, bodies rigid boards. They were watching. This was my chance.

The line judge handed me the ball.

Come on, Lorali. One more. The night belongs to you. You can do this.

When the whistle blew, I gritted my teeth, tossed the ball, and served. The ball shot from my hand, a bullet straight into the net.

My missed serve burst our momentum. We lost 15–9.

As the home crowd erupted around us, pouring onto the court to celebrate, I fisted my hands. Another loss. A blown opportunity. I worked so hard and had nothing to show for it but bruises on my elbows and an empty feeling in my gut. Acid burned my throat, threatening to choke me. Why did God give me this drive, this desire, only to fail? How could I serve Him if I couldn't even serve the ball?

Emily pushed me. "Stop beating yourself up, Lorali."

Ignoring her, I shot a dark look at their team. "The way they're celebrating, you'd think they'd won the National Championship instead of barely beating a team everyone expected them to slaughter."

"Lorali!" Emily grabbed my shoulders. "Snap out of it. It's just a game."

I tried to shrug her off, but she held on, relentless as a bulldog. "Hank says to trust in the Lord with all of your heart. Lean not on your own understanding."

Those words grounded me like a slap. Bowing my head, I

released my pent-up adrenaline and grief. A dull ache settled in its place. "You're right. I'm sorry."

"I'm always right." Emily loosened her grip. "Besides, I bet that 6'5" girl is relieved they pulled it off. Look at those sharks circling her."

Sure enough, the two recruiters had cornered the girl with her parents. Heads nodded and business cards traded hands. The girl held herself with easy, confident grace. Her parents hovered beside her, probably interrupting to supply her impressive stats. The coach, oily pride restored to her smug face, seemed to bask in the limelight.

"You know what you need?" Emily poked me. "Food. C'mon, let's see if the concession stand is still open. Sometimes at the end, they sell the sandwiches cheap to get rid of them."

"You go. I'm not hungry."

Emily shrugged. "Your loss. Or your second loss tonight since we already lost. Or third since that coach lost her patience. Or fourth since you lost your cool. Which, by the way, doesn't make you a loser, just a winner who lost face." She cocked her head and grinned. "Which would be the fifth loss. And now sixth since I just lost my train of thought. At least, I think so." She paused, gaping at the ceiling, then snapped her mouth shut. "I need food."

As she tromped off, I sighed. Why did I take defeat so much harder than Emily? I remember when we were younger, we both went to a birthday party. I tried with all my eight-year-old strength to reach the ribbon dangling from the bottom of a helium balloon in the living room, but no matter what I did, it floated beyond my reach. I stewed over that balloon all afternoon, even abandoning the Bingo game to try different retrieval maneuvers.

But Emily? She took a few swipes at it, then laughed it off

and went for the cake. Just like now. She moved on while I still reached for the unreachable balloon.

Habit sent me to fetch my gear. My phone vibrated, and I checked the screen.

Taylor: Terri's team won in three sets. How did your team do?

Without answering, I tossed the phone back into the bag and lowered my head into my hands. *Dear God, why does everything I want always seem so unobtainable? Please help me discover what I need to do to be successful.*

While we gathered up our supplies, Coach talked to one of the recruiters. An old friend maybe? They looked about the same age.

My phone buzzed again. Taylor had sent a selfie of him doing the Heisman pose in front of the nets.

I took a deep breath. *Trust in the Lord. Move on.*

Me: Did you win the knitting MVP award?

Taylor: Of course. Call me later?

The hard spot in my stomach didn't move.

Me: Too tired.

Taylor: <frown face>

Me: But I can't wait to see you!

Taylor: Tomorrow. <smiley face>

Me: Talk soon.

On the bus ride home, no one spoke. No one laughed. No one took selfies.

When my phone buzzed again, I muted it. I plastered my face against the unyielding pane of the window and fell asleep.

CHAPTER FIFTEEN

TAYLOR TIPS

The next day came too soon.

"I'll pick you up at 2:30," Mom called through the open car window. "Where is this *friend* you're meeting this morning anyway?"

Shifting my backpack, I checked the area. "Taylor texted that he was at the sand courts."

Mom squinted past me at an approaching figure. "Is that Taylor?"

I whirled around.

My new trainer sauntered closer, dressed in baggy shorts,

a tank top, and sunglasses. Without thinking, I waved, then yanked my hand down. I didn't want to seem overeager.

To my relief, Taylor waved back.

Relaxing, I glanced at Mom. "Yes, that's Taylor. Do you want to meet him?"

Mom shut the motor off. "Absolutely."

We climbed out of the car and intersected him on the footpath.

"Hello, Lorali's mom." Taylor extended his hand. "Nice to meet you."

"Ms. Mathews is fine. Are you ready to play?"

"I am." A broad smile dimpled his cheeks.

My heart may or may not have beat faster. I'm not telling.

Mom held her purse in front of her like a shield. "Lorali says you're teaching her setting skills."

"Yes. My sister plays volleyball for Jefferson, so I picked up a thing or two."

"And you also go to youth group at our church?"

"Wouldn't miss it."

Mom smiled. "Wonderful."

We spent ten more minutes talking about everything from his favorite school subject—literature apparently—to the politicians in his old state.

Finally, Mom sighed. "I'll let you two go. Thanks for helping Lorali. You'd think she'd had enough volleyball this week, but sadly, no. After this, she's got a team bonding event."

"She warned me already." Taylor nudged my shoulder.

Heat tingled down my arm and settled in my fingertips. I stepped away from him so the rest of my body didn't burst into flames. But not too far away. I can handle a little heat.

As we headed for the court, I licked my lips. "Sorry my mom grilled you."

"I can't blame her." Lowering his sunglasses, he winked at me. "She probably wanted to make sure it was safe to leave you with a boy she's never met."

I chuckled. *Wait! I'm chuckling again? Why isn't that out of my system?* "Since I'm investing my time here instead of studying, she's probably more concerned about whether or not you know your way around a volleyball court."

That seemed to amuse him. "Lucky for you, I look good on paper."

"Yeah." Then, after an uncomfortable pause, I cleared my throat. "I'm sorry I didn't call you after the match last night. It's been a long week."

"Translation: You lost."

"Yup."

"Did you have fun?"

For a moment, I couldn't breathe. Did he read my mind? "My aunt always used to ask me the same question." A twinge of sorrow pricked my heart, and I paused to let it pass. "My answer was always yes. And it's still yes, a compulsive yes. I can't get enough. But honestly—" I swallowed. "Sometimes I want to scream when we keep losing no matter how hard we work."

"Hey, I know what you mean," Taylor said. "Sometimes football was like that too. It's not that volleyball's not *not* fun. But sometimes it's not fun."

"Exactly." I stopped at the edge of the first court. "Are we using this one?"

"Yes. This one. Not *not* that one," he said, straight-faced.

I couldn't help it. I burst out laughing.

When my giggles subsided, he offered me a water bottle. "It sounds like you have an interesting relationship with volleyball."

Shaking my head, I tried to explain my feelings. "Volleyball is like a roller coaster ride. The dips and loops can rip your insides out, you dread each slow incline because you know the big drop that follows, and you wonder what you were thinking when you locked yourself in. But as soon as the ride's over, you hop in line and go again. Because as traumatic as a roller coaster ride is, you love the rush."

"Until you vomit?"

I nodded. "Until you vomit." Not sure what to say next, I pulled my sweatshirt over my head, swishing my ponytail to free my hair.

Taylor watched me, rolling the ball between his hands. "I get your frustration. But that doesn't explain why you didn't call me last night."

"I was physically and emotionally exhausted." I stretched my arms over my head, then folded them behind my back. A twinge forced me to relax my muscles.

"Any sport takes a lot out of you." Taylor pushed the sand with his toe. "I remember our extreme summer football sessions. I'd get up before five in the morning five days a week for cardio and weight training. Then we had mid-day practice in the hottest part of the day, and scrimmages after that. At least we didn't wear full pads until August."

Football wasn't the only demanding sport. I'd played in volleyball tournaments where pool play lasted from eight in the morning to ten at night—and then bracket play started bright and early the next day. Still, even running on six hours sleep and adrenaline vapors, I couldn't get enough of the game. "You sound just like me and volleyball. I live and breathe it."

Peeling off his sunglasses, Taylor rubbed his eyes. "Enjoy it while you can. My whole life revolved around football. And then the concussions came, and poof! Gone."

The end of his football career was probably like getting an arm cut off. His life had to change. His routines. His eating habits. Maybe even his friends. How did Taylor deal with losing something he loved so passionately?

I searched his eyes for regret but found only hooded shadows. Shielding my face with my hand, I squinted toward the sun. "I bet you miss it."

"Sometimes." He slipped his sunglasses back on. "Every fall I get an itch to grab a helmet. I scratch the itch with season tickets and body paint."

With awkward hesitancy, I reached out and patted his shoulder. "I'm sorry."

For a moment, he leaned into my touch, as if absorbing my sympathy.

Before things got weird, I pulled back and grabbed the ball out of his hands. "Ready?"

"You don't mess around with small talk, do you?"

"We can talk and play at the same time." I juggled the ball with one hand, mentally tracking each tap "I want to see if you're as good in real life as you are on paper."

"I am. I thought I already established that fact."

"We'll see." I held the ball, feeling playful. "Warm up first?"

"Always." He rubbed his hands together. "Then *I'll* see what *you've* got. My skills are not in question here."

His sudden animation sparked my competitive instincts. Maybe this guy wasn't all dimples and talk. Maybe I could learn a thing or two from him. "Based on what?"

He snorted. "Based on my reputation as an incredible knitter."

Laughing, I flicked the ball toward him.

We peppered for fifteen minutes, and then he pushed me through a series of drills. Slogging across the court reminded me why I preferred indoor to sand volleyball. A vat of molasses would have been easier to navigate.

Meanwhile, Taylor cut through the court with ease. And he was good. His sister didn't own a fraction of the skill he possessed. If he knitted as well as he played, he'd be the Picasso of potholders.

Finally, he called for a water break.

I plopped down next to him in the grass. "So what do you think?"

He took a swig from his water bottle. "You have a lot of natural athletic talent and a hard work ethic."

"But...?" I paused. "I feel like there's a *but* coming." My face grew hot. "I mean, not a *butt* but, but a *but* but." Yeesh. I really couldn't form sentences today.

Taylor capped his bottle. "There is a but. You're talented, *but* your sets are slow."

I plucked a piece of grass and twisted it. "Sets can be slow?"

"How fast the ball comes out of your hands involves your wrists." Lifting his arms, he demonstrated while he explained. "Basically, you 'catch' the ball, bend your wrists, and then let the ball spring out of your hands. If you bend your elbows too much, it affects your speed and accuracy."

I studied my fingers as if they'd betrayed me.

"Try using your legs and wrists more. Bend your arms less. Do it enough times, and your body will develop muscle memory."

Groaning, I flopped backwards. "I've got so much more to learn."

"Don't be too hard on yourself." Taylor sprawled out next

to me, stretching like a cat, which I found oddly attractive. Even though I'm a dog person.

"You've been setting for…how long?" he asked.

"Not long enough, apparently."

"You'll get better. Do you want a turn at hitting now?"

"Really?" I rolled over, waiting for confirmation.

At his nod, I jumped to my feet and ran to the imaginary ten-foot approach line.

Taylor took the setter spot at the net and motioned for me to toss the ball. After I lobbed it to him, his perfect fingers pushed the ball in a perfect arch to the outside corner of the court.

Barely able to hold contain my frenzy, I powered through my approach. The ball lingered right above the woven grid until I spanked it. With a thud, the sand cushioned my spike.

I clapped. "You have no idea how good that felt."

Grinning, he hunched under the net to fetch the ball. "Oh, I have *some* idea. Again?"

"Yes!"

Taylor held up a hand. "Calm down! Once Gwen raises her grades and comes back, you can hit your heart out."

I wrinkled my nose. "What do you mean?"

"I mean—" He paused. "You sound mad."

"Just tell me what you mean," I repeated, voice level.

He scrunched his face like a child caught stealing a cookie. "I know you embraced the role of setter to help your team. But I assumed when Gwen came back, you'd go back to what you do best. Hitting. Are you still leading the team in kills?"

Shifting my eyes down, I shook my head. Strange how my stomach dropped.

Taylor stepped closer. "No offense, you're a decent setter. But you are an amazing hitter. When I watched your game against my sister, I couldn't keep my eyes off you. Those line shots. So tough to defend. Explosive. You were like..." He paused, rubbing his chin.

"Like what?" I prompted.

"A crazed airborne piranha shredding the net."

That image tickled my imagination. I kinda liked it. But still. "I want to set."

His face stilled, and he moved closer, his breath warming my cheek. "Why?"

I flushed, searching his face for any signs of mockery. But he seemed sincere. Of course, an athlete or top-rated knitter would understand the kind of physical, social, and sleep sacrifices you had to make to excel.

"I want to play Division One volleyball." The sudden admission rushed out. "And the best chance I have of getting recruited is as a setter. So, I'm throwing everything I've got at it."

Holding my gaze, he smiled, slow and languid. Then he stepped back, scooped up the ball and gave it a determined slap. "That's exactly the way I felt about football. So, if that's what you really want, I'll help every Saturday as long as you need me. But for the record, I think you could make it as a Division One hitter."

My face burned at his unexpected compliment. "It would take a miracle."

He sighed. "Oh, ye of little faith. Okay, setting it is. Let's make a plan."

"I have a plan." I tilted my head. "Why do you think I'm here this morning?"

"I-I thought you might be interested in—" He slid his sunglasses on top of his head. Gulped. "Never mind."

What had he been about to say?

After blowing out a breath, he started over, this time with a lighter tone. "I mean, obviously, you're here because besides befriending an amazing, incredibly interesting, and talented new kid like me, you want to tap into my vast expertise as you plot to take over the volleyball world."

"Volleyball universe," I corrected.

"Universe? Whoa." Taylor took a step back. "You give me a lot of credit. What if I've already taught you everything I know about setting?"

"Then you're useless to me and should leave now," I said, deadpan.

His eyes widened.

"Kidding. Honestly, it's nice to talk to someone who understands. Besides, it's not often I get to hang out with a world-class knitter."

That ready smile returned. "You got that right."

"And yes, I'll take that Saturday lesson offer."

"Right. About that. What's in it for me?"

I considered the offer. "I bake decent chocolate chip cookies. How about a dozen cookies for each lesson?"

"What if I don't want cookies?" His eyes held a mischievous glint.

I scoffed. *"Everyone* wants cookies."

"What if *I* want you to go to a movie with me tonight?"

My brain stalled like an old car.

"And you make me cookies," he added.

I found my voice. "That's a tough bargain."

He shrugged. "I'm worth every chip."

"You'd better be."

A car honked from the parking lot. Michelle and Emily's voices carried our way. Had it already been two hours?

Taylor followed my gaze. "Sounds like your team is showing up. I should go. See you at six?"

I cocked my head. "That's dinner time at my household."

"Wow, and you said I drove a hard bargain!" Taylor pocketed his keys.

"What?"

"It's fine." He waved a dismissive hand. "I get your hint. I'll join you for dinner before the movie."

"But—"

He touched a finger to my lip. "Say no more. I'll see you tonight."

I froze, mouth gaping. I'm not used to being taken by surprise like that. I'm sure his vision of me as a piranha lost to the image of me as a floundering fish.

I was just as articulate as one too.

CHAPTER SIXTEEN

GODZILLA

Even surrounded by my teammates, I couldn't get Taylor out of my head.

Meanwhile, Emily polished off two hamburgers, a hot dog, and a plate crowded with what looked like the aftermath of an explosion in the snack aisle. She even squeezed in extra dessert—a birthday cake for Gwen dubbed "Death by Chocolate" because of all its gooey richness.

Later, we played a game called *Heads Up!* One player held Coach's cell phone on her forehead and faced her team. A word popped up and teammates shouted clues to describe it. In sixty seconds, the player guessed as many words as possible. On

Emily's turn, her first word was *Einstein.* We yelled scientist, crazy hair, E=MC2, great inventor. She guessed *Frankenstein, Mark Twain, R2D2's mama,* and *the guy who created M&Ms.*

No points for her, except for scoring laughs.

Our picnic was the first time in a long time I breathed stress-free air.

When it ended, I grabbed Emily and Michelle and took a happy selfie to send Taylor. He should see my fun side before our date.

* * *

On the ride home, I told Mom about the bargain I had struck with Taylor. And, of course, asked permission to go out on the date. She hesitated, chewing on the inside of her mouth. She finally agreed but insisted on recruiting Emily and Em's cousin Mark to tag along.

Talk about mortifying. Not one, but two escorts!

Still, the idea of having Emily with me soothed the butterflies that insisted on camping out in my stomach. After all, if the conversation lagged, she'd fill in.

When Taylor arrived, Emily threw open the door with a cringe-worthy bang. Without pause, she yanked him inside. "Taylor! I can't believe you're going with us to *Godzilla 16.* This is going to be so much fun!"

A frown creased his brow. "Us?"

"Uh, surprise." I smoothed my shirt. "Group date."

His eyes narrowed. "Wait. Did you say *Godzilla 16?*"

Emily prickled. "Please don't tell me you wanted to see *Romaine-E-O and Vinaigrette* instead. I like comedies, of course, who doesn't, because, duh, they're funny, but I crave action slash adventure. Besides, did you see the *Godzilla* trailer? The CGI in the movie is so good. Godzilla looks real. I mean, actual mucus comes out of his nose. Plus, there's a new monster, some type of mutant beetle. Except I can think of a lot scarier bugs than a beetle, can't you? Like a walking stick. Those things give me the shivers. So long and skinny and sticky. And my cousin Mark, he's over there someplace, he's coming with us, but he has been *dying* to see *Godzilla* for like two whole days."

"One." Mark didn't lift his eyes from the electronic game in his hand.

"See?" Emily pointed. "He can't wait."

Taylor laughed. "Oh, Lorali, I like this girl. We are going to have a blast."

My legs sagged with relief.

Mom took charge. "I'm treating tonight to thank you for helping Lorali. She's got money to cover dinner, and the movie passes are on her phone."

Shaking his head, Taylor met my eyes. "Thank you. That's very generous."

I leaned close. "I hope *Godzilla's* okay."

"If that's what *you* want to see," he whispered.

"Yes, she wants to see *Godzilla,*" Emily whispered, linking an arm through mine.

Taylor straightened, putting space between us. "No problem. Ms. Mathews, may I give you my phone number in case you need to reach me?"

A smile warmed Mom's face. "Of course."

Following ten more minutes of awkward niceties, we piled into Taylor's Honda Civic and headed out to Arnie's Pizza Parlor. We ordered their famous Maui Zowie pizza with ham, pineapple, BBQ sauce, and cheese. While we waited,

Emily summarized every Godzilla movie ever made. She only stopped when platters with steaming, gooey pizza arrived.

Taylor separated out pieces. After lifting one onto a plate, he passed it to me, then sectioned off another slice for Emily. "How was the team picnic?"

Between the two of us, we relayed all the craziness of the day. Emily got louder and more animated with each passing moment until she suddenly stopped like a bird smacking into a glass windowpane.

"The end," she said.

"Wow." Taylor wiped his fingers on a napkin. "My sister's team never does fun activities. They practice like it's a low-paying job."

"A *no*-paying job." I scooped up a fresh slice of pizza and plopped it on Taylor's plate.

He nodded his thanks and reached for the Parmesan cheese. "It's okay. My sister is like you, Lorali. She wants to play at a Division One school as a setter. And that doesn't come without a lot of hard work."

Emily cocked her head. "Lorali's not a setter. She's a hitter."

"She kills it," Mark agreed, eyes on his game.

Taylor snapped his fingers and then pointed at me. "That's what I said."

Face heating, I looked down.

Suddenly quiet, Emily examined her pizza crust, rolling it between her fingers. "A college scout is interested in me."

A jolt shot through my body. "What? Who? When? Why didn't you tell me?"

"You forgot 'where' and 'how,'" Mark muttered.

"One of them talked to Coach after the Weatherford game." Emily's nostrils flared. "Apparently they were shocked someone could dig Miss 6'5" spikes."

"I can't believe you didn't tell me!" I cried.

Gnawing on the crust, Emily grunted. "It doesn't matter. The recruiter's school doesn't have the academic program I need. I'm not going to give up my plans to be a dentist just so I can play volleyball for a few more years."

Taylor choked on his soda. "You want to be a *dentist?*" He coughed back his laughter, taking big, gasping breaths. "I'm sorry, but I can't imagine that."

"That's why she's always pushing candy," I said. "She'd trying to build a future generation of customers."

"I'm happy to give you a root canal any time." Emily's smile was all sweet innocence.

While Emily giggled over her own joke, a combination of emotions ambushed me. Recruiters noticed Emily. My heart warmed with genuine happiness for my friend. But I wished I could hear the same news. And I worried that my window of opportunity would close.

Taylor seemed to sense my warring reactions. Eyes trained on me, he elbowed Mark. "I'll give you ten bucks to try those old arcade games in the back room."

Mark's thumbs hovered mid-air. "They're classic. But outdated."

Leaning closer, Taylor waved the money. "Exactly. How often do you get to experience the pixilation and sounds of the original Pac-man?"

Raising his eyes, Mark set down the device. He reached for the bill like a zombie coming to life. "Okay."

As Mark headed toward the change machine, Taylor bumped Emily. "Can you beat him?"

In response, Emily grabbed her soda and then scrambled out of the booth. "I will pulverize him."

As soon as they were out of earshot, Taylor cocked his head. "You seem like you're in shell shock. Are you okay?"

Nodding, I twisted my napkin between my fingers. "I don't know how to react. I'm proud of Emily. But she doesn't seem to care about something I'd give anything to be offered. Which makes me feel...I don't know. Anxious? Afraid? Desperate? And then I feel bad about feeling that way because I know I should feel happy. Does that make sense?"

"Actually, it does." He raked his fingers through his hair. "When my old football team won the conference championship, I was happy for them, but sad too, because I wasn't truly part of the victory. It was a warm joy mixed with a hollow kind of longing. Like sand slipping through your fingers."

A fleeting frown crossed his face, and he shifted in his seat as if the field still haunted him. "Anyway, my dad noticed, and he suggested I help to train Terri, maybe to keep me busy. So I did. That's when I discovered there's more to life than football."

Lifting my eyes, I smiled. "Like knitting?"

He grinned. "Something like that. My point is, God obviously had a different plan for me. Maybe God has a different plan for Emily. Maybe God has a different plan for you too."

Though I'm sure he meant his comments to reassure me, doubt bubbled up instead. Was I making a mistake pursuing setting?

As if sensing my inner turmoil, Taylor pushed away his plate and leaned close. "Give your fears and feelings to God. In the meantime, enjoy some pizza and a movie. We'll celebrate Emily's success and keep hoping for yours."

"What if no one wants me to play for their college?"

Mischief raced across his face. "There's always room in the Knitting Club."

He rested his hand on top of mine. A chill ran up my spine at his touch, the kind of rush I get before a game starts.

I traced his knuckles with my fingertip. "You're right." I sighed. "I guess I'll keep working my hardest and hope for the best. Gwen's kind of in the same situation. Working hard on her math. Hoping to get back to the court." It was weird, empathizing with her.

"Maybe she'll give you some setting tips."

"She's more likely to stab me with a fork," I said.

"Then you're stuck with me. Every Saturday, remember?" He tucked a stray hair behind my ear, then cupped my chin. "Do the best you can, but don't stress over it. Just make sure your heart is in the right place, and then follow it."

A soft, musky smell filled the space between us. My skin prickled.

Emily and Mark chose that moment to return. Blushing, I sat back.

"We're out of money, and it's time to go!" Emily clapped her hands. "Come on, come on, come on, people. Godzilla awaits. And I don't want to miss anything. Maybe they'll show a preview for that new documentary *Scar Wars: An In-depth Look at Plastic Surgery.*"

"I want to see the preview for *Ice-SCREAM,* the cool horror movie," Mark muttered, head again buried in his electronics.

Lucky for us, the theater showed both previews.

And for the record, there was a giant mutant walking stick in the Godzilla movie. It worked like a radio antenna drawing in all the Titan monsters. When it crawled onto the screen, Emily's shriek made my heart stop.

I'm sure she'll experience nightmares for months.

CHAPTER SEVENTEEN

NEW PRESSURE

After two more weeks of the daily grind, Gwen showed up at practice. Our tutoring sessions had paid off.

When she stepped into the gym, our team crowded around her, high-fiving and hugging her.

As usual, Emily bubbled with enthusiasm. "Yay, you're back! Why didn't you tell us at lunch? Oooh, I bet you wanted to surprise us."

"I just got used to the timing of Lorali's sets." Brianna crossed her arms. "Now I'll have to readjust to yours again."

"Don't worry." Gwen pulled Brianna to her side the way she might a lap dog. "It'll come back to you in a snap."

Brianna broke out in a wide smile. "Glad you're back! I missed that sass."

Lingering in the back of the group, my heart ached. Even though Gwen's reinstatement meant I could get a proper opportunity to hit, I longed for my teammates to embrace my setting the same way. Such an odd mixture of emotion bred uncertainty in my heart.

God, please help me discover what I need to do to be successful.

Success. I shook my head. Any athlete knows, when challenges come your way, positive thinking equips you to overcome them and leads to success. As Aunt Tina once said, "Believe in yourself. Trust your training. Play with confidence."

And work even harder I added squaring my shoulders.

With Gwen on board, we shared the setting duties in a 6–2 offense. Coach started Gwen in her regular position and sent me to my old spot in left front. That lineup put Audrey back on the bench rotating in for Gwen in the front row when I moved into the back row as setter.

Audrey didn't complain, but she didn't look happy either.

As practice progressed, my eyes followed Gwen's moves. She hadn't lost a step. I hadn't fully found mine yet. She was flat stone skipping across the water and I was a boulder lodged in quicksand. Maybe I should give up setting and return to the more comfortable role.

No. Not yet. Not while I still had a chance to pull it off.

I threw myself into practice. My chest heaved. My muscles tensed. When Gwen moved, I moved, matching her footing and motion.

Gwen seemed to notice my efforts and, with a sour look, pushed herself harder.

So did I. I didn't execute my sets as well as she did. Yet.

The pace didn't ease until Gwen got caught in another campfire moment.

Coach puffed her cheeks. "Gwen! You've got to pick those up. Ask Lorali to give you tips on defense."

That suggestion earned me a face-melting glare from Gwen. By now, I knew her well enough to interpret it. Coach had called her out. And Gwen hated admitting she needed help, especially from a sophomore.

If we were going to turn this season around, we had to heal this tension. Change started with me. I decided to talk to her.

Catching Gwen alone proved tough since Audrey clung to her side most of practice. But finally, during our water break, I pulled Gwen aside.

"Let's help each other. I'll give you a hitter's insights on reading offense if you give me tips on improving my setting."

When she hesitated, I sweetened the pot. "Plus, you get one day off of lunch tutoring each week. You pick the day."

The way her eyes lit up, you'd think she'd hit an oil well. Her smile, even though it still seemed calculated, didn't hold the same hint of malice as usual.

"Deal," she drawled, sounding as if she were the one doing the favor.

For the remainder of practice, I held up my end of the bargain. Advice came in brief moments as I modeled or explained what to look for. *Watch the angle of the hitter's shoulder. The position will give you an idea of the direction they plan to hit the ball. Pay attention to patterns. Hitters fall back on habits, which makes them predictable.*

That kind of thing.

She held up her side...sort of. "Stick with hitting." Long pause. "I'm not kidding."

Frustration toyed with my emotions, but I held my tongue so I wouldn't say something that would set our tenuous relationship on a downward spiral.

If she wouldn't offer advice, I could still learn by watching and imitating.

I zeroed in on Gwen so much that everything else seemed to disappear.

Maybe that's why I noticed how pale she looked when she headed toward the locker room at the end of practice. Maybe that's why I noticed how her spandex revealed a slimness that her loose-fitting day clothes concealed. Maybe that's why I noticed her hands shaking when she pushed open the locker room door.

Why did spitfire Gwen look exhausted? Maybe she was rusty after those weeks off. That might explain her fatigue, but not her thinness.

Cinching my eyebrows, I mentally reviewed last week's study sessions. I tried to recall what food I had actually seen her put in her mouth, but I couldn't think of anything she ate.

But she *did* have plenty of excuses for not eating. An upset stomach. A late breakfast. Too busy. Hated the school mystery meat. Food too hot or too cold or too spicy or too bland. Sometimes, she pushed, mushed, or squished things around her plate, but never brought the fork to her mouth.

Something didn't add up.

"Stop daydreaming, Lorali." Emily snapped her fingers in front of me. "We've still got an extra fifteen minutes to go. Let's do this!"

Frowning, I turned away from Gwen. An unsettled tension filled my heart. I sensed Gwen was hiding something. But what? Or more importantly, why?

I couldn't address my misgivings though. I still had my own commitments and a load of homework to deal with.

Finally, the day drew to a close. As I lay in bed exchanging texts with Taylor—some soulful enough to warm my cheeks and some cheeky enough to warm my soul—my dark musings resurfaced.

Me: What do you know about eating disorders?

Taylor: Nothing. Why?

Me: Worried about a friend.

(I deleted friend and typed "teammate".)

Taylor: Emily? That girl could out eat a 300-pound gorilla.

Me: No. She's a high energy girl. That's normal for her. She never stops eating.

Taylor: Who then?

Me: Gwen.

Taylor: ? Didn't know you were hanging out with her.

Me: Lunch. Tutoring. Practice.

Taylor: Oh, yeah.

Me: I don't see her eat. And I get a weird vibe from her.

Taylor: So?

Me: IDK. Something is off.

Taylor: Is there someone you can ask?

Me: I'm asking you. <smiley face>

Taylor: Ha-ha! Because I'm an expert on stuff like that. NOT. I view scented markers as a potential food source. Ask me about knitting. I've got a yarn for you.

Me: Should I say something to Coach?

Taylor: Maybe. But what happens if you're wrong?

Me: Gwen would get mad. It could cause a rift. The whole season could fall apart.

Taylor: But what if you're right?

Me:! IDK. Same thing?

Taylor: Tough choice. I don't know. I'll pray for Gwen. And for you.

Me: Thanks.

After we texted good night, I pulled up a search engine and typed in one word: Anorexia.

* * *

On Tuesday, Gwen once again completed her math homework under my supervision. On a hunch, I tracked what she ate. It was no easy task since Emily made a habit of polishing off whatever Gwen left on her plate.

Today's excuse for not eating? The food smelled funny.

But I came prepared. While Gwen worked out a word problem, I guided the conversation.

"We play West Side tonight. Someone told me their outside hitter is amazing. I bet she fuels up before the game. My Aunt Tina always claimed that diet affected performance. She said carbs were a main source of energy for athletes." I glanced at Emily. "Although I don't think she had Doritos in mind."

Though Gwen said nothing, she quirked an eyebrow. At least I knew she was listening.

Crumpling her empty chip bag, Emily leaned toward Michelle.

"No, you can't have my PBJ sandwich." Michelle pushed her away. "I want to establish that before you ask."

Emily pursed her lips. "Did your aunt's menu include peanut butter?"

"Yes." I wracked my brain. "She also listed lean meats like turkey. Protein helps with muscle recovery and repair."

"No corn dogs?" Emily asked.

I shook my head. "My aunt ate a lot of 'clean' food."

"Clean food?" Emily licked a splatter of ketchup off her plastic fork. "That sounds scary. And complicated. Like my own love-hate relationship with food."

"Love-hate?" I cocked my head. "Explain."

With a carefree wave, Emily said, "I love food, and I hate it when it's gone."

Gwen snorted.

"I read something interesting in a blog." I rested my chin on my hand. "The writer said that volleyball players move in bursts of energy and use up tons of calories. So you see Gwen's whole lunch right there?" I swept my hand over her tray. "Wait, what am I saying? Of course you do. You're always eyeballing her food."

Crunch. Emily bit into a potato chip. Wait, that girl had a backup bag stashed away? "What's your point?"

"If Gwen ate every morsel on that tray, she'd burn all the calories off in one game. It'll be like she never ate a thing. As if the meal never existed."

Gwen lifted her eyes to mine.

Holding up my apple, I smiled. "Here's to fuel for the win."

"The win!" Emily hefted her chip bag.

"The win!" Michelle repeated, lifting her PBJ.

We paused, waiting for Gwen to join in. Sighing, she lifted a cracker. "The win."

We toasted each other and took a bite of our offerings.

Gwen watched us with veiled eyes. After a moment, she popped the whole cracker into her mouth.

By my calculations, that's all she ate.

We played at home that night. Even before the visiting team showed up, the gym was packed. Simply putting two schools' JV and Varsity teams in the place filled it to near capacity, let alone piling in opposing crowds of parents, a truckload of rowdy high school students, and twelve cheerleaders per school.

In the middle of the chaos, Audrey's dad sat in the bleachers. As he watched us take the court for warmups, his eyebrows crept lower and lower over narrowed eyes.

From the doleful look on Audrey's face, she had probably fed him a healthy serving of whatever perceived injustice she felt over the lineup change.

But the way I pounded the ball told me there was something *right* about Gwen setting me again. I stood on the court like Thor getting his hammer back. Even though I would be more marketable as a setter running a 5–1, a 6–2 offense lowered my stress level. Now I could spike the ball off an actual set instead of pushing the ball into the hands of others.

As the game progressed, the Rally Cats found their rhythm. Once again, Emily dominated. The way she protected the floor, you'd think the ball was a rare flavor of donut she didn't want contaminated.

No wonder she caught a recruiter's eye. Like my aunt once said, *It's the intangibles, like hard work, the competitive drive, and grit, that make players great.*

We won the first two sets, but after we lost the third, Coach pulled us together. "Girls, we've been down this road before, starting strong and then losing momentum. We can do it. Remember your training."

"Nothing hits the floor!" Emily yelled.

Brianna mimicked a block. "Six inches tougher."

"Rally Cats," Michelle cried. "Rally Cats!"

My teammates joined the chant, working themselves into a frenzy, ready to boil over onto the court.

Everyone but Gwen.

Nostrils flaring, Gwen raised her chin. Her stare hardened

and bore into the crowd as if penetrating a cloud of darkness Despite the noise, my ears picked up her quiet, fierce words. "Be ready."

Be ready? I followed her line of vision. Her uncle hovered in the doorway. Even from the huddle I recognized the stubble of his unshaven chin.

Not good. When he had shown up at practice, his presence seemed to throw off her game. We couldn't afford to let her lose focus again. *I* couldn't afford it. Time to redirect.

"Gwen." I grabbed her arm to draw her attention. "I'll be ready. Set me."

She nodded curtly. For once, I didn't mind the intensity etched on her face. In fact, I embraced it and every abrasive thing about Gwen she could bring to the court. We needed her fire to win.

An image of Gwen's thin legs popped unbidden into my mind, followed by three words: *Pray for Gwen.* So I did. A two-second prayer for my cantankerous teammate. It's all I had time for.

Dour determination brought our front row back with a vengeance. Gwen's sets kept the defense guessing. But mostly, she fed me balls. And I kept putting them down. We won 25–18. Match over.

I left the court elated. Another win under the belt, and me back on top as lead hitter. And Gwen? I figured whatever dark clouds threatened to consume her could wait.

CHAPTER EIGHTEEN

A WALK IN THE PARK

G ritty sand clung to my feet. A quick swipe in the grass loosened the grains, but I rubbed sore fingers over my toes to free the rest. "How was my setting today?"

Taylor lounged in the grass next to me, forehead slick with sweat from our Saturday practice. "Better."

Slipping on my flip-flops, I pursed my lips. "Better as in I could pass as an actual setter?"

"Bad choice of wording." He tilted his head. "Pass as a setter? C'mon now."

Smiling, I lifted my chin. For a moment, I let my gaze drift upward to the creamy blue sky. A light breeze cooled my skin. I'd been so busy I'd forgotten what it was like to breathe.

"Hmmm," I murmured, coming back to reality. "Am I all *set* now?"

"Clever." Taylor raised an eyebrow. "I think you'll pass."

That earned him a playful shove.

Laughing, he fended me off. "I mean, you're an ace! A chip off the old block! People will dig your setting. You'll be a hit on the court."

"Stop!" I grabbed his hand. "A girl can only handle so many bad puns on any given day."

In one smooth motion, he rose to his feet and pulled me up with him. The sun haloed his head. "It's still early. Have you ever explored the trails here?"

"A few times with my mom when I was younger. One time we spotted a Tiger Swallowtail."

"I've seen one before." He raised a finger. "A yellow and black striped butterfly, right?"

I nodded. "We pretended it was a fairy on the way to a masquerade ball and followed it. Until I decided that with a name like *Tiger,* it was more likely to be a ferocious predator out to destroy the nearest village. The only way to stop its evil plot was to charge at it with a stick sword."

"You attacked a butterfly?"

I scoffed. "I protected my mother from a vicious beast. But yeah, I chased it away."

Lowering his sunglasses, he let his eyes meet mine. Mirth danced in them. "Are you up for more butterfly hunting then?"

I couldn't resist an opportunity to spend more time with

him. "Yes. Let me change out of these flip-flops though. I left a pair of sneakers in my bag."

After he scooped up the ball and his keys, he crooked his elbow. I laced my arm through his, and we retraced our steps to his car where I'd left my gear.

"How long is the trail?" I asked.

"That depends. The park has three trails. If you have enough time, we should try the first one because it's longer—about four miles—and part of it goes past the river." Releasing me, he clicked the remote and opened the passenger side. "It also has a fire pit that overlaps the second trail."

"Ohhhh, I like the idea of a fire pit." I rummaged around in my bag and produced a pair of Converse. "Do you have any marshmallows to roast?"

"I should have thought of that." He rubbed his forehead "But that's what I get for being spontaneous."

"I like spontaneous." I slipped my shoes on. "As long as I'm prepared for it."

"In that case, I'll keep an assortment of tools in my glovebox. Like marshmallows."

I finished tying my laces. "Technically, a marshmallow isn't a tool."

"Tell that to Emily," he said. "Ready now?"

Standing, I dragged off my ponytail holder and ran my fingers through my hair. A breeze teased a few strands, blowing them across my face. "Almost. I guess I need to pull my hair back up."

"No, leave it down. You look nice. And it won't be as windy on the trail."

Warmed by the compliment, I slipped the stretchy band around my wrist. "Okay. So, the first and the second trails are decent, and we can hit the fire pit either way. What about the third trail?"

Leaning against the car, Taylor snorted. "Short and boring. Like a documentary about candle wax."

I pushed my foot into one of the shoes. "In that case, I pick the first trail."

Once I tied the laces, we set out in the direction of the wooded section of the park. The trailhead lay past the sand courts and beyond the picnic area.

Midway there, the sound of heavy metal music and the smell of BBQ wafted our way. My stomach rumbled, but I ignored it. Maybe Taylor and I could grab a burger on the way home.

Ahead, a gang of rowdy adults clustered under the picnic shelter. The enticing aroma obviously belonged to their cooking, as did the eardrum-busting song. Beer bottles and trash littered the area. Raucous laughter cut through the music.

As Taylor and I approached, a gruff voice called out. "Hey! Ain't you Gwen's friend?"

Eyes wide, I turned my head toward the source of the question. A familiar bulk lazed by one of the green tables. Greasy hair framed the face of Gwen's uncle. A girl young enough to be his daughter pressed against him, and his beefy hand rested on her waist.

His eyes traced the contours of my body before giving a low whistle. "Bet I know what you're heading into the woods to do." Smirking, he lowered his hand from the girl's waist to her backside, then he made a lewd thrust with his hips.

Feeling sick, I pulled the edges of my shorts lower and quickened my pace.

"Go on, little worm!" he yelled. "Make your mama proud."

Not even the wind could disguise the nasty in his coarse words.

Once a safe distance away, Taylor glared back at him. "You know that guy?"

Stomach queasy, I nodded. "I recognize him from the gym. That's Gwen's uncle. But I've never talked to him before." I shuddered. "And I never want to again."

"Forget about him." Taylor squinted. "We're well beyond his reach."

Swallowing, I slowed my breathing. "Yeah, you're right. Besides, who would bother me when I've got this big knitting champion to protect me?"

He quirked a grin. "Hey! Respect the yarn. It keeps me from coming unraveled."

My discomfort evaporated. Taylor always found a way to make me smile. "How long have you been waiting to deliver that line?"

"I thought it up last night," he admitted, cheeks coloring, "and then waited for the right moment to weave it in."

Groaning, I looped an arm through his.

At the base of the hill, we came to the trailhead. A soft clay-and-pebble surface with wooden signs invited us to adventure.

We paused to study the trail map. Taylor drew a finger along a blue line representing trail one. "Each path has its own colors to follow. They use that marking system since sections of each route overlap, and they don't want people straying the wrong way."

His finger stopped at a blue and red circle. "That's the fire pit. See where both paths intersect?"

Stepping closer, he reached down and took my hand.

Rough calluses from years of sports gave his fingers a sturdy, comforting feel. I didn't trust my voice to speak, so I nodded.

"That's where we're headed." With a gentle tug, he pulled me forward. "Stick with me. I don't want you off chasing butterflies."

No need to worry. They had all gathered in my stomach.

For about twenty minutes we followed the path. As the trees swallowed the sun, Taylor pushed his sunglasses to the top of his head. The density of the foliage muted the external noise and blocked the industrial landscape, allowing me to focus on the surrounding nature.

Branches arched above the walkway creating a fairytale castle. Birds twittered overhead, darting from branch to branch in an endless game of hide-and-seek. Damp moss mixed with the sweet decay of fallen leaves flavored the air with a woodsy fragrance. Taylor's own musky smell blended right in.

The serenity calmed me, especially after the encounter with Gwen's uncle. After a few cleansing breaths, I broke our silence. "I've been so busy with volleyball and school lately, I forgot how beautiful the world could be."

He squeezed my hand. "It has its perks."

My heart sped up wondering if I was one of them.

The further we got down the trail, the more my body relaxed. Had I always carried such tension with me? My coach's expectations. My friends' expectations. My mom's expectations. My aunt's expectations. My expectations for myself. Each of those stacked one on top of the other in a confusing pile until I hardly knew which expectation belonged to me or someone else. But right now? In this gentle place, they didn't matter.

Several curves in the path later, Taylor stopped. "The fire pit is to the right."

A footpath leading to the stony circle branched off the main course. In two dozen steps, we reached it, and from there we could see the second trail angling up from the other side. Wasting no time, I lowered myself onto the closest rock. Taylor settled in next to me.

"Hold a minute." I fished out my phone. "Selfie."

Smiling up at the camera, I leaned into him. Three snaps later, I had a decent shot. I noticed the way one side of his lips curled higher than the other and how the muted light danced in his eyes. He looked happy. Was he?

"Do you miss your old school?" I asked.

He picked up a pebble and rolled it between his fingers. "A little. But it was a small town. Basically, the whole thing fit in the middle of a cornfield. The highlight of my day was counting the cows in the field next to the school. Although that got tricky when they moved around. I like this area better. No corn. No cows. More than one movie theater. And you've got four-laned roads."

For a fleeting moment, his lips turned down. He paused, then tossed the pebble into the weeds. "What I miss the most is playing football."

Shifting to get a better view of him, I considered his words. "But you said God had other plans for you. Doesn't knowing that make it easier?"

Stooping his shoulders, he reached for another rock. "It does. Except it doesn't take away the urge to throw on some pads and tackle somebody. I think that's why I liked Hank's message last Wednesday."

I hated to confess I'd missed most of the message because watching Taylor proved too much of a distraction. Instead, I plucked a short stick off the ground and dug it into the soft dirt. "What did you like about it?"

"That part when Joseph's brothers showed up."

Using the twig, I drew a star shape on the ground. "The ones that tried to kill him and then sold him into slavery. Right?" I guess I had listened to some of the story.

Taylor nodded. "Like, dude, they treated him horribly. After all they did, if I were Joseph, I would have thrown them in jail or made them slaves. Sweet revenge, you know? A Hollywood ending. But what did he do?"

"He forgave them."

"The plot twist no one saw coming." Taylor sent the second stone flying. Turning his head, his eyes searched mine. "At first, I wondered how Joseph could let go of a *wrong* like that. His brothers destroyed his plans for the future. Why wasn't he mad? But when Hank read that verse about 'your actions were meant to harm me, but God used it for good,' it got me. God did have a plan. Enduring those hardships gave Joseph a whole different perspective. About humility. Trust. Faith. Forgiveness. Lessons he needed to learn in order to rule effectively. Maybe I needed those lessons too."

Frowning, I shook my head. "I still think it would be hard to forgive someone who treated you so bad."

Taylor placed a hand on my knee. "Sometimes bad things happen. That doesn't mean we have to let those things control us or continue to hold us back. It just means there might be a different path to travel."

I studied his face, seeing nothing but contentment there. "Maybe so," I murmured.

His upbeat attitude made me like him even more. An almost dizzying feeling of attraction swept through me quickly followed by the nauseating recollection of Gwen's uncle's last leering words. Suddenly uncomfortable with how close we sat, I jumped up. "We should probably get back. Mom will worry."

Rising with slow grace, Taylor stood. Eyes lowered, he smoothed his shirt down. "Sure, no problem. I'll take you home."

My heart dropped. Had he misunderstood my sudden mood change?

I needed a save! "We should do this again sometime. I liked it. Only next time, let's bring marshmallows."

A smile broke across his face. "Deal."

The hike back to reality passed faster on the way out. The trees thinned and more industrial sounds replaced the chirping of birds. Our conversation swam from deep waters to shallow reflection pools. Life returned to its normal pace.

At least Gwen's uncle was gone when we approached the picnic area. His crew had left behind the beer cans, trash, and a smoldering grill. The lingering smell indicated it hadn't been long since their departure.

I quickened my step. The fear of running in to him again brought bile to my mouth.

CHAPTER NINETEEN

WINNER, LOSER

"How does it feel to win?" Taylor asked.

I'd called him after the Tuesday game to share our success. "Amazing! Like discovering I can now leap over buildings in a single bound." I bounced on my toes. "I want more!"

"You and my sister both."

"Did Terri win tonight?"

"Weatherford beat us. That tall middle shut us down."

"I think the fact that we played them so tough last week made your sister's job harder." Holding the phone with my chin, I waved goodbye to Emily and Michelle. "The humiliation of almost losing to what they view as roadkill probably shook them up. You should have seen the fit their coach threw. She exploded like an egg in a microwave."

"Not surprising. Teams like Weatherford aren't used to losing."

I eased my locker open so it wouldn't rattle. I had clean socks in there somewhere. "For sure. Everywhere we go, people see our size and dismiss us as a second-rate team."

"It's their own fault if they underestimate you."

"I guess. At least Terri's team will probably make playoffs."

"Don't give up too soon. Your team won tonight, against all odds. That shows courage. Bet it felt good too."

I laughed. Tonight's victory still tickled every spot of happy in my body. "Yeah, our win column is bulking up, so there's hope."

"You can thank me later for the setting lessons."

"I'm sure you'll remind me. But listen, I have another reason for calling." I lowered my voice. "As of eight o'clock this morning, I graduated from a learning permit to a provisional driver's license."

"Dude!" Taylor's booming voice made me wince. "Congratulations. I thought you were waiting to take the test until after the season because you were too busy."

"Mom surprised me with the keys to her old car and got me into the Motor Vehicle Center before second period," I smiled into the phone. "I'm driving myself home from the game tonight."

"Wow. I'll be on the lookout for your car weaving through traffic." He paused. "You still have restrictions."

"I know." I savored my knowledge as I recited our special state rules. "According to the state laws, until I turn eighteen,

I can only have one non-related passenger under the age of twenty-one in the car with me."

"I call dibs on the first ride," Taylor said.

My heart fluttered. "Of course."

"Is that all? We had more rules in Indiana."

"I wasn't done." I hardened by tone. "I can't drive between midnight and 5 a.m., and I can't use my phone while driving."

"Pfft," he scoffed. "Same in Indiana. That's just common sense. What happens if you cheat?" His voice took a flirty edge.

Thinking about my aunt, I tightened my jaw. "No chance. I'll crawl home before I break the rules."

The locker room door creaked, and I glanced up to see who came in.

Gwen. *Pray for her.*

Turning away, I cradled the phone so I could whisper. "Hey, let me call you back when I get home. I need to talk to someone really quick."

"A boy?"

I grunted. "In the locker room?"

"Kidding. No problem. Later!" The line went dead.

After tucking my phone away, I cleared my throat. It seemed God kept prompting me to pray for Gwen. Maybe I should try harder to connect with her too. "You played well tonight."

Gwen glared at me. "Don't pretend you're glad I'm back, Loser. I know you liked being the only setter."

Her words slapped me in the face. After all the time we spent together during lunch and all the help I gave her in math, how could she lash out at me like that?

Learn from Joseph. Get a new perspective.

Maybe she wasn't attacking me. Maybe she had something else on her mind.

Taking a deep breath, I squared my shoulders. "I did like running a 5–1 offense. But I'm still glad you're back."

Uncertain of how she would react, I paused.

Gwen raised an eyebrow, seemingly interested.

With her unspoken permission, I continued. "I never realized how hard a setter worked, especially when the passes are bad. The problem is, it doesn't matter where the ball goes, you're still expected to put up a good set. It's exhausting."

She inclined her head. "No kidding."

"Add the pressure of keeping the sets consistent and mixing up the offense, and it's enough to make your mind spin. Plus, don't forget defense. Dinks are a killer."

"Now you know why I get frustrated all the time." Gwen shrugged. "I feel like I've got to be everywhere. Every play."

"Don't you love the hitters who complain they don't get enough sets?" I asked.

"They don't understand that sometimes our options are limited." Gwen shrugged. "Example—if the pass is off, it's hard to set the middle."

"Sometimes I lose where I'm at on the court if the hitters don't talk."

"Exactly." Gwen slapped her hands together. "Hello, hitters! We need to hear you to pinpoint your position. It's not like we have psychic abilities."

I noticed her response changed from *I* to *we*. Interesting.

"I hate it when we're going for the ball, and we're right there, ready to make the play," I said, following suit, "and then BAM! Someone steps in front and sets the ball because they don't think we'll get it."

Gwen made a face. "They need to trust us. C'mon, people. We'll call for help if we need it."

"I know." I gritted my teeth. "And then when we manage to pull off this incredible set from a broken play, who gets all the credit for the point?"

"The hitter," we said together.

Gwen's eyes widened. For a moment, we stared at each other. Then her lips flattened into a line. Turning her back, she opened her locker. "So what's your point?"

"I get it now. Why you love setting so much." I spoke low and even. "The job isn't easy or glorious. It's not high profile. But it's vital. Passing is critical, hitting makes highlight films, but nothing else works unless the setter does."

Her hand paused over her bag, then she nodded stiffly. "It's nice that someone else understands. I guess." Her body swayed slightly, thistle in the wind, fighting to hold itself erect.

Did we have a moment there? Could I build on that?

I stepped next to her so she couldn't avoid looking at me. "I really, really, *really* loved winning tonight."

A grin quirked Gwen's mouth as if uncertain which way pointed up. "Me too."

"What felt even better was pounding the ball again." My chest swelled in response to the memory. "I didn't realize how much I missed it."

"We connected well." Gwen lowered her eyes. "You can put the ball down."

"And I love your sets. With Caroline out, I need to improve so I can set as well as you. For the team's sake."

"You are pretty lame," she said, but her words held no sting. Or did I imagine a playful tone?

"What if we kept winning and made it to district

playoffs?" I fisted my hands. "Our team hasn't made it that far in forever!"

Shaking her head, Gwen stuffed a pair of socks into her bag. "Our division has a lot of big programs. I don't see how we get past them."

"All we gotta do is win."

"Duh." Gwen smirked.

Okay, so maybe we weren't ready to be best buddies yet. But I couldn't give up yet. I'm too stubborn for that. Steeling my resolve, I met her gaze. "I think if we work together, we might pull this thing off."

The silence that followed my blatant request made my mouth go dry. Had my eagerness somehow undermined our tenuous connection?

But Gwen finally nodded. "Okay."

With a hiss, I released a breath I didn't realize I held. "You'll help me then?"

Licking her lips, Gwen shot a furtive glance around the room. Closing her locker, she sized me up. "I'll help you with setting but...I need help too."

I nodded. "Math, of course. I can keep tutoring you during lunch. I know it's tough, but as long as we—"

"No." Her brusque voice cut me off. With another surreptitious look around, she hefted her backpack. "I mean yes. Sure. Math. Whatever. I gotta go."

As she spun to walk away, she stumbled. Her thin frame seemed to fold in on itself. I suddenly remembered my earlier suspicions. The words left my mouth before I could hold back. "I know what you need help with."

Gwen stopped in her tracks. Wanting to ease the words I needed to say, I put my hand on her shoulder. She tensed at my touch, eyes straight ahead, jaw set.

"I notice how little you eat. How thin you are. The excuses you make."

Her body stiffened. "I'm fine," she choked out.

I shook my head. "No, you're not."

Flint colored her eyes. I could almost see her mind reviewing our interactions from the past few days.

"I researched eating disorders to make sure I wasn't imagining things." I paused, unsure if I should continue. But I owed her some honesty. I took a slow breath, then let it out. "After that, I tested you. Those conversations we had about calories and food? How one game burns up an entire meal?"

"You tricked me into eating." Her words lashed like a whip.

I backed away. "I needed to know."

Gwen's tiny frame vibrated like a flag caught in raging wind. "Know what? What about my life is any of your business?"

Her reaction put me on edge. Was I jumping to conclusions? "Nothing. I'm sorry if I overstepped. But I'm worried about you."

"Why?" she shot back. "Because you need me?"

"No. Yes." I shook my head. "Look, if I didn't care about you, I wouldn't say anything. I just...am. Worried."

"Liar. You've never liked me." Venom laced her words.

My hands curled into fists. But was there some truth to what she said? After all, this was Gwen, the teammate that antagonized me. Frustrated me. Angered me.

But she also pushed me to be a better player, if only to prove her wrong.

Pray for Gwen.

I tried brushing the thought away, but it clung to me like a cobweb. "Look, I'm trying to be a friend. You don't make it easy."

"Yeah, you like easy. You've got this perfect family and perfect friends and perfect grades and perfect everything," Gwen snapped. "All I've got is volleyball. And now you want to take that away too."

My mouth dropped open. "I haven't taken anything from you. And my life isn't perfect. I'm tired and..." My voice trailed off when a look of outrage crossed her face.

"You're tired? Is that the worst thing in life you deal with? Well, how's this? I failed math. My parents got a divorce. My uncle lives with us now, but he's a pig. My friends don't like him. I don't like him!" Her tirade became shrill. "My whole world is falling apart. And there's nothing I can do about it. Everything is out of my control. And you're *tired?*"

Her words stung, but this verbal attack wasn't about me. It was about Gwen—her pain, and her inability to cope with it. Her desire to control it.

My research showed that many eating disorders stem from people needing power over something, anything in their lives. Often the only thing they could monitor was the food they put in their mouths, and they guarded that ability fiercely.

It all made sense.

"You have anorexia." I wasn't asking.

"You don't know anything!" Gwen snapped. Her lips twisted in an ugly way. "You're just a selfish brat."

Facing her rage forced me to do the hardest and bravest thing I'd ever done. Stand my ground. Meet fire with fire.

"A moment ago, you said you needed my help," I said. "Tell me why."

"For math." The words came out clipped, sharp.

I didn't back down. "No. Not for math."

"Yes, for math." Gwen's voice took on a murderous edge.

"NO!" I shot back, getting right up in her face. "Tell me the truth. Why do you need my help?"

Gwen's mouth snarled open, then went slack. Her face blanched, and she crumpled forward. Only the closeness of my body kept her from toppling.

"Gwen!" We sagged to the ground, me bearing her weight. She struggled to push herself away from me, but her effort only flopped her onto her back. A waxy sheen coated her cheeks and her eyes lost focus.

"I can't do this," she whispered, speech slurring.

"Do what?" My voice shredded the air.

"Help me." Gwen lifted a shaky hand, then let it drop. "Promise me...our secret...promise."

"What secret?" Nausea churned in my stomach. "Is there something more going on?"

"Don't tell Audrey. Don't tell...anyone," she mumbled. "Especially...don't tell Coach. Secret. Our secret."

Secret? No. Someone asking you to keep a secret was a red flag in all the crisis classes our school counselors made us sit through. "I can't promise," I said.

"Yes." Her eyes rolled backward, showing their whites. She blinked the pupils back in place. "You have to."

Gripping the front of her shirt, I pulled her closer. Her limp body didn't resist.

"Gwen!" Ice shot through my veins. "Wake up! I promise. I promise!"

Her rag doll head lolled my direction. The effort seemed to exhaust her. "Okay. Besides...those crackers...at lunch...I... haven't eaten...all day."

And then she passed out.

CHAPTER TWENTY

GWEN

My whole body shook. My throat thickened. I didn't know what to do.

Heart racing, I yanked off my sweatshirt and pillowed it under Gwen's head. Leaving her cradled there, I flew out of the locker room to find help.

The gym stood vacant. Sticky garbage cans lined one the wall, their guts overflowing. A cloth broom sprawled nearby like a forgotten carcass.

Coach's voice drifted out of her office. From the rapid-fire chatter, it sounded like she was on the phone sharing the happy news of our victory.

Desperation drove me her direction until the memory of Gwen's words slammed into me. *Promise me...our secret...*

She didn't want Coach to find out.

Maybe I should call 9-1-1. Or my mom. Or Emily. Or Taylor. I rushed back to the locker room and snatched my phone.

Promise me...our secret...

Wanting to scream in frustration, I squeezed my phone like a bottle of old glue.

She didn't want *anyone* to find out.

But didn't this secret need to be found out? How else would Gwen get help?

From me? *I promised.*

I couldn't call Mom. I couldn't involve Coach. I had to find a solution on my own.

Think, think.

Nothing came to mind.

Beside me, Gwen lay in a heap. Pale. Lifeless.

My chest tightened.

Trembling, I took a deep breath to steady myself.

Think, think.

What was the right thing to do?

The phone weighed heavy in my hand. I typed 9-1-1. My finger hovered over the "send" button. *It will expose her.* I paused, glancing at Gwen. Her eyelids fluttered as if in protest. So she wasn't completely out of it. Yet.

Growling, I deleted the number.

Think, think.

One time at youth group, a visitor got dizzy. Like Gwen, the girl had slurred speech and uneven walking. She claimed to have low blood sugar and asked for apple juice. Fifteen minutes after slurping it down, she acted normal again. Would that work for Gwen?

Think, think.

My head swiveled from Gwen to Emily's locker. If anyone had food stashed away, it would be her. And I'd stood next to Emily enough times to learn her combination.

Seconds later, I rummaged through the landfill that made up Emily's locker. My breath caught when my hand landed on juice pouches stashed under a stray sock. I pulled them free. Three had been drained dry, but one remained untouched.

"Thank you, Emily and your food-grubbing way of life," I whispered, clutching my prize. Rushing back to Gwen, I freed the tiny straw, shoved it into the opening, and lifted her head.

Gwen groaned, a small, pathetic whimper. She seemed to have trouble keeping her head upright.

I pushed the straw between her teeth. "Drink."

Without further protest, Gwen took a feeble sip. Then her eyes rolled back in her head again.

Health class taught me that you don't give liquids to an unconscious person. But Gwen wasn't quite there yet, was she? Taking a more aggressive approach, I held her chin and pushed the straw again. When she resisted, I knew she wasn't completely gone.

"Drink." I put force behind my command.

It took eight minutes to pump the liquid into her.

Now all I could do was wait. And pray. And hope I'd done the right thing.

I kept guard over her, chewing my fingernails until she finally opened her eyes. Just to make sure she was normal again, I poked her, and she swatted at my hand. "Ah, there you are," I said. "I missed you."

I never thought I'd feel so happy watching Gwen transform from meek incoherency back to her regular surly self, but I did.

Still groggy, Gwen propped herself up on one arm and rubbed her head with the other. Her eyes widened as she took in the sight of me, the floor, and the empty container. She scooted up against the wall. "What happened?"

"You barely ate anything all day and then burned off energy you didn't have." I lifted a brow. "What do you think happened?"

She lowered her gaze. "Did you tell anyone?" she whispered.

Rattling came from outside the locker room followed by Coach's voice still chattering on the phone. Footsteps came our way.

In one sweeping motion, I stood and stepped away. "Not yet."

The steps came closer, and Gwen struggled to her feet. A look of panic raced across her face. "Don't," she warned. And then, after a nervous glance at me, added a quiet, pleading, "Please?"

The door swung open. Coach reached toward the light switch, then stopped when she spotted us. "Hang on, let me call you back."

After clicking off her phone, she studied us for a few seconds. "Why are you two still here? I thought everyone left."

As if in slow motion, I fumbled to find an answer. I couldn't lie. I can't even pull off a practical joke because it feels dishonest.

But I couldn't tell the truth either. Not until I sorted everything out.

So I froze, open-mouthed, Gwen's secret right on the tip of my tongue.

Gwen sidled next to me and snaked an arm around my shoulders. Her face smiled up at Coach, but her fingers pinched me. Not hard enough to hurt, but hard enough to snap my mouth shut.

"Sorry, Coach." Pink dotted Gwen's cheeks now, and her voice sounded steadier. "We were making a plan to keep winning and lost track of time."

True, thankfully.

Leaning against the door frame, Coach crossed her arms. "What's the plan?"

"I'm going to help Lorali with setting." Gwen released me and smoothed her hair with a shaky hand. I wondered if Coach noticed or not. Gwen's demeanor remained haughty, although how she pulled it off in her weakened state, I'll never guess. "I know you're working with her on improving, but I'm giving Lorali tips too since she's still not very good."

When I winced, Coach raised her brows. If I didn't know better, I'd say she was amused. "That's generous of you, Gwen. And it will definitely help the team."

"Yup." I bit my lip, not trusting myself to say more.

Coach checked her phone, a look of impatience flitting across her features. "Even so, it's late, and I need to lock up. Do you two have a ride home?"

"Lorali is going to drop me off."

Gwen's quick answer threw me. Taylor had dibs on that ride.

"What?" I'm sure my eyes bulged.

Tilting her head, Gwen shared a meaningful look. "We still have lots to talk about."

With a snort, Coach leaned in. "You're driving now, Mathews?"

Swallowing, I fished my keys out of my pocket and jingled them. "Yup."

Coach lifted a finger. "Thanks for the warning. And since you're in the helping mood, Senior Night is coming up in a few weeks, and I need underclassmen to spearhead it. I considered asking Michelle, but since you two plan on talking tonight anyway, I just now volunteered you to organize it. We need a theme and decorations. Now, get going. I'm ready to go home."

At first, Gwen and I both stood there gaping at her.

"This is unexpected," I finally said.

"I'm sure you can handle it." Then Coach clapped her hands twice, all business. "Now, out, out!"

That snapped us into motion. Gwen grabbed her bag, and I swung mine around my shoulder. As we stumbled through the door into the cool night, I wondered if Gwen was thinking what I was thinking. What had we gotten into now?

* * *

"I need very clear directions to your house since I've never, ever in my life been there before." I kept my eyes glued to the road. "And the next time you need a ride, ask first."

I'd already texted my mom to let her know the change in route. She'd worry otherwise. I didn't need nightmares of Aunt Tina's accident haunting her all night.

When Gwen didn't reply, I glanced over. She leaned her head against the window fogging up the glass with her breath. Proof, at least, that she still lived.

We had our differences, but I hated to see another person suffer. Especially not if I could help. Tightening my grip on the wheel, I pressed Gwen. "Look, I kept your secret. Something is wrong. Life is hard. You're not eating. But you owe me some kind of explanation."

She sighed, and I risked another sidelong glance. Listening to her *not* talk, sensing her unease churning below the surface of her skin, left an uncomfortable knot in my stomach. And did I see a tear running down her cheek?

My heart broke.

"Turn here," she mumbled.

Slowing down, I turned on my signal, its quiet *click-click* filling the awkward hush. Streetlights lined one side of the road, their dome-shaped light making it easier to spot the speed limit sign. 25 MPH. Must be a neighborhood.

We drove past darkened driveways and brick mailboxes, the silence a wide river. This was a version of Gwen I didn't recognize, vulnerable and weak. If we weren't arguing, I wasn't sure what to say. I decided a quick prayer might be in order, and mentally asked God's wisdom for me, and guidance for Gwen.

"Take a right at the stop sign," she said, voice hoarse. "My house is halfway down the street in front of an annoying speed bump. There's probably a Pontiac in the driveway."

Pontiac. Wasn't that her uncle's Trans Am? Why didn't he pick her up tonight?

After turning onto the road, I stopped by the curb and shut the engine off. Gingerly, I sat back. I didn't want to leave without some sort of resolution, but Gwen kept her head turned away from me, tilted down at her feet.

"I want you to know, I actually *do* care. About you," I said, surprising even myself by the realization.

Squeezing her lips tight, Gwen twisted the string on her hoodie.

"And I understand if you don't want to talk about your problems yet." I tried to catch her eyes but gave up. "I hope you will sometime though. Because if I'm the only one that knows your secret, then I'm the only one who can help you. So let me help."

She huffed. "I don't want to talk about this."

"Okay," I soothed, using a calm voice. How could I bridge the wall between us? *Coach's assignment!* "Until then, we can at least plan Senior Night. With food. Otherwise, Emily will probably eat the decorations. She'll start with the balloons, claiming they're not much different than grapes. She'll stuff them into her mouth one by one. And they'll pop. B*ang, bang, bang!*"

This brought a snort from Gwen.

"Next, she'll call the glue on our posters 'frosting' and lick it off. Then she'll move on to the streamers. She'll pile them up like noodles and throw spaghetti sauce on top." With exaggerated outrage, I shook my fist at the sky. "For the sake of Emily and all that is decent, we can't delay our Senior Night planning!"

A smile played on Gwen's lips as if battling for dominance. She looked so funny, it made me laugh.

That broke the tension. For the first time since we left the gym, Gwen seemed to relax. "Okay." She puckered her lips, face serious. "Let's tackle Senior Night. But leave food off the list."

"Speaking of food…" Leaning forward, I popped open the glovebox and pulled out a granola bar. Acting casual, as if it weren't a big deal, I pushed it her way. "I keep this stashed in the car in case of an emergency. The emergency being Emily someday ending up in the passenger seat, of course."

Gwen didn't take it, so I dropped it in her lap. "Please eat.

The juice revived you, but it won't last. And I don't want you passing out on me ever again."

Just like that, the tightness in her attitude came back like a smothering blanket, its heaviness threatening to choke off all hope of connecting.

Please, God, I prayed. *Touch her.*

Maybe a bribe would work. "If you eat it, I'll leave the food out of our planning."

Frowning, Gwen lifted the offering. With slow fingers, she unwrapped the bar. After wrinkling her nose at it, she broke it in two, then curled one half back up. Sighing noisily, she nibbled on the other half.

Relief swept over me.

It would do. For now.

We spent the next thirty minutes planning a theme, decorations, and gifts. We didn't mention what had transpired in the locker room, but I feared it would resurface soon, like a shark in shallow water.

When Gwen ran out of steam, I said goodbye.

She thanked me—a shock even now, trust me—and climbed out of my car. Instead of slamming the door like any normal teen, she leaned against it to close it with a quiet click. Then, shoulders stooped, she plodded toward her front door.

Stomach churning, I watched Gwen's slow progress. Where was her fire? Where was her steel? Who was this stranger?

And what could I do about it?

Nothing. I wasn't a hero. I was barely a friend. And I only knew as much about anorexia as I'd read on the internet.

Blinking back tears, I turned my wheel toward home, my soul as empty as the passenger seat.

CHAPTER TWENTY-ONE

RESEARCH

Bleary-eyed, I roughed a hand across my face. Even though I went straight to bed when I got home, I couldn't sleep. An unsettled feeling, the kind you get when you eat something rotten, soured my stomach. I needed answers—answers Gwen wasn't giving me. And answers came from knowledge, which I lacked. So, I tucked another pillow under my head and thumbed through articles on the internet.

I read that anorexia developed as a coping mechanism to deal with unresolved conflicts or painful experiences. Gwen's parents got divorced, so that qualified.

The profile also included having a thin appearance, fatigue, checking the mirror often, and denial of hunger. All symptoms I'd seen firsthand in Gwen. And all things easily overlooked given the strenuous demands on a diva athlete.

Groaning, I set my phone aside. I knew Gwen's secret, I knew the possible source of the problem, but I didn't know how to help. And even if I did, I was sworn to secrecy. My emotions were leaden feet caught in a campfire moment, longing to respond, but unable to move.

God, all I asked for this volleyball season was to learn what I needed to be successful. But I can't stop thinking about Gwen. Please bring someone, anyone, to help her. Just, not me. I am not equipped for this.

As fitful sleep pulled me under, one thought remained.

Pray for Gwen.

✱ ✱ ✱

Coach dismissed the seniors from practice fifteen minutes early so Gwen and I could present our ideas for Senior Night to the rest of the team. Gwen let me do the talking while she stood, arms folded, like my supervisor.

"Senior Night falls on the last home game of the season," I said, "so that night has to be extra special. Heroically special. We decided to take a comic-book style approach to decorations and gifts. The theme is *Superhero.*"

Emily raised her hand. "What kind of gift goes with superheroes? Pajamas and bedsheets? Actually, I'd be totally into that."

After fishing my phone out of my sweatshirt, I flipped it around to show her a picture. "Fierce-looking female action figures flood the market these days. We buy one for each senior and put miniature volleyball charms inside the box with the weapons. It'll be a memorable gift."

Emily passed the phone around, letting everyone peek at the merchandise. Several heads nodded approval.

"As for decorations, I'm going to take headshots of each senior and blow the images up bigger than a desk. And then Michelle, our artist celebrity"—I jutted my head toward her, and she blushed—"we'd like you to paint life-sized superhero bodies we can paste the heads onto. Once they're done, we'll hang them up around the gym. We even picked out names for them. There's Auto-bot Audrey, Bionic Brianna, and Captain Caroline."

"Ohhh." Michelle groaned. But I could tell from the gleam in her eyes she didn't mean it. "What about the other wall decorations in the gym?"

"Other?" I glanced at Gwen.

She shrugged, looking like she cared about "other" as much as she cared about the plight of desert snails.

"What did you have in mind?" I asked.

"Classic comic metropolis landscape." The ideas poured out of Michelle. "Use butcher paper to line the walls with black skyscraper silhouettes. Hang Christmas lights in the window slots to mimic the city at night. Of course, our constantly overflowing garbage cans fit right in with the motif, so we leave them alone. And use posterboard to add taxi cabs and police cars and villains like The Ref-inator. Then cut out big cartoon bubbles that say *POW* and *BAM*—"

"Whoa, whoa, whoa!" I stopped her. "That sounds like a *ton* of work."

When her shoulders slouched, I reconsidered. After all, I gave up sleep to practice more, and Michelle loved art.

I caught her eye. "Unless you want to oversee the gym decorations while the rest of us tackle the locker room?"

Michelle gave a quick nod.

"All right." I clapped. "Who wants to stuff balloons into lockers while Michelle does everything else?"

Every hand shot up in the air.

Raising an eyebrow at Michelle, I nodded. "Have at it."

The way she beamed you'd have guessed we qualified for playoffs.

"The other thing we decided on," I said, "was buying masks and plastic tablecloth capes for the whole team to wear during warmups. Together, we make the League of Wildcats."

Emily pumped her fist. "Not as catchy as the Justice League, but I love it!"

Gwen straightened her back. "I have one more idea to share. You know those mailing labels you buy at the store? I plan on recruiting our cheerleaders to print individual senior pictures and names on them, then they can wrap the labels around water bottles in the concession stand. I bet parents will want to collect them since it's a novelty of sorts." She lifted a bottle off the floor and handed it to Emily. "I used a picture of me as a sample."

Emily turned it over in her hands. "This is *so cool*. I want one with my face on it. I know my mom would buy a million of these if it had my picture. But she's not going to want to drink out of an Audrey bottle, you know?"

When Michelle gasped, Emily winked at her. "Hey, being honest here. I love Audrey, of course, as much as an all-you-can-eat smorgasbord, but I want to see my own brand image when I hydrate this amazing body."

I cleared my throat. "I have to admit, I'd like featuring

everyone." Maybe I could give Taylor a dozen Lorali labels. "Consider it done. Anything we forgot?"

"Food!" Emily blurted.

Flattening my lips, I avoided looking at Gwen. I knew she didn't want to be surrounded by something she obviously had a problematic relationship with. In the car, she had eaten the granola bar on my promise to keep food out of Senior Night, and I had kept my word by not bringing it up. But I had no control over Emily.

Before I could respond, Gwen shot it down. "We're honoring the Seniors, not having a dinner party. We need to keep it simple."

Emily narrowed her eyes. "What's simpler than a box of cream-filled donuts with chocolate frosting and sprinkles? Except maybe an ice cream cake, which combines two of my favorite ingredients. Ice cream. And cake."

From the corner of my eye, I saw Gwen stare daggers at Emily. But since she almost always looked mad about something, I doubted anyone noticed.

Still, if I dismissed the idea, Emily would probably bargain more adamantly, and I didn't want Gwen agitated over that either.

"Okay." I waved a hand as if it were no big deal. "Bring a cake."

"*Ice cream cake,*" Emily corrected.

As the team talked about the details, I caught a whiff of sour smoke. Odd. Wrinkling my nose, I searched for the source.

Gwen's uncle lurked in the doorway of the gym again, arms folded and face taut, his stench closing the distance. I turned away, resisting the urge to pull on sweats to cover my legs. Instead, I focused on answering questions about our plans.

The longer we lingered in the gym, the more Gwen glanced his way until, finally, she grabbed my arm.

"This is taking too long," she hissed. "Can we work things out later?"

I guess we had gone overtime. Her uncle probably had somewhere to go. "Guys, are we good now? We've got two weeks to pull this off."

"We're good." Emily answered, bouncing on her toes.

On the way to the locker room, I fell in stride with Gwen. "I think that went well. I can't wait to see how it turns out. It'll be a lot of work though."

"GWEN," a rough voice bellowed across the gym. "Let's GO."

Gwen flinched, but locked eyes with me. "Whatever. You did it to yourself by adding all those extra decorations and food."

A slap in the face would have hurt as much.

"GWEN."

Without grabbing her bag, she turned a one-eighty, and fled out the gym door.

The hair on my arms rose. *Pray for Gwen.*

I'm not sure how long I stood gaping after her with prayers flitting through silent lips. My phone buzzing in my pocket snapped me out of meditative zone.

Taylor: Sand courts on Saturday! Bring the cookies!

Me: Yes. But no cookies. No time to bake.

Taylor: Remember the fire pit?

What I remembered was the way my heart raced when he sat next to me. How my words came out in a jumbled mess whenever I talked to him. How the heat rose to my face when he leaned close. How his musky scent haunted me after he left. How much his easy smile distracted me from focusing on my goal.

And how much I craved that distraction.

Me: Yes, and?

Taylor: Lunch there instead of cookies?

Me: <Thumb up> With you?

Taylor: <Laughing face> Yes.

Me: Fast food? Taco is my love language.

Taylor: <smiley face> Tacos it is.

Taylor: Wait—how did it go from you baking cookies to me bringing tacos?

Me: IDK. But taco 'bout fun. See you Saturday!

Smiling broad enough to make my cheeks ache, I scrolled through the latest photos of Taylor and me. I'd see him soon. So cute. So silly.

And wow! Pictures from our team building picnic. I stopped on my favorite one. It showed Emily shoving two cookies in her mouth at once. Next to her, Michelle, polished as ever, had one arm around Emily and the other toasting me with her designer metal water bottle. Did she use a Wildcat sticker on it?

I zoomed in on the image and froze. At the table behind them sat Gwen. No plate. No food. Just a sucker in her mouth.

My smile wilted. I wasn't sure when it started, but this eating disorder wasn't something new. The signs were there all along. I just missed them.

Everybody did.

God, please send someone to help Gwen. While pocketing my phone, I amended my prayer. *"Someone qualified."*

Until then, maybe I could appeal to the aggressive streak in Gwen.

CHAPTER TWENTY-TWO

INSIDE THE TEN-FOOT LINE

"Y'all gotta hear this." I cued a video on my phone. "I found it last night when I was searching for ways to achieve optimum sport performance levels. It's a podcast discussing what to eat to fuel up for a game. I think my mom was on to something with the kale chips."

"You mean that grassy stuff you always throw out?" Emily asked. She reached across the table to swipe a roll off Gwen's tray.

"Yes." I shifted to block Emily from snagging anything else. "But I eat everything else she packs. Just listen."

When I pressed play, Gwen quieted and leaned forward. I hoped hearing from experts instead of me might inspire her to eat better—or at all—before tonight's game. After all, at the core of most athletes' hearts is a deep desire to reach your potential. So, between her need to control life and her competitive streak, I banked on her competitive streak winning out.

When the podcast ended, Gwen took a bite of banana and nibbled on a few chicken nuggets. Not a feast. But not a famine. Considering her struggle, I counted it as a victory and a bridge between us.

The connection proved short-lived. When lunch ended, Gwen shut me out again. On the bus ride to the game facility, she hunched up with Audrey, whispering in her ear and glaring at anyone close enough to overhear.

Oblivious to all these theatrics, Emily lounged on the seat next to me. I couldn't tell if she was using her phone to take selfies or pictures of the bus ceiling. Either would be typical Emily.

With nothing else to do, I almost texted Taylor, but the upcoming match crowded out that impulse. I needed to concentrate on my game. The rival team's lineup featured elite players, increasing the likelihood of college recruiters watching from the stands. Last time, Emily got noticed. Beating a team everyone expected to roll over us might get me noticed this time. Best to run mental rehearsals in my mind.

Closing my eyes, I settled into a comfortable position.

One calming breath. Two. Three. *God, help me learn what I need to be successful.*

I envisioned myself on the court. The crowd. The sounds. I

executed flawless jump sets. Serves. Spikes. A certain dimpled boy with a crooked smile. Gwen in a deep pit, dressed in a multicolored coat. Her uncle, leering over her. And dancing kale chips.

Something jabbed me and my eyes snapped open.

"Stop snoring," Emily said.

I sat up and wiped drool from my cheek. "I was visualizing a Wildcat victory."

"Yeah." Emily wrinkled her nose. "In your dreams."

Before I knew it, the bus rolled into the parking lot. In tandem, Emily and I hefted our bags and headed into another building that, once again, made our school look like a dystopian junkyard.

When we entered, an overflow of people crowded the court, filling the space with energic chatter. Nibbling on my thumbnail, I glanced across the gym to the visitor side. Fans dotted the section, pieces of driftwood in the vast ocean of bleachers. Above them sat three recruiters, their college shirts and attitude evident in every move.

I put on my game face. *Let's see what they think of me now.*

As luck would have it, tonight was our rival's Senior Night, and the event was laced with an almost Hollywood level glitz.

During team introductions, the announcer fawned over their superstars. Each senior received a sash with *Queen of the Court* written on it and a large bouquet of roses. Wearing tiaras that looked like they had real jewels, the seniors walked a red carpet surrounding the court. A dozen underclassmen and twenty-four cheerleaders flanked their stylish parade.

As they strutted forward, a parent on each elbow, the loudspeakers broadcast their future plans. "After Graduation, Miss Six-foot-four Giantess will play volleyball for University of Amazingness and study Elementary Drizzle." Or "The

Master-of-All-Things Kneepad Woman will play volleyball for University of Wealth and Prosperity and major in Creative Whatever." Or "The Amazonian Beast Girl signed to play at Out-of-Your-Price-Range College and major in Blah, blah, blah." That kind of thing.

Did all their players earn scholarships?

A searing desire to join them seized me. *I want to play in college too.* Swallowing, I glanced at the recruiters. They came because they had an opening to fill. I may not be their target, but they still might notice me.

Coach called us over. Her eyes flashed with an inner fire greedy to consume all in its path. "Last time we played this team, they trounced us in three sets. But I lost that paperwork long ago. Shredded it into tiny pieces and fed it to dogs. They may expect another easy victory. They may expect us to roll over for them. What they don't know is that every time we roll over, it will be in pursuit of another ball. Because we are not the same team they conquered earlier." Coach's voice lowered, drawing us in. "Ladies, shall we re-introduce ourselves?"

"Yes!" we screamed.

With a grunt, Coach held our eyes. "This game belongs to us. We will earn their respect. And I suspect by then, it will be too late for them to realize they've already lost."

Gwen aced her first serve, and my team exploded with cheers. But like all strong teams, our opposing team barely flinched. Point by point, the intensity ratcheted up into an all-out battle—their height and coaching versus our grit and scramble.

Emily tore up the back court in a good way. She proved Coach's claim that a team can't score points if you never let the ball touch the floor.

And me? Taking my cue from Taylor, I went into piranha mode.

As the level of competition rose, so did my spirit. All that practice. All that training. I let muscle memory take over and drank in the joy of the game.

Because I both hit and set, their blockers often tracked me, which left holes in their defense. Even if our strikes weren't as powerful, they were still effective enough to score.

We won the first set 25–23.

Perhaps mortified by their loss to an "inferior" team, they pounded back hard, winning the next two sets 25–16, 25–18.

Coach rallied us for the fourth game. "They may tell themselves that they're in control, that they'll finish us off now. They may believe the first loss was a fluke, but we know better. We earned round one. This one is ours too. Prove to them you can play. Prove it to yourself."

We dug in and took set four 25–21. Putting us, once again, into a fifth game.

While the captains met to call the coin toss for the final serve, I noticed Gwen stumble. Her hand shook as she reached for her water bottle. Classic low blood sugar symptoms, according to my research. I feared this might happen. But because I knew her secret struggle, I came prepared. I fished around in my duffle bag until I located a pouch of apple juice.

More concerned than I cared to admit, I pulled Gwen aside. Somehow, I'd grown to care about the girl. Prickles and all.

"Are you okay?" I folded my arms. "You look dizzy."

Ducking her head, Gwen's eyes darted. "Shhh."

Following her gaze, I saw Audrey turning her head our direction, brows furled.

I shifted my body to shield Gwen and protect her secret.

"It's okay. It's just us." I hesitated, then gently pushed the pouch into her hands. "Drink this. You're our number one setter. We need you to win."

Focusing on me, Gwen's eyes widened. Then she nodded, stabbed the straw through the silver lining, and took quick, tiny slurps.

Lowering my voice, I spoke with urgency. "Time is a factor. You still need a recovery period. We could try to drag out this break somehow. How slowly can you tie your shoes?"

Gwen didn't respond. Instead, she finished her juice and crumpled the pouch. Straightening her back, she took a deep breath. "Don't worry about it. I'll be fine."

Behind us, Brianna's whoop brought reality back. Bouncing on her toes, she rushed to the bench. "We won first serve!"

That was a huge advantage in a 15-point game. But it meant Gwen served first. Was she up to it?

She bit her lip.

I narrowed my eyes.

With seconds clicking off the clock, Coach called us together.

Before Coach could talk though, Gwen spoke up. "I have a risky idea. It could backfire, but it might surprise them."

Frowning, Coach met her eyes. "We won the last game. Why would I want to change anything?"

"Because they won't expect it."

Coach quirked an eyebrow. "I'm listening."

"Take me out and run a 5–1 with Lorali setting."

My eyes widened as if all air got sucked out of the room. Gwen always played with self-centered ferocity, and now she volunteered to remove herself from the game? She must feel worse than I realized.

Coach split a stare between the two of us. "You want me to take out our best setter and limit our best hitter?"

I lifted my hands to show I wasn't in on that particular idea.

With a quick dismissal, Coach shook her head. "I don't think so. Same lineup. Dig deep into your reserves and steal this game."

As we took the floor, I sidled up to Gwen. We stood close, right inside of the ten-foot line. Friend to friend. Or something that closely resembled it.

Turning to keep our conversation private, I leaned in. "Hang in there. I'm going to stall for more time."

Lifting my hand, I signaled for someone to wipe the floor. One of the ball boys rushed over with a rag in hand and worked on the area I indicated.

"Pulling yourself out of the match?" I whispered. "Are you crazy? You're our best setter. We need you."

Gwen tucked a loose strand of hair behind her ear. Her hand still trembled, but less than it had five minutes ago. "I–I don't want to let the team down. I feel drained."

Sensing her distress, I patted her shoulder. "We're all drained. But here's the cool thing. We're a team. Win or lose, we're in this together. We share the pain together. We share the joy together. If one stumbles, the others step up." I paused, letting the words sink in.

She lifted her chin. "You're still stalling for me, aren't you?"

"Maybe." Grinning, I raised a brow. "Remember. You're not alone. I'm right here with you."

Something seemed to spark in her eyes. Determination? Gratitude? I wasn't sure.

"Is that something your Aunt Tina said?" she asked, her voice almost playful. Almost.

The ref circled us, checking our lineup numbers.

Ignoring him, I snorted. "Nope. That's something Lorali Mathews said to the teammate she's going to rely on the most."

This time, a genuine smile broke out on her face, although she quickly concealed it behind her hand.

It wasn't the Gwen I was used to seeing. But it was a Gwen I could get used to.

I knelt and retied my shoes in slow motion. "Should I find another imaginary wet spot for the ball boy clean up?"

"No." Gwen took a breath. "I'm ready."

Brushing back her ponytail, Gwen took her place behind the serving line. The whistle blew. After three infinite seconds, Gwen served. Maybe it was low energy or maybe it was by design, but the ball barely cleared the top of the net, a difficult shot to receive. And, as it turned out, an ace.

After that, there was no holding us back. Each point we won sent a shot of adrenaline through me. I tapped inner strength I didn't know existed. We played like a horde of crazed zombies. Unstoppable. Overwhelming. Hungry.

In the end, I'd like to say we won, but I won't.

Instead, I'll say that the bus ride on the way home carried champions as rowdy as midnight on New Year's Eve.

Not only that, but a recruiter talked to Coach after the game. In the madness of the match, I'd forgotten about them.

Maybe one had noticed me. But more likely the recruiter was asking about Emily. Once again, her rabid, Tasmanian devil defense kept the ball in the air, proving that a team can't score if the ball never drops on their opponent's side of the court. She deserved a scholarship.

She was amazing.

We were amazing.

We were a team.

And we had our sights set on playoffs.

CHAPTER TWENTY-THREE

THREE EVENTS

The days leading up to Senior Night flew by. Other than pushing myself to improve every day, three awkward events took place. None of them were related.

One day, I dealt with Audrey drama.

It had started when her dad visited Coach at the beginning of the season to complain about Audrey rotating into the game instead of starting. As a senior, he expected favoritism. But despite his threats, Audrey didn't get what she wanted.

Until, through unfortunate circumstance, she did.

However, since Gwen's return, Audrey once again spent

the first three rotations on the bench. I suspected Audrey missed the spotlight.

I couldn't fault her for that longing. Everyone wanted to play.

But I still believed that privilege should be based on each player's own merits.

If I were in Audrey's place, I'd channel my disappointment into effort. I'd work harder in practice, soak in any learning I could, and push myself to do better. And if I failed, then I'd work even harder.

Even Judy's decision to quit the team made sense to me. Sometimes when I'm frustrated, I'm tempted to throw in the towel. Good thing I'm too stubborn to let that idea stick around for long.

But the way Audrey and her dad acted made no sense to me at all. Convinced of their correctness, they harbored resentment. It boiled and blistered and blackened inside of them, and then burst out again in all its Frankenstein glory.

I suppose that's why I wasn't surprised to discover Audrey lounging alone in the locker room before practice. An arrogant lift of her chin and a curled lip told me something was up. Down the hall, I recognized the abrasive timbre of her dad's voice assaulting the air from behind closed doors.

As the uncomfortable outburst continued in the background, I bobbed my head at her. "Hey."

Audrey smirked and raised an eyebrow. Was she that confident her dad's ploy would pay off? That Coach would yank either me or Gwen in favor of her?

Tensing under her scrutiny, I considered how to respond. My relationship with Gwen had started rocky too. Our tenuous bond only improved after I prayed for her and purposely set aside my animosity and tutored her in math. God had done something unexpected with that softer approach. Like it or not, in that process of friction between us, somehow the irritating grain of sand called Gwen had transformed into a treasured pearl of a teammate.

As that realization sank in, I studied Audrey as she loitered within earshot of Coach's office.

Lifting her chin, Audrey stared down her nose at me, contempt marring her smile.

Maybe Audrey deserved the same kind of effort I gave Gwen.

Closing my eyes, I blew out a slow breath. *Okay, God. Your turn. I'm just going to start talking and hope you'll give me the right words.*

Ignoring a sour taste in my mouth, I spoke. "Sounds like your dad and Coach are having a loud discussion."

"Uh-huh." Audrey stretched out her fingers and examined her nails. "Daddy is reminding Coach that I deserve better."

Pausing, I collected my thoughts. Audrey had a self-centered approach to most situations. What if I helped Audrey realize how our current lineup benefitted her?

Letting my posture relax, I slid onto the bench. Following my normal routine, I dropped my duffle bag onto the floor. In the split second it took to unzip my sweatshirt, I sifted through a dozen responses until landing on a safe and truthful one. "Yes, I agree. Our team deserves better."

Audrey widened her stance. "I didn't say our *team* deserves better, I said—"

Cutting her off, I pulled an Emily and kept talking. "I mean, look at you." My hand swept toward her. "You've been so flexible, filling in spots no one else on the team could fill. It's awesome."

Frowning, Audrey blinked at me. Had the compliment robbed her of speech?

Leaning over, I untied my shoes. "And now we have a winning record. Can you believe that? A winning record."

With a quick flip of the wrist, I pulled a shoe off. I hefted it like a weight and cocked my head at her. "Who knows? If we win these next three games, we might even make playoffs. Whatever we're doing, it's working, don't you think?"

Wide-eyed, Audrey licked her lips. "I suppose."

Shaking my head, I reached for my other shoe. "I compared our conference record to the other schools in our district. We're close to making the bid. And going to playoffs for the first time since 1983? Think of all the hype that would go with that. Social media would go nuts. Do you think the local news would pick up the story too?"

Audrey folded her arms across her chest. "Probably."

"Cool," I said. "I bet the principal would hold a special pep rally for us. We'd go up on stage in front of the whole school and stand right next to the cheerleaders. The upperclassmen like you should get extra applause of course."

Sitting back, I sighed. "Ah. But maybe I'm dreaming. I mean, one single loss could make the difference between making playoffs and getting sidelined again. One little change could throw everything off course. Although I truly believe that as long as we finish strong, we have a chance."

Swallowing hard, Audrey shot a quick look toward Coach's office. The noise coming from behind the door had risen to a volcanic rumble.

Time to hit it home. "You're so lucky." I beamed at her. "I can't imagine going to playoffs my senior year."

Audrey grimaced and shifted her body. "Yeah, we're on a roll. Do you think we could really make playoffs?"

"Don't you?"

She cleared her throat. "I'll, uh—catch up with you later. I'm going to check on, uh—my dad. He, uh—lost his wallet at the last game."

I raised an eyebrow. "No wonder he's so upset. I'm sure Coach can help him."

"Of course."

A cockroach couldn't have scrambled away more quickly.

Five minutes later, Audrey escorted her dad out of Coach's office. Red-faced and tight-lipped, he tromped out the door.

As for Audrey, she didn't mention "I deserve better" again. In fact, she seemed downright content for once.

✳ ✳ ✳

Audrey's new attitude helped practice run stress-free. It remained that way until the last thirty minutes when Gwen's uncle came early to pick her up. Instead of waiting in his car, he made himself comfortable in our tight bleacher area. In any of our opponents' facilities, he would have been an ant in a desert. But the size of our gym made him appear more like an alligator in a sandbox.

I avoided his side of the gym. If a stray ball rolled his way, I let it go. After our encounter in the park, being around him creeped me out. I couldn't shake the memory of how he had undressed me with his eyes and fondled the young girl by his side. Every time I bent over to pick up a ball or squatted for serve receive, I felt him watching me.

But as uncomfortable as his unwanted attention made me, Gwen's game suffered more. Her movements became jerky, and her sets missed their mark. The longer he watched from the bleachers, the more she stole glances his way and wiped her hands on her shirt.

When Michelle tossed Gwen a free ball and it hit her in the face, Coach called her out. "Gwen, get your mind on the game. What's up?"

Lowering her eyes, Gwen scowled. "Nothing."

"Then quit daydreaming," Coach snapped.

Gritting her teeth, Gwen called for the next ball and sent a quick set to the middle hitter. Meanwhile, Coach glanced at Gwen's uncle, her face expressionless but her eyes calculating.

I took that opportunity to prod Coach a little. "We don't normally have an audience during our practices."

"No," Coach murmured. "We don't."

Then she sucked in a breath and called for a five-minute water break.

While players cooled off, Coach squared her shoulders and approached Gwen's uncle. I slinked closer, hoping to hear what they were saying. I only caught the tail end of the conversation.

"It's a free country," Gwen's uncle snarled. Eyes twitching, he swiped the back of his hand across his nose.

Coach balled her hands into fists and stood to her full, considerable height. After a moment of tense silence, she fished her phone out of her pocket. Pausing with her finger over the screen, she lifted her eyebrow. You could have chopped wood with the look on her face.

A few seconds later, Gwen's uncle cursed and stomped out.

Audrey sidled over to Gwen and whispered something.

Red-faced, Gwen nodded.

✳ ✳ ✳

The last notable event happened at youth group. Since I'd taken too long to get ready, Michelle, Emily and I arrived late. As soon as we stepped beyond the threshold of the doorway, Emily swooped for the snack bar.

Apparently, she discovered that someone had donated boxes full of what looked like gourmet frosted cupcakes. I say "looked like" because it turns out they weren't actually cupcakes. They were those popular bath bombs sculpted to look like the tastiest offering of the local bakery.

Emily grabbed one in each hand before clambering to the couch. "Can you believe my luck?" she giggled. "Look at these handfuls of heavenly bliss!"

Before anyone who knew better could warn her, she bit into a pink one. And I mean a Godzilla-sized bite.

As soon as her saliva hit the fake frosting, it foamed up. Dropping them like the bombs they were, Emily shot out of her seat. "Ewww! Ewww! Ewww!" Tears streamed down her cheeks, and she spat into a napkin. "It's *soap?* This is so wrong in so many ways."

Unable to keep a straight face, Hank apologized for putting the gift so close to the food table and excused Emily to collect a different snack. Wiping her tongue with a napkin, she flounced back to the table of treats. Scooping up the first thing available, she shoved a brownie into her mouth and chewed like an angry goat.

Joel rushed to join her, bearing an unopened soda. Without even glancing at him, she accepted it.

Hank allowed them to camp out there. He pointed out that having Emily and Joel sit apart from the rest served as a great visual for his lesson on how the Pharaoh provided Joseph's family a separate land within Egypt to live in.

Of course he had a connection.

Meanwhile, Taylor claimed Emily's spot next to me on the couch, and I didn't mind one bit. The side of my body that pressed against him heated up like a kiss of sunshine on the beach. You could have baked real cupcakes on the warmth of my skin. But they wouldn't have smelled half as amazing.

I remember frowning when that food image seared my heart. God still hadn't answered my prayers to bring along someone to help Gwen. And I still didn't know what to do with her—I mean our—secret.

Chapter Twenty-Four

SENIOR NIGHT

Emily kicked her way through the sea of blue and yellow balloons littering the floor. A string of helium-filled ones bobbed along behind her like so many ducklings. Each had a long ribbon tied around it, which Emily fastened to the arch framing the locker room door.

"I'm dizzy," Gwen complained. She sagged on the locker room bench surrounded by more of the orbs. "Can I use the helium too?"

"No," Emily said. "We don't want your balloons to float."

Gwen's lip turned down. "How many more do I have to blow up?"

"That's probably enough." I scooped up a handful. "Let's stuff them into the seniors' lockers now."

Thanks to Emily's snooping, we had the combinations to all the seniors' lockers. I tried shoving balloons inside, but they kept clinging to my sleeves.

Mouth set in a hard line, Gwen helped me shepherd them back in place.

"Look, Gwen." Emily pointed. "Your hair is standing up."

"Mine too." I squeezed the latex orb in my hand. "Static electricity."

A mischievous glint sparked in Emily's eyes. "You know what this means?" She snatched a balloon off the floor and rubbed it on her head. The hair-raising effect was immediate. "Time for selfies!"

Michelle frowned when she walked in on us posing. "Finished in here?"

"Almost." I pulled Michelle into the group. "One more shot."

I flashed peace fingers. Emily puckered her lips. Gwen rolled her eyes.

"What am I supposed to do?" Michelle asked.

"Tell us about your decorations," I said.

Immediately, a smile lit Michelle's face, and I snapped us all with my phone. "Now we're done." I checked the image. "Nice pic, Michelle. Makes me curious about what you did."

Michelle quirked a smile. "Let's go look."

A minute later, we stood in a transformed gym. String lights glowed through windows in the city skyline. Senior superheroes with comical speech bubbles crowded the walls. Street signs and car cutouts completed the busy metropolis scene.

Squealing, Emily scrambled off to explore the landscape. After a moment's hesitation, Gwen shadowed her.

Mesmerized, I turned a slow circle. "Michelle, you are a wizard."

Michelle blushed. "Thanks. I had fun. I still need to hang these posters at the entrance." She pointed to an area decorated like a marquee.

Tilting my head, I lifted the nearest one. "More of your amazing artwork?"

"No, the parents of each senior made these scrapbook features." She ran a finger down the edge. "I provided artistic suggestions, of course."

From across the court, Emily yelled, "I'm adding graffiti to this skyscraper. Where's the spray paint?"

Face blanching, Michelle pushed duct tape into my hands. "I gotta stop her. Handle the posters, please!"

While Michelle bolted, I studied the poster I held. A timeline with Caroline's grade school pictures traveled across the top. Underneath the images, blue ribbon framed two sections—a list of her favorite things, from sports team to song, and a paragraph about her plans for after high school.

Caroline plans to attend Baylor University and earn a degree in Social Work. She feels called to work with underprivileged students and—

I skimmed the rest.

Interesting. No mention of volleyball. Curiosity piqued, I flipped to the second poster. It belonged to Audrey. Timeline shots showed her living large with a collection of name-drop worthy students. Curly print highlighted her post-high school plans. *Audrey is interested in Public Relations and all related fields, including voice acting. This summer, she hopes to get an internship managing social media accounts for a local recording studio. She will attend Texas A&M and major in Communications. Follow her on Instagram @QueenBeeAudrey or visit her web—*

Blowing a huff of air, dropped the poster back in the pile. Communications, huh? Guess she'll have to stop letting her dad talk for her then.

I lifted Brianna's poster last and studied her timeline. In one picture, Brianna stood in a kitchen. A bald child sat on the counter next to her. Both held popsicle sticks and stuck out blue tongues at the camera, the obvious aftermath of an encounter with their frozen sweets.

Our fierce middle hitter and blood-thirsty captain had a soft side? I frowned. Brianna rarely talked about her family. Seeing that side of her was like discovering a house with a hidden room full of treasures.

What valuables might someone find in my home? Or would they only find a closet empty of all but a handful of cheap medals and trophies?

When Brianna graduates, she will major in biology at Purdue University. One day, she hopes to become a pediatrician and work with cancer patients. She dedicates her final home game to her eight-year-old cousin Abigail, who is currently battling leukemia, and to her Aunt Linda, a breast cancer survivor.

Shocked, I lowered the poster. Such heartache, but such spunk. And again, no mention of volleyball. Giving up the sport never occurred to me. I assumed everyone felt the way I did about it.

Swallowing, I swiped my sleeve across my eyes. Aunt Tina loved volleyball. She would have played forever. She was my hero. And she died.

My eyes traveled to a poem taped at the bottom of Brianna's poster. "Equipped." Apparently, she wrote it herself.

You undermine yourself each day
By what you think and what you say
And blame your loss on destiny
Instead of seeking actively
To use your blessings, one by one,
And then, when all the work is done,
To know God gave you what you need,
But let you *choose* to go succeed.

Puzzled, I reread it. What did Brianna mean, choosing to succeed? What did success look like to her anyway?

I ran a finger along the edge of the poster. *Did you have fun? Because if playing the game is fun, then losing means nothing. But if playing the game isn't fun—*

"Then winning means nothing," I whispered. My words faded, absorbed by the walls.

What about volleyball captured my heart? A sense of pride? Satisfaction? Or was it the exhilaration of the challenge? I could play a rec league, of course. But it wouldn't be the same level of competition. Why did I crave more?

And what would I do if I lost it all to injury the way Taylor had? If all my work meant nothing? Uncertainty oozed into my gut and coated my stomach. What would life look like without volleyball?

Fighting the urge to bite off a nail, I curled my hands into fists. Volleyball connected me to Aunt Tina. We shared a dream. And I'd do anything to reach it.

Including hanging these posters in the hallway to help boost team unity.

After letting my momentary doubt leach away, I broke off large pieces of duct tape and pressed them on the back of each poster. Michelle left an obvious gap on the wall where they would go, and I slapped them up there.

My phone buzzed in my pocket.

Taylor: I'm coming to your game tomorrow night!

Me: Yay! What about your sister?

Taylor: She won't care. They already made playoffs.

Me: <Hand clap> Congrats.

Taylor: How is Gwen?

I promised Gwen secrecy.

Me: I'm keeping an eye on her.

Taylor: Much better than keeping an elbow on her.

Me: Or a toe.

Taylor: Or a chin.

Me: <Laughing face> When you come, ask for me at the concession stand.

Taylor: ???

Me: You'll find out.

Taylor: No fair!

Me: You'll live. Can't wait to see you!

* * *

Except for the rain, which started sometime the next day between the end of school and the start of the JV game, Senior Night turned out magical. Even though I'm sure our seniors mourned the end of their high school sporting career, during warmups, they bounced higher and hit harder with their plastic capes streaming behind them.

Our bleachers, which normally overflowed and forced people to sit on the floor, seemed even more congested. The outdated speaker system struggled to voice music over the noise of the mass.

When Taylor arrived, I laughed. He had taped the word "Rally Cats" to the front of his black t-shirt. At his side stood Joel. I'd have to tell Emily.

After a quick wave, I pointed toward the concession stand. Showing his palms, Taylor shrugged. Widening my eyes, I pointed again with emphasis. He flashed a smile and headed toward the counter.

While in line during our warmup drill, I watched for his reaction. He and Joel emerged hoisting water bottles into the air like trophies. Grinning wide, Taylor waved before the two squeezed into the bleachers.

During introductions, the crowd cheered as each senior escorted her parents down a black carpet runway—Michelle suggested that the long dark strip looked like a street and so fit our theme. Each clutched a bouquet of flowers and our super-amazing gift bags.

Without a hitch, we transitioned onto the court. We were confident. Unrelenting. Strong. Unified. Our play had improved so much over the course of the season, the game was over in three quick sets, and, just like that, we added another win to our belt.

As the throng cleared out, I scanned the gym for Taylor. I spotted him and Joel hovering near my mom. With animated motions, Taylor showed her his water bottle. She opened her oversized purse for him to peek in. No doubt it was stuffed to the top with "Lorali" merchandise.

When I joined them, Mom swept her arm around my waist. "Great game. For once, I think the referees did a decent job. Your weekend coach here asked me if it's okay to take you and Emily out for a milkshake to celebrate. I told him sure. But be home before eleven."

"Mom, it's a Friday night."

"Okay, midnight then." She stepped back, still holding my hands. "But if you ride with Taylor, how are you getting your car back?" My stomach dropped. I was so used to being chauffeured everywhere that I'd forgotten about my trek home.

Mom squeezed my fingers. She must have understood the look on my face. "I guess you can take separate cars to your restaurant, right?" She glanced at Taylor.

"Of course," he said.

Nodding, Mom turned to leave. "Perfect. You and Emily have fun. And remember, drive slow."

"Thanks, Mom," I called after her. She waved.

Taylor cleared his throat. "Actually, Joel hasn't asked Emily yet. He's hoping you will do it for him." He shoved Joel on the shoulder.

With a sheepish look, Joel held up his water bottle with Emily's feral face plastered on the label. "She's amazing. Do you think she'll come with me?"

I laughed. "Don't worry. If there's food involved, Emily will be there."

Quickly, I texted Emily. Then, hefting my bag, I backed away. "Emily said yes. If you give us five minutes, we'll change."

Taylor raised a thumb. "I'll give you ten."

Right before reaching the locker room, a hand jerked my elbow and spun me around. Gwen stood there, her eyes wide. "I need a ride home. Now."

A wave of panic hit me. Did this have anything to do with anorexia?

Eyes locked on me, Gwen inclined her head towards a

figure hulking on the far side of the gym, a black stain against the dirty wall.

"Your uncle?" I wrinkled my nose. "Why don't you go home with him?

Her gaze seemed to increase in intensity. "I won't get in the car with that man," she whispered. "I won't let him near me ever again."

The way she said it made my chest tighten.

Nerves tingling, my eyes shifted to Taylor, hands in his pockets, waiting. Then back to Gwen, hands clenched, waiting. I didn't want to disappoint either one, but Gwen's pale face and wide eyes helped make up my mind.

"Okay." I frowned. "But I promised a friend I'd go out with him too. I'll drop you off at home, but I can't stay."

"I didn't ask you to stay," Gwen hissed. "Just get me out of here."

CHAPTER TWENTY-FIVE

REVELATIONS

Gwen didn't move.

"I said yes." I snapped my fingers in front of her face, breaking whatever spell she was under. "Let's go."

"Right." Gwen's lips drew back in false-looking smile. Swinging around, she called, "Thanks for coming, Uncle John, but you can leave now. Lorali is driving me home."

She flinched as he stepped toward us. Then Taylor laughed, loud and sharp. Gwen's uncle hesitated, and Gwen dragged me into the locker room.

Before the door swung shut, I peeked over my shoulder. Her uncle was retreating to the darker recesses of the gym.

Once inside, I pulled free. "What's going on?"

Ignoring me, Gwen flattened her lips. Her eyes narrowed.

I followed her gaze. Emily. Audrey. Brianna. Michelle. All still here. Finger to her lips, Gwen scuttled to her locker. She worked the lock, opening it in short jerks.

Puzzled, I opened my own locker. Gwen's actions didn't make sense. Did they somehow involve her eating disorder?

"I'm happy to help, but why didn't you ask Audrey?" I whispered.

"No. Only you." Hands trembling, Gwen lowered her knee-pads. They had hidden a dark bruise I suspected she picked up during the game. Emily would be sure to celebrate it.

"O-k-a-y." I drew the word out.

Gwen threw the pads into her backpack and quickly yanked on sweatpants.

"Take your time." I folded my arms. "I'm going to clean up before we leave."

Tight-lipped, Gwen nodded, pulling out her phone.

After waving goodbye to Brianna and Michelle and nodding at Audrey, I hit the showers. Turning the water on full blast, I lifted my ponytail to wash the nape of my neck. The warm spray hit me, sweeping away grime and soothing my aches.

While wispy steam cocooned me, I prayed. *God, please send someone to help Gwen. Something is bothering her, and I still feel inadequate to deal with it.*

Emily's calming words popped into my mind. *Trust in the Lord with all of your heart. Lean not on your own understanding.*

Was that an answer? If so, it sure seemed like all I had to do was play chauffeur tonight. If not, well, tomorrow was another day. Either way, Taylor waited for me on the other side of the door. I shut off the water and toweled off.

While I dressed, Gwen sat on the bench, back stiff, staring at nothing. Her phone sat beside her, pulsing with each new text she got. She remained motionless while I touched my lashes with mascara.

"Done!" Emily shouted. "With—" she checked her phone. "One minute to spare."

"I need every last second." I shoved my feet into a dry pair of socks.

"You look fine," Emily said.

Grunting, I knotted the laces on my Converse. "You'd say that even if I wore a gorilla costume."

"No." Emily sniffed. "I'd say you looked bananas."

Gwen snorted. The sudden noise startled me. At least her reaction showed that words could penetrate her outer barrier.

Only a handful of people remained in the gym when we exited the locker room. Gwen shadowed me, skittish as a stray dog. The boys lifted their heads as we approached and started our way. Joel stumbled to keep pace with Taylor's confident strides.

Halfway there, Emily slowed. "Wait, are you going too?" she asked Gwen.

"No. Lorali is dropping me at home."

"Don't be silly." Emily sidestepped. "Come with us."

Gwen didn't seem to hear her. Instead, she craned her neck, looking around the room. Then her shoulders relaxed, and she shifted into her usual swagger. A mask of indifference washed across her face. "Huh?"

"Come with us," Emily repeated. "I call dibs if you don't finish your milkshake. And let's be honest. We both know you won't. So order chocolate, would ya?"

I tensed. With her eating disorder, I knew the last thing Gwen wanted was food.

"No." Gwen shook her head. "I need a ride home, that's all. No big deal."

"Milkshakes are always a big deal," Emily said, followed by, "Pizza boy!" She leaped at Joel and hooked an arm through his. Total hyper-active move.

Joel's face turned pink up to his ears. "Hello, Emily. Remember me?"

Emily beamed. "How could I ever forget the man who saved me from the bath bomb disaster with a Dr. Pepper?"

Taylor turned his eyes to my one-plus. "You must be Gwen." He held out a fist.

"Hello?" Gwen fist-bumped his hand. "Do I know you?"

Grinning, Taylor shook his head. "No, but I know you. My sister is a setter too, so I make it a mission to study her competition. Especially the good ones."

Ill-concealed pride colored Gwen's face. She crossed her arms. "Scoping our team tonight?"

"Nah." He winked at me. "Just cheering for a cute friend from youth group."

I shifted, feeling suddenly awkward.

"I heard Emily talking," Taylor said. "She's right. Join us."

Gwen licked her lips. "Thanks, but I need to go home."

She didn't want to be surrounded by food again. Protecting Gwen, I interrupted before anyone else pressured her. "It's fine, really. I'll drop her off. You can follow me, Taylor, or I can meet you there. Sorry, Emily, but you'll have to go with the boys. The law says I can only drive one other passenger."

"No problem." Emily's stomach rumbled. "And I vote we meet you there. I'm ready to order now."

I touched Taylor's arm when we reached the doorway. "Are you okay with my side trip?"

Questions lingered in Taylor's eyes, but he nodded.

"I won't be long." I smiled. "I promise."

Beyond the entrance, rain still poured, flooding the sidewalk and spewing rivulets of water down the street. Using our duffle bags for protection, we made a run for our cars.

Ahead of me, a squealing Emily ducked into Taylor's vehicle with the boys close behind. Seconds later, Taylor's car headlights snapped on, countering the darkness.

Gwen and I splashed through the remaining puddles. In the extra time it took to throw our bags in the back seat and climb into the car, we got soaked.

Blinking away the rain from my lashes, I turned my key in the ignition. Warm air kicked in from the vent.

"Ugh." Gwen dotted her cheeks with the sleeve of her sweatshirt.

"Tell me about it." I wiggled my toes. Cold water seeped between them. "And gross. My socks got wet. Now they're all squishy and cold. I'm changing."

Straining against the seatbelt, I groped around in the backseat until my fingers landed on my wet duffle bag. Grateful that my flip-flops were still inside after last Saturday's sand session with Taylor, I pulled them out. "These will work."

As I struggled out of my shoes in the cramped car, my phone buzzed. Gwen peeked at the message. "Emily wants to know what to order for you."

"Tell her a number two meal with a chocolate milkshake."

Gwen tapped the screen. "There you go."

"Thanks." I put the car in gear and switched on the windshield wipers. As I eased forward, another pair of headlights popped to life across the parking lot. "Guess we weren't the last to leave," I said.

"Is that a Pontiac Trans Am?"

Turning into the street, I shrugged. "It's black. That's all I got."

"Pull over," Gwen ordered.

Her urgency made me comply. Wipers *swish-swishing,* I paused by the curb.

Gwen gaze laser-focused on the street outside, watching the car pass. Then she relaxed back into her seat. "It's a Chevy. Keep going."

Baffled, I checked for traffic, then pulled out again. "You're acting weird. In the locker room, you said *only I* could take you home. Now you're checking out cars. Will you please tell me what's going on?"

Silence stretched between us, broken by the bark of thunder. Finally, Gwen took a deep breath. "Don't tell anyone. Promise."

My heart skipped. "I haven't mentioned your eating habits to anyone, if that's what you're worried about."

"No. This is different." She said nothing more.

Sighing, I slowed to turn onto the main road. The ticking of my turn signal was lost in rattle of the storm. "At least tell me why you went home with me instead of Audrey."

Gwen slumped. "You've already met my demons. For everyone else, I have an image to maintain, you know?"

"Fair point," I said. "But there's more, isn't there?"

Silence again. *Trust in the Lord.*

"Fine." Her voice came out strangled. "You saw the bruise on my knee?"

"I assumed it was from the game."

"It wasn't. My uncle slammed me down." Gwen shuddered.

"I have matching bruises on my arms and shoulder. And a bump on my head."

A prickly sensation enveloped me, like ants crawling up my leg. *Lean not on your own understanding.* "What happened?"

"I had an argument with my uncle."

I waited two heartbeats before pressing her. "About what?"

"About my mom," Gwen whispered. "He hurts her."

My stomach twisted, and my thoughts plunged to a dark place. I wouldn't jump to conclusions. Not yet. "What did he do?"

Gwen shifted as if sharing my unease. "Nothing much at first. He lost his job four months ago, about the same time Mom went through the divorce." Gwen plucked her sweatpants. "I've never seen her so broken. So lost. So desperate to hold on to whatever semblance of family she could. A person like that's bound to make a mistake. Like inviting an abusive leech to move in with us."

My heart ached for her. I understood loss and brokenness. My mom still hadn't dealt with Aunt Tina's death. Honestly, I hadn't either. "I'm sorry," I said.

"For what?" Gwen suddenly iced over.

Keep her talking, Lord. I don't know what else to do.

"I'm sorry for not being a better friend."

"What makes you think you're a friend? I needed a ride home."

Ouch. She doesn't want my sympathy. Or maybe she does but fears it.

"Call me your teammate then, if that makes you more comfortable," I said. "I'm here for you either way."

Again, the splatter of rain and quiet *thunk* of windshield wipers filled the space between us.

Finally, she spoke. "My mom didn't want him loafing

around the house all day while she worked full time and paid all the bills. She insisted that he at least run errands for her."

"Like picking you up from practice?"

"And other things." Gwen cleared her throat but didn't elaborate. "He agreed, but he made her pay for every 'favor' she asked."

"How?"

"It started with criticism and put downs. He called her a worthless piece of crap. But he used a nastier word. Then it escalated. He forced her to sell some of her jewelry because he wanted beer money. Made her cry. Things like that. And whenever I asked her about it, she still made excuses for him." Gwen threw up her hands. "'Johnny hasn't been himself lately. Be patient, he's going through a hard time too. Things will get better. We can't put him out, he's the only family we've got.' That kind of stuff."

Realization set in. "That's when you stopped eating, isn't it? When he moved in. Because you couldn't control your mom. Or your uncle. Or your life."

"Yeah." Gwen folded her arms. "That's my story. It sucks."

"Verbal abuse," I said. "No one ever sees those wounds, do they? That's how men like him get away with it." I turned onto her street. "But what about your bruises? That's physical abuse. Was it a one-time thing?"

"No." Her words came out quiet. Hesitant. Ashamed. "Mom too."

A lump formed in my throat. "How bad?"

For several minutes, Gwen didn't answer. Then she drew in a ragged breath. "When his drinking got worse, he grew more violent. He threw a television remote at my mom like a bullet. He punched a hole in the wall right next to her face.

And I didn't see it, but sometimes at night when I was in bed, I'd hear him slap her. It terrified me."

My mouth went dry. What else might have gone on that she didn't witness? "That sounds bad."

"It was. It is." Gwen rubbed fingers on her head. "He's a ticking bomb. And I don't know when he's going to explode next."

"Did you tell anyone about what he did to your head?" I asked. "Your neck? Your legs?"

"My mom, but she didn't believe me. She thought the bruises came from volleyball. Got defensive. Called me a liar trying to get rid of her beloved brother." Gwen huffed. "Even after all he did to her, she's so afraid of losing him, she denies it."

An ache grew in my chest. "I can't even imagine."

"Volleyball keeps me sane," Gwen said. "I don't have to think about him while I'm on the court. And if I win a scholarship, I can escape to a college far away."

Guilt twinged in my heart. Gwen and I both loved volleyball, and we both seemed to own an unquenchable desire to play the sport. My reasons for wanting a scholarship were more complex than that. But still, that wasn't the whole story for Gwen. She played to survive. Her low-grade suspension earlier in the season must have hit her like a tsunami.

Uncertain of how to respond to her revelation, I said nothing. In a way, I understood her dreams. And her heartache. I guess everyone struggles with darkness at some point in their lives. The difference between us? I had hope to light my way.

When we approached her house, I pulled to the curb and idled there. I sensed Gwen had more to say if I had the patience to listen. Headlights winked on from a car a few driveways behind us, brightening the interior enough to study

Gwen's face. The dark lines under her eyes held new meaning for me. "Maybe you should talk to a counselor."

"I don't need some feel-good fraud telling me what to think." Gwen shook her head. "I did threaten to go to the police. Except Uncle John didn't like that. Which is why I'm avoiding him now."

"Won't he be waiting for you in the house?" I asked.

"He'll be drunk, passed out on the couch by now." Gwen shrugged. "He's predictable that way. I'll sneak past him and lock myself in my room until my mom finishes her shift. When she gets home, I'll talk to her again. Convince her to get out of there before he wakes up."

"That doesn't sound safe. Let me stay with you. We can figure something else out." I picked up my phone. "I'll text Taylor and tell him I can't come."

Her brows furrowed, a sad expression. "But Emily already put your order in."

"Oh, that's not a problem. You know Emily will eat it for me."

Gwen sighed. "Okay. Thanks, Loser."

"Any time..." I narrowed my eyes. "Winner."

Gwen snorted, but her lip curled into a grin.

I grinned right back.

Me: Sorry, something came up. You'll have to take a rain check. Rain. Get it? <Laughing face>

Taylor: <Frowning face> What's up?

A car door slammed. Gwen jumped and hunched her neck toward the noise.

I checked my rearview mirror. A shadowed figure stood by the car behind us.

Gwen gasped. "It's my uncle! Drive!"

CHAPTER TWENTY-SIX

CHASE

My fingers hovered over the phone as I tried to process the panic in Gwen's voice.

"Relax," I said. "It's probably your neighbor. We took ten minutes getting dressed, and fifteen more talking to the boys. That means your uncle should have beaten us here by at least twenty-five or thirty minutes. Besides, *you* claimed he'd be passed out on the couch by now."

Gwen ducked. "His Trans Am isn't in the driveway. I bet he waited on the curb for me to get here."

"Not likely." I refreshed my phone screen. "Besides, nothing's happening back there."

"But—"

I held up a hand to stop her. "Gwen, why would your uncle sit in his car for a half hour waiting for you to get home? It doesn't make sense."

Frowning, Gwen stayed low. "So, it's not him?"

"No."

"Okay." Gwen squeezed her eyes shut. "Because I didn't tell you the rest."

The hair rose on my neck. "There's more?!"

"I left out a few things. See, when he started tongue lashing my mom a few days after he moved in, I called in a domestic violence complaint." Gwen stared straight ahead as if purging her soul. "Mom should have thrown him out. She should have protected herself. Protected me. Except she didn't do anything. So I did. When the police showed up, it turned into a *he said, she said* situation, and—" Her voice hitched. "My mom took his side. When the cops left, Uncle John said he'd make me pay." Tears welled in Gwen's eyes. "So, it's my fault things got worse. I put us in danger."

My heart sank. Once again, I could only imagine how betrayed she felt. How helpless. How angry. How alone. And no one knew.

"I'm sorry," I whispered.

"Quit apologizing," she snarled. "You couldn't change anything anyway."

The raw harshness of that truth cut me.

"Maybe not then. But I can change something now." I leaned back into the seat. "I don't think you should stay here tonight. Come home with me. We'll figure something out."

"And leave my mom at his mercy? I can't do that." A

wildness touched her eyes. "Besides, she'll have to believe me. Because now I have proof. I have bruises. This time, the police will arrest Uncle John. And he knows it."

"Then you've already called the police?" I asked.

"No. I just—" A wistful look clouded her eyes, like a sick child with her head pressed against a frosty window on a snowy day. She wrung her hands. "I didn't want all hell to break loose until after Senior Night. I couldn't let him spoil that too."

I put a hand on her knee. "You don't have to do this alone anymore. We can deal with this together."

Whatever vulnerability her eyes held evaporated, and a mask of indifference took its place. "Like you could handle it. He threatened to kill me."

My jaw dropped. Gwen stated it so coolly. "Say *what?*"

A hand slapped her window, startling me enough to drop my phone. Damp flesh pressed against the glass. Uncle John's face. His bloodshot eyes bulged like two ravenous sharks, roving the dark interior of my car.

"Gwen!" he shouted, voice distorted by the rain. "Why aren't you getting out of the car, Gwen? Why aren't you going into the house?"

His other hand smashed against the window. It hit with a metallic thud.

The blood froze in my veins.

He had a gun.

One milli-second. He lifted it.

Two milli-seconds. Cocked it.

Three milli-seconds. Pointed it.

We were dead.

"Drive!" Gwen shrieked.

Pulse restarting, I dropped the phone and threw the car

INSIDE THE TEN-FOOT LINE

into gear. I slammed the gas pedal. The tires squealed in protest, unable to find a solid purchase on the wet surface, then fishtailed forward.

Lightning flashed. Gwen's uncle fell backward, and the gun exploded. Glass shattered like cheap diamonds and a *whoosh* sucked the oxygen out of the car. Gwen slumped.

A hundred feet ahead, I screeched to a halt. "Gwen! Are you okay?"

She touched her face. "I think so."

Ears ringing, I blinked at the gap in my car. The beast had struck the back window, passenger side.

That would have been the front window if I hadn't reacted.

Gwen's window.

Gwen's *head*.

My hands shook. The shot had to be an accident, right?

In the rearview mirror, I watched Gwen's uncle stumble to his car. She had been right—his were the headlights on the curb behind us. Was she also right about him wanting to kill her?

This situation was not covered in my Driver's Education class.

Panic threatened to choke me. "What do I do? Which way do I go?"

"I don't know. Just drive!" Gwen snapped.

Holding my breath, I peeled out, fought to control my steering. I turned right, bumping over the curb, and accelerated, determined to put distance between us.

Long shadows darkened the road. The unfamiliar streets disoriented me. Taunted me. The broken window made the air pressure in the car wail a painful *whum, whum, whum*.

Seconds later, two rapidly approaching lights winked into my rearview mirror.

Bile rose in my throat. I sped up.

Narrow streets. I couldn't avoid puddles. We plowed into one. Water sprayed, wrenching the steering wheel in my hands. The tires momentarily lost their grip on the road.

Hydroplaning. Mom had warned me about this.

Pulse racing, I yanked my foot off the gas pedal.

"Call 9-1-1," I ordered. My tongue moved thick and slow.

Scrambling, Gwen snatched her bag and tore through its guts. "I can't find my phone!" Her voice rose several octaves. "I think I left it in the locker room."

"What?" I cried. "You're inseparable from that thing until now? Check the floor for my phone. I dropped it when your uncle jumped us."

With a jerk, Gwen bent over. The headlights behind me drew closer.

White-knuckling the wheel, I pushed the gas pedal again and squealed onto another street. *Careful. The car might flip. Like Aunt Tina's had.*

Images of her broken body sent me into a momentary panic.

I had to get away. I had to find safety.

The speedometer spiked to forty, forty-five, fifty.

"I found it!" Gwen lifted my phone.

I glanced her way. The move brought a reflective yellow line into my vision.

"Hold on," I screamed, slamming the brakes.

The jolt from the speed bump sent my car flying. The underside landed with a jarring scrape. Gwen's head slammed the dashboard. The phone shot out of her hand and smacked into the windshield. I overcorrected and clipped a mailbox.

In my rearview mirror, I saw Gwen's uncle. That leech hit the same speed bump. His car soared like a metal demon, tires spitting water. The Trans Am hit the pavement with a sickening crunch.

"The phone?" I yelled, speeding ahead.

Groaning, Gwen retrieved it. In her clutches once again, she punched the screen a number of times.

A great number of times.

A great, great number of—

"What's wrong? 9-1-1 is only three numbers!" I cried.

Gwen rubbed her forehead. Her hand came back bloody. "The screen broke when it hit the windshield. Hey, Siri."

My chest tightened. "Siri is disabled. My mom's afraid the government uses it to spy on us."

Gwen tossed it into the cup holder. "Great. Now what are we going to do?"

"I don't know!"

Lord, I need an idea.

The highway loomed ahead.

"I have an idea," Gwen's voice shook. "Take the highway to the police station."

Fear crippled me, and the car responded with a wobble. A vision of my aunt covered in a white cloth on that very stretch of road hit me. *Lord, please, is there any other option than that road? I can't go that way. Won't go that way.*

"He's getting closer!" Gwen screamed.

Adrenaline kicked in. I blew past the next stop sign, yanking the steering wheel hard left. The tires lost traction again, sending the car into a spin.

We came to a complete stop on the frontage road with Gwen's uncle's car bearing down on us. Gritting my teeth, I slammed down the accelerator.

The leech careened after me, swerving wide before correcting his trajectory.

"You can't go this way!" Gwen cried. "It's a one-way street."

"Doesn't matter! You said go to the police station."

"Which is that way." Gwen pointed behind her.

I gulped, fighting panic. "I'll take the next ramp, cut across the highway, and turn around."

"Great. In the meantime, avoid head-on collisions," Gwen muttered.

I hit a pothole. The car bucked. I pressed my foot down anyway. The speedometer climbed. Seventy. Seventy-five.

My phone lit up.

I sucked in a breath. "I thought you said the phone was broken,"

"It is. I can't dial. But maybe the speaker function works." She picked it up and pressed a button. "Hello?"

Taylor's voice came through. "Lorali! You never answered my text. Is everything okay?"

"Call 9-1-1," I shouted. "Gwen's uncle is chasing us in his car. He has a gun."

The line went dead for a second. "You're kidding, right?"

"Call 9-1-1, you idiot!" Gwen shrieked. Then, "Watch out!"

Laying it on the horn, I swerved out of the way of an incoming car. Behind me, Gwen's uncle ran it off the road.

"Stay on the line so I know what's happening." Taylor's voice had a sharp edge. "Emily, stop taking selfies. Call 9-1-1."

My lights reflected off a sign indicating a half mile to the ramp. I floored it.

Gwen put the phone to her mouth. "Hurry. Lorali can't keep going like this. She's a horrible driver!"

Sudden doubt filled me. Gwen was right. I was a horrible driver. I had no business getting on the highway. My aunt died there. With my amateur driving, we could too. And my mom, she'd have to relive that nightmare all over again.

No, Mom wouldn't relive it. If I crashed on the highway, it would kill my mom.

An idea popped into my head. I *did* have another option.

This frontage road came to a "T" at the entrance to Echo Park. My sand court park. Beyond the courts and the picnic area were the trails Taylor and I had hiked. It was lined with trees. We could ditch the car and hide there. No more dangerous driving for me.

I had to make a choice. I had to rely on my strengths, not my weaknesses. "Taylor, send the police to Echo Park," I ordered.

"What?" Gwen said. "Didn't we agree on going to the police station?"

"Change of plans. Taylor, we're going to abandon the car at Echo Park and run for it. Tell the police we'll be on trail one."

"Roger that," he confirmed.

Gwen's hand shook. "T-T-Taylor. Start praying."

"Always." His voice sounded tight.

Prayer. A request I never expected from Gwen.

The cabin flooded with light. I'd been so distracted, I'd slowed. With a crunch of metal, the Trans Am rammed me. My neck whipped. The car shuddered but somehow kept going.

Treat him like a player. Show a predictable move.

I gunned it toward the highway ramp. Uncle John followed, close enough to kiss.

Plant a seed and *then change.* At the last moment, I split right.

Gwen's uncle overshot onto the ramp. With a screech, his car lurched to a stop. Over the pounding rain, his engine sputtered. His car must have stalled.

This was the break we needed. My tires ate up the road

speeding toward the park. When we skidded to a stop in the open lot, Gwen threw open the door. She staggered toward the sidewalk.

That's when I realized the flaw in my plan.

I had on flip flops.

"Wait!" Terror spurred me on, groping for the shoes I'd tossed in the back seat.

Gwen paused, wringing her hands. "I see his headlights coming our way!"

Deserting my hunt, I flip-flopped after her. My footing was slippery on the thin rubber soles, just like my tires had been on the road.

A car door slammed behind us when we reached the sand courts.

"Can't you go any faster?" Gwen snapped, staggering with an uneven gait.

I yanked off the cheap rubber sandals and threw them into the sand. Barefooted, I raced to catch up. We sprinted past the picnic area. Had he seen us? As we flew down the slope, the unyielding sidewalk tore my skin. The trailhead waited at the bottom, its landing slick with rain.

"Gwen!" Uncle John's voice cut through the downpour.

Gasping, Gwen looked back, and I followed suit. A bulky silhouette crested the hill.

"No!" Gwen gasped. She bolted for the nearest trail. Trail two.

I lagged behind, feet slapping painfully on the path.

A hush enveloped us as we crossed the tree line. Thick branches filtered out most of the rain and light, leaving the air congested. I slowed while my eyes adjusted to the darkness. My breath came in ragged puffs.

Ahead of me, Gwen lifted my phone. It glowed.

"Lorali! Are you safe?" Taylor's voice crackled over the speaker.

Leaping into action, I spiked the phone away. It disappeared in the weeds, taking its light and noise with it. Then I grabbed Gwen's arm, leading her forward.

"What did you do?" she hissed.

"Your uncle can track the light and the sound of that phone," I said.

She yanked herself free from my grasp. "I could've hung up—after I told Taylor we didn't take trail one. Now the police won't know where we are!"

My stomach clenched. I made a deadly mistake. Maybe. "The trails overlap. The police can still find us." *Please, God, let them!*

I couldn't see well, but I could feel the path under my bare feet. I picked my way forward, trusting the gloom to hide us.

"Gwen." Uncle John's voice echoed oddly in the woods. "I know you're here, you lying little brat." He actually used a coarser word.

A beam of light crisscrossed the tree line. Of course, leave it to the crazy guy to come prepared with a flashlight.

We stole ahead. When a branch snapped somewhere behind us, I reached out an arm to stop Gwen.

The faint sound of sirens reached my ears.

Gwen trembled beside me. She'd faced Uncle John alone. But no more. I had to be strong for her. "You hear that?" I whispered. "The police are on their way."

"But...I can't... keep going." Gwen shoulders curled up like a leaf. "It's...too dark. My head hurts. I have... no...energy."

She swayed.

The hackles rose on my arms. I'd seen this before. "No, no, no, no…"

I wrapped an arm around her, dreading what might happen.

And it did. For the second time that year, Gwen fainted on me.

Chapter Twenty-Seven

BAIT

My phone was gone, darkness cloaked the path, the rain made my steps slick, I didn't know where I was, and a terrible, vengeful man stalked us. Still, I had to protect Gwen. She needed me.

The hairs on my arm stood on end. *Vengeful man. Or murderer?*

How long would it take for Gwen's uncle to scour the area behind us? We needed to keep moving.

I snapped my fingers near Gwen's ear. "Come on, come on, come on."

Gwen groaned, eyelids fluttering. For a moment, she focused on me. Then her pupils rolled back, and her head flopped.

Shaking her, I whispered, "Wake up!"

Her unresponsive body sagged into me.

Biting my lip, I surveyed the gloom. *What are my options? Leave her? Hide her? Carry her?*

Carry her. Slipping one hand under her armpit and the other under her knees, I lifted her. The weight hunched me over. I shifted Gwen's body to get a better grip. "It could be worse," I whispered. "You could weigh more."

A dozen steps later, I realized I couldn't stay ahead of her uncle this way. That left two choices—leave or hide her.

I'll die before I leave Gwen unprotected. So, I'll hide her.

I'd have to go off path, risk the noise, and conceal her in the trees. Except, would I be able to find her again later? If we survived?

Leading with cold feet, I tested the ground before transferring my full weight through the thick foliage. A snapped twig might give away my location.

One step. Two. Three. Four.

A loud curse stabbed the night. A shot ripped through the air, its sound distorting as it traveled. It ricocheted behind me, in front of me, all around. My throat tightened. Had he shot an animal? Or my phone?

Holding my breath, I moved on. Sweat crowned my lips, leaving behind a salty taste. In the distance, Uncle John's angry bellows covered any inadvertent noise I made. When his tirade ended, and the woods quieted again. I imagined Uncle John moving up the path, a slow prowler. A hunter stalking his prey.

My progress was slower. The hunted.

Gwen grew heavier in my arms. *Dear God, give me strength. Give me courage. Give me wisdom!*

An owl screeched overhead, spooking me. I staggered and stepped on a branch. Dread cramped my breathing. My legs shook under the strain.

Don't think about it, Lorali. Keep moving. One more step.

My toe scraped something hard. A brick? I tapped it with my foot. No, a rock. A big one. Sliding Gwen to the ground, I reached out. My hand traced the crooked contours of one rock, then found another wedged next to it, about the same size. And then, traveling farther, another.

My pulse quickened. This was the fire pit, the one Taylor and I visited with our bag of tacos. I'd found the intersection between the trails.

A plan formed. The pit provided space to hide Gwen. Her black sweats would make her more difficult to spot. And I would know where to find her.

Lifting her over the nearest stone, I eased her into the ashy interior. A groan escaped her lips.

"Stay quiet, Gwen," I whispered. With my fingertips, I spread mud across her cheeks to darken them. "Stay safe."

Grim claws of pale moonlight broke through the branches, allowing me to discern the ring of stones that sheltered Gwen and my muddy footprints leading there. She might be hard to spot, but if Uncle John used the flashlight, he'd be sure to spot the indentations in the ground. The tracks would lead him right to her.

Could I use my sweatshirt to wipe the prints? That worked in movies, right? I unzipped my top, but my t-shirt underneath was white, a dead giveaway. So, I checked Gwen. She wore a dark long sleeve tee-shirt.

"Sorry, but I'm gonna borrow this," I murmured. Working

quickly, I threaded her limp arms out of the sleeves and rolled her over to free the other side.

Something dropped to the ground. I reached after it, my fingers probing its smooth surface.

"You've got to be kidding me," I breathed, lifting it.

A juice box. I could revive Gwen. I ripped the plastic straw off the side but hesitated. Would she recover fast enough to escape? Probably not. And the lost time waiting made both of us sitting ducks.

But what if she woke up alone and freaked out? Then leaving her might be just as dangerous.

What to do? Stifling a growl, I touched my fingertip along the edge to find the groove for the straw hole. When I found the indention, I speared it. Lifting Gwen's head, I forced liquid into her mouth. This time, I met no resistance. But the juice dribbled out.

Freshman first aid class. She was unconscious. She could choke.

I dropped the box. *Great.*

Snaps and crunches echoed in the woods.

I tensed, crouching low. I'd lingered too long.

God be with you, Gwen, I prayed. *I can't stay here any longer.*

Grabbing the sweatshirt, I retraced my steps. After I passed one, I patted the ground and swept fallen leaves over it. Fast. Quiet.

Halfway back to the path, a light trickled around a bend. "Come out, Gwen." Her uncle ground out each word.

My nerves tingled. Bile soured my mouth. With Gwen's uncle near, getting back on the path and making a run for it was no longer an option. But if I stayed put and he spotted me, it wouldn't take long for him to find Gwen either.

Squatting, I turned sideways. No more covering our

tracks. From this point on, I would create a new trail leading away from Gwen.

I quickened my pace. I had to put space between us, even if I made noise.

My eyes searched the forest for a safe path. My breathing pounded in my ears, so I took shallow gulps. A sharp burr stabbed my tender arch, and I winced. Balancing on one leg, I dropped Gwen's sweatshirt and pried the stickler out.

At least I didn't step on a snake.

Clouds must have smothered the moon again. What little light remained crept through the branches like a faltering candle. Hesitating, I surveyed the gloom. Farther back, I could make out Gwen's uncle, black against black. His flashlight stopped moving. I let out my air slowly, waiting to see what he would do.

A bead of sweat trickled down my forehead mixing with the damp rain.

Waiting. Waiting.

He stepped off the path. He must have spotted my footsteps. Which meant I might not only lead him away from Gwen, but sneak past him on the trail.

Moving like a shadow, I eased out of the trees. On the path again, I poised, ready to flee the moment John committed to following me.

The light lowered. Bobbed left and right, like a scanner.

A moment later, the light rose. "You're not very smart, Gwen. Dumb, like your mom," he boomed. "Two sets of footprints entered at the trailhead. One barefoot. One with shoes. And over there—" the light moved. "I spotted tracks indicating someone went down."

Trembling, I sucked in more air.

"From here, I see only one set of footprints, traveling off

the path. Barefoot. That means the one with the shoes is injured somehow. Probably hiding nearby." His light swayed over the ground. "The other person kept going through the woods. By the size of the print, I think your friend is the barefoot one. And I think you, Gwen, my dear helpless niece, are the one hiding."

With a guttural laugh, his light moved toward the fire pit. "Come out, come out, wherever you are."

My stomach dropped.

I thought I'd been so clever.

I thought I'd tricked him.

I thought leaving Gwen behind and hiding her would keep her safe.

Instead, it doomed her.

Her uncle would find her.

Kill her.

I had to distract him.

I had to make him want me instead.

I had to expose myself. Like my net play, I had to be the bait.

"Hey!" I screamed. "Hey!"

The light stopped.

"You must be the shoeless one." His voice tore through the leaves. "You're not the one I'm after. Yet."

Think fast!

"You're right, I'm barefoot." I clenched my hands to stop their shaking. "But you're wrong to think I'm not the one you want. Because Gwen told me all your dirty little secrets. But unlike her, I have no reason to keep them."

The leech cursed.

Branches snapped.

My eyes could barely make out his lethal mass, oozing back onto the path like tar. Every instinct in my body screamed to run. But if I was the bait, I couldn't pull out of the water too soon.

"Whatever she told you was a lie," he growled, unmoving.

Did he see me, or was he waiting for me to talk and give away my position?

No matter. I had to lure him forward. "She said you lost your job."

John moved toward me, his pace measured, steady. I back-pedaled, matching his speed. I stopped when he stopped.

"That's not a secret," he snarled, swinging the light side to side.

My muscles tensed, not daring to move.

He hawked a spit. "You're a liar. Like Gwen."

The darkness that defined his body shrank. Was he headed back to Gwen?

Don't let him go. "She told me you criticized her mom!"

He paused.

Every muscle in my body quivered. "You yelled at her," I called out. "Threatened her."

"That's not a crime." He ground out each word.

My mind raced. "What about Gwen's injuries? She told me you *beat* her."

"More lies," he hissed.

"She showed me the bruises."

He snorted. "Those were from volleyball."

No." I steeled myself. "They were from YOU!"

My last word ricocheted around the trees and back to me, empty. After the echo died, silence reigned long enough to sharpen my tension. A heavy foreboding needled my spine.

Was that a rustle? I strained my ears. Where did he go?

"Now you've ticked me off."

The moon chose that moment to escape from behind a cloud, spilling milky light on everything. Including me.

"Gotcha, worm!" He thundered up the path.

I bolted, but my feet slipped in the slick mud. Before I could regain balance, the leech was on me. He clamped onto my sweatshirt, a jaguar sinking its teeth in. I squirmed. My sweatshirt went taut, then tore.

The sudden release of fabric upset our footing. John reeled backward, pulling me toward the ground. Tucking my head, I rolled and sprang to the balls of my feet. My elbow stung. I'd scraped it, but I was loose.

I took off.

The gun blazed, sending a spray of wood onto my cheeks from a nearby tree. I changed direction, arms pumping, but my toe caught a root. I stumbled, arms flaying.

Another clip whizzed past, striking above my head. The stagger had saved me.

"Don't move. You're in my sights. And I'll pull the trigger again."

Despite the strong flight instinct vibrating through my veins, I froze, hunched over like a scarecrow.

Gwen's uncle circled me, gun cocked, his smug grin of crooked teeth visible in the feeble moonlight.

Heart pounding, I followed him with my eyes.

"My worm." His lips spread in a leer. "My wicked little worm."

Fast as a viper, he backhanded me in the face.

Yelping, I fell to my knees. The world spun. I gagged on the blood in my mouth.

"I hate worms!" He stomped on my hand. I screamed again and cradled my fingers.

Gripping my ponytail, Uncle John twisted my head back.

I thrashed against his vise-like grip. Pain seared down every vertebrate.

Lowering his face, he leered at me. His hot breath burned my cheeks. It reeked of alcohol.

"Your mouth looks sexy when you're not talking." He licked my muddy cheek, spat out the dirt. "I'm going to enjoy this."

I was going to die. And the most ridiculous thought crossed my mind. I would never get to play Division One volleyball in college. This man would take that away from me.

After all my hard work? No. Way. "Get off!" I screamed, elbowing him.

A figure burst out of the darkness and tackled John. My neck wrenched as the impact tore John's fingers out of my hair. The gun dropped, its muzzle wedging in the mud. Roaring, John bucked his attacker, his boots clawing the slippery surface.

On one side, the path of escape snaked ahead, leading toward the parking lot and distant sirens. On the other, two men grappled.

My mysterious rescuer leveraged his grip. Mud coated his clothes. His familiar mop of hair paralyzed me. My nerves shrieked at me to run. But my legs, trapped in a spell, wouldn't respond.

Taylor.

As if in slow motion, he struggled to restrain Gwen's uncle.

From the bundle of arms and legs, one meaty hand broke free and clocked Taylor on the head. The blunt force sent Taylor sprawling. Gwen's uncle rolled on top, using his weight to pin Taylor down. Grunting, he pressed his knee onto Taylor's neck.

"Lorali!" Taylor rasped. "Run!"

The spell broke. I ran. I ran while the leech choked the life out of my boyfriend.

Chapter Twenty-Eight

RUNNING

ran straight at Gwen's uncle and hurled myself at him. My body slammed into slick flesh. I barely made an impact against his bulk, but at least the force shifted his knee off Taylor's throat.

"WORM!" John pushed away from Taylor and snatched at me. Tucking my head, I rolled out of his reach. My volleyball dive brought me back to my feet.

Beside Uncle John, Taylor sat up, coughing, and gasping for air. In one violent move, John sent him sprawling again. When Taylor groaned, John kicked his curled body until Taylor fell silent.

Eyes trained on me, Uncle John squatted. His beefy fingers lifted Taylor's limp arm and then released it. It fell without resistance.

John's coarse laugh cut through the air. "Another worm. This one even more worthless than you. Cuz he's dead."

Dead? No!

Grunting, John raised to his full height and cracked his knuckles. Panic threatened to overwhelm me. I edged back. He circled left, I circled right.

Within spitting distance, he squared his shoulders. "Scared yet?"

He no longer had a gun. And I could outrun him. I bluffed. "No. I'm angry."

Coach's voice rang in my head. *Keep your body low. Watch the hand position. Look for patterns. Anticipate.*

The tenseness in his shoulders betrayed his lunge before he moved. As he swiped, I ducked and spun toward the open path. Something struck me hard in the back, and I stumbled.

He grabbed me again, crushing my skin with his grip. "I don't need a gun. I'm good with rocks too." He held up a baseball-sized one, and I cowered. "This one is going to take out those lying teeth of yours."

A shadow rose behind him. I tensed, my breath caught in my throat. A sickening thud broke my mounting terror. The leech's eyes rolled into his head, and he toppled to the ground. Behind him stood Taylor holding a hefty branch in one hand. His other hand clucked his ribcage.

Relief weakened my knees. "Taylor!" His shirt was torn, one eye was swollen, and mud splattered the rest of him. He looked like an angel. Whimpering, I threw myself at him.

"Ow, ow, ow!" he said, pulling away. With careful slowness,

I lowered myself to my knees. Huge, heavy sobs poured out of me. "I thought you were dead."

"Shh! Shh!" Taylor crouched by my side. "It's okay. I guess I forgot to tell you about my acting career. When I was in fourth grade, I starred as Wise Man number three in the church Christmas play."

A sniffling laugh dribbled out of my mouth. I buried my face in his chest. For a moment, the thrum of his heart drowned out all other sound.

Releasing me, Taylor approached the crumpled body, bearing the branch like a sword. Cautiously, he poked the leech's body with it. There was no response.

"I should've played baseball." Taylor dropped his makeshift weapon. "My brilliant football tackle clearly didn't work as well as my home run swing."

Beams of light crisscrossed around us. "Hands in the air," someone yelled.

We lifted our arms—Taylor with a visible wince—as a half dozen men stepped into the clearing and positioned themselves around us.

A flashlight shined in our faces making me squint. "Police! Can I see some identification please?"

Taylor cautiously pulled his student ID card out of his back pocket and held it out. The stocky officer nearest us holstered his gun and took it from him. After an intense study of it, he looked at me. "And you, miss?"

"It's in my car. I was being chased and—"

A groan issued from Gwen's uncle. The officer held up a hand, and I choked back my words.

A jerk of the officer's head sent two policemen to approach the heap. The shorter one kneeled and lay two fingers on the leech's neck.

My mouth went suddenly dry. "He attacked us."

"He's unarmed," the short cop answered.

"He dropped a gun somewhere over there." I pointed.

A bald officer swept his light across the area trampled by our struggle.

The man in blue refocused on me. "I'm Officer Ty. We were dispatched to find some girls in danger. Do you know anything about that?"

Swallowing, I nodded. "I'm one of those girls."

"What is your full name?"

"Lorali Mathews. And there's another girl here, Gwen. She's hidden in the fire pit off the trail maybe two hundred yards back. And she needs medical attention. Or at least apple juice. She passed out, probably from low blood sugar. Although she did hit her head on my car dashboard too."

Officer Ty arched a brow. "Is the girl diabetic?"

I shook my head. "No. Just hungry."

Officer Ty lifted a walkie-talkie and relayed that information. Then he blinded me with his light again. "We'll need statements from both of you. But it looks like you need medical attention first."

The additional light revealed Taylor's swollen and bleeding lip. A purple bruise colored his neck. His injuries were worse than what I suspected.

My own face had a tender spot where I'd been backhanded. I was afraid to move my injured hand, and my feet were a mess of scrapes and cuts.

All business, a trim policewoman stepped up. "I'll escort you to the ambulance. Follow me."

My body trembled as I fell in step. We paused partway, allowing medics with a portable gurney to crowd past us. Apparently, my message about Gwen had gotten through. I grabbed Taylor's hand with my uninjured one, an anchor in the middle of all this confusion. He squeezed it and held on.

"How did you get here before the police?" I asked, leaning into him.

He shrugged. "I don't know. I guess I was closer to the park. But I didn't see any signs of you on trail one. Then I saw a light near the fire pit."

"That's because we panicked and took trail two instead," I said. "But it worked out. You found us at the overlap."

"It took forever though because I had to travel the longer path to get there."

I considered how the whole scenario had played out. "If you had arrived sooner, you might have found Gwen's uncle before his full attention was on me. Which would likely have resulted in you being shot. No, the timing was perfect. Surprise worked in your favor."

"I never considered it that way," he said. "But that still doesn't answer why I beat the police here."

Our guide cleared her throat. "Flooding. And there was an accident on the highway. A firetruck tried to get through the median, but the tires got stuck. Blocked us all off. One patrol car risked going around it, and it's still stranded. We had to take an alternate route."

She inclined her head toward Taylor. "That was brave of you to go after the girls. Brave, but dangerous."

Taylor lowered his eyes. "Not nearly as dangerous as what Lorali did. Good thing she's as tough off the court as she is on it."

I blushed at the unexpected compliment. "Have they found Gwen yet?" I asked to deflect the officer's measured stare.

The cop's eyes softened. "I'll check." She unsheathed her

walkie-talkie and clicked it to life. "Ty, did you find the other girl?"

After a moment, Officer Ty's bland voice crackled back. "Affirmative. Alive but unresponsive. Medics started an IV."

The rain had completely stopped by the time we reached the end of the parking lot. The moon, no longer hindered by persistent clouds, guarded the sky. I spotted Emily, Joel, and my mom, her face pasty white, standing outside the yellow-taped police line. Another woman—maybe Gwen's mom— hovered by the ambulance wringing her hands, deep worry lines marring her face.

When we stepped closer to the crowd, my mom wailed and rushed forward. Emily shoved Joel aside and added her body to my mom's embrace.

"Ouch!" I cried, keeping my injured had free. "Be careful."

"You're alive!" Mom's body shook with gasping sobs. If she squeezed me any tighter, I'd be on the other side of her body. "Thank you, Jesus, thank you, Jesus, thank you, Jesus."

Then questions rushed out, one after the other, with no time to answer before the next flood came. They made an odd tag team, Emily with her demanding voice, and my mom, seemingly desperate for reassurance. My head swam like it was underwater with the sounds stretching and humming in my ear. *Are you okay? What happened? Where are your shoes? Where's Gwen? Why was that man after you? You look terrible. Does it hurt? It looks like it hurts. How did you get away? I don't know what I'd do if something happened to you! Where's your phone? I tried calling a million times. Your car is missing a window. Where are the car keys?*

And finally, "I saved your chocolate milkshake. Do you still want it?"

I blinked at Emily. She held out a Styrofoam cup with a red straw. "Because if you don't want it, I'm drinking it," she said.

With a sigh of relief, I took the offering. "Thank you."

"Good, because I need two hands to videotape you." Emily held up her phone.

"Why?" I asked.

"The whole team, including Coach, is praying for you, and they need an update. Pictures speak louder than words. Do you think you can wipe some of that mud off? You look awful. Or no! I have a better idea. Let's smear some more on. It's more dramatic that way." She snapped her fingers. "Get me some mud, Joel."

Joel obediently leaned toward the ground. I shooed him away. "Ignore her, Joel. Remember, less is more, Emily." I swiped my face with my wet sleeve. "Just don't post it on every social media site."

Emily turned, capturing a panoramic view of the police, the flashing blue and red vehicle lights, and our ragtag crew. "No promises." Her fingers danced across the screen.

Taylor's phone buzzed in his pocket. He checked it. "A video of me. Right now. Covered in mud. Uh...thanks, Emily."

Medics came out of the trail carrying Gwen on a gurney. A tiny cry escaped her mother's lips when she appeared.

As they loaded Gwen into the ambulance, an EMP approached us. Mom hovered over me while the woman gave Taylor and me a quick check. She attached a splint to my ring finger and put Taylor's arm in a sling. "You both seem stable, but I'd like you to see a doctor. There's room in the ambulance."

"No, I'll drive them." Mom's voice shook.

The medic nodded and excused herself.

"Thanks," Taylor said. "I appreciate the ride. I'm pretty sore. I'll ask Joel to drive my car back."

I nodded, sending him on his way. When we were alone, I studied my mom. She clung to my good arm, stroking it as if I might suddenly disappear. Her eyes were puffy and red from crying, her cheeks slack, her hands trembling. I'd only seen her in this nightmare state one time before, the night my aunt died.

Memories flooded back.

A pizza box on the counter. Melted candles on a chocolate frosted cake. Gifts on the table. Mom, in the other room, on the phone, her voice drifting back to me.

"It's a recreational league. It's not every day your niece turns fourteen, you know."

Silence followed by angry words. "The rain held you up? That's another excuse. You skipped my fortieth too, and that was a sunny day as I recall. I've never been a priority for you. Never! Where were you when Mom died? At a tournament. Where were you when Steve left me? On the court. I needed you. And you weren't there."

More silence. Then, "You can tell yourself that if it makes you feel better. I think the only reason you spend so much time with Lorali is because of volleyball. Yes, I know she loves it too, and I'll give her all the support she needs. But don't think for a minute that I'm going to let her make the same mistakes you did."

Shuffling sounds as Mom paces the room. "I don't care how tired you are. You promised. Don't keep Lorali up all night waiting for you."

Mom comes back into the kitchen, her eyes flashing.

"Is Aunt Tina coming?" I ask, pretending I didn't hear her conversation.

A tight smile. "You bet, sweetie. On her way right now."

Except she never made it. That night, as Aunt Tina sped to my party, her car slid off the road and wrapped around a tree. I never got to say goodbye.

CHAPTER TWENTY-NINE

WOUNDS

om's face seemed bleached of color, and she took several deep breaths while transferring volleyball gear out of my car and into her trunk.

"Mom, are you okay?" I asked, pulling my blanket tighter.

"Oh, I'm fine." She paused to examine my injured hand. "Those fingers look swollen. Can you bend them? Or no, don't bend them, wait for the doctor."

Pulling my hand free, I gingerly tried curling my fingers anyway, then winced. "Yeah, I should wait."

"Lorali!" Mom huffed. "I told you to wait. You could make

it worse. You're just like Tina, taking risks without thinking about the consequences. Like wrecking your car and running around in the woods on a rainy night."

"Mom, stop," I said. "You don't even know the whole story. I took a risk to save Gwen. Wasn't that worth it?"

"No." Her voice rose to shrill. "No risk is worth this."

I swallowed. "I'm sorry about the car. I'll help get it fixed."

"No!' She threw her arms around me and squeezed. Great gasping sobs wracked her as she clung to me. "No, Lorali, no! It's you. I can't risk losing you too. I can't."

"It's okay, Mom." My throat tightened. "I'm right here. I'm safe."

She wept until Taylor returned.

"Joel agreed to drive my car," he said, "and Emily promised she'd let your coach know what was going on. They'll meet us at the hospital, along with my parents." He pulled at his wet shirt. "Mom's bringing me dry clothes."

Calmer now, Mom opened the back door of her car, and we climbed in. The blankets protected the seats, but our feet made smudges on the floor mats.

"Wait here a moment." Mom glanced behind her. "I'm going to speak with that officer before he leaves. Legal matters, of course. Be right back."

After she closed the door, Taylor took my healthy hand in his. "I'm still shook up. Can we pray?"

Swallowing, I nodded. "I'm shook up too."

His eyes studied my face, then he closed them. "Dear God, thank you for protecting us tonight." His voice was laced with humility and gratitude. "Please watch over Gwen. And help me and Lorali recover too. We're not on a stretcher, but we're still not out of the woods yet. I mean, we are literally out of the woods, but not figuratively out. Anyway, you know what I mean. Thanks for being so good to us. Amen."

"Amen." Raising my head, I sighed. "Although 'good' feels oddly painful right now. I think I'll be scarred for life."

Taylor quirked a smile, and then winced. No doubt he overstretched his split lip.

"Sometimes I think it's the scars that make us beautiful. Remember what Hank told us about Joseph after all those horrible things happened to him?"

I nudged him. "Remind me."

Looking at the ceiling of the car as if hoping to find the quote there, Taylor said, "He read that verse. You're doing evil, but it's actually good. Or your evil is good." He threw up his hands. "Never mind. I forgot how it went."

"Use your phone and look it up."

"Oh, duh." Releasing my hand, he pulled his phone out of his pocket. It lit up, casting shadows on his face and highlighting his fresh bruises. "Found it. 'As for you, you meant evil against me, but God meant it for good in order to bring about this present result—'"

Putting a hand on his arm, I stopped him. "You mean the present result where even if our team qualifies for playoffs, our main setter is heading to the hospital, the other has her leg in a cast, and my feet are so cut up, they might not fit back into my shoes?"

"Well, yes. I believe good will come from this. You just can't see it yet."

"Because my eye is swollen." I traced the puffy edges to prove it.

"A few minor scrapes—"

"*Major* scrapes." I lifted my hand.

Taylor inclined his head. "Okay, a few major scrapes still

aren't as bad as being betrayed by your brothers, sold as a slave in Egypt, and then thrown into jail on false charges."

I slouched. "Touché."

Cupping my chin, his eyes searched mine. "God is in control. You know that, right?"

"I do. But sometimes it's hard to believe that. Especially when things go wrong, and my prayers go unanswered." I sighed. "I guess I don't understand the way God works."

"If we did understand, we might not have the courage to walk the path we need to take," he said. "Do you think Joseph would have volunteered to go into slavery?"

"No." But my aunt would have. She was tough. A competitor. She would have walked the path even if she knew how hard it would be. And she would have strapped my mom on her back and carried her along with her.

I glanced out the window. Apparently, Mom had finished her discussion because she was marching toward the car.

Worry lined her face. I shook my head. With Aunt Tina gone, was Mom where she needed to be? Joseph was pulled from the pit. Mom was still in it. She never forgave herself for what happened, never grieved.

Was there good in store for her?

"Taylor," I said. "I need to talk to my mom. Alone. I know your ribs hurt, so don't feel like you have to get out. Stay in the car and rest." I pulled headphones out of the seat pocket and pressed them into his hands. "But wear these and don't interrupt."

"Oh. Okay." Blinking, he slipped them on. "I'll just sit here and look pretty."

"Thank you," I whispered.

When Mom slid into the front seat, I climbed into the passenger side. "I'm going to ride up front with you."

Eyes glowing, she reached out to slick a stray hair behind my ear. Her hand lingered there. "Of course. Buckle up."

"Mom, Aunt Tina loved you," I blurted.

Mom stiffened.

Not quite the opening I had hoped for.

But still. No going back now.

"I know you had a fight the day she died. About her priorities. About me. But you're stronger than you think you are, and Aunt Tina knew that. She knew you could walk the path God laid out before you. And when she played volleyball, that's what she was doing too. Following God's leading. The court was her mission field, just like the courtroom is yours."

Frowning, Mom glanced at Taylor in the rearview mirror. He smiled back, looking pretty, like he said he would.

"Lorali..."

"He can't hear you." I pointed at my head. "He's got headphones on."

Mom shifted. "This isn't a good time to talk about it."

"But that's the thing," I said. "It's never a good time. We never talked about what happened. Aunt Tina simply disappeared, and we buried her, and that was that. We didn't talk about her laugh. Her playfulness. Her fierceness. Her passion for life. Remember how much fun we had that time we went sledding together?"

"Yes." Mom's eyes went unfocused, as if contemplating the scene. "I didn't want to slide down the hill because there was only a sprinkle of snow on the ground, and the bottom of the hill fed into the street. You might have wiped out and broken your arm. It was a lawsuit waiting to happen. But Tina talked me into it."

"We didn't have sleds, so you grabbed cookie trays, one for

each of us. And we flew down the hill." I pushed her shoulder. "You screamed the whole way."

"It was terrifying." Mom smiled. "And lovely too."

"And then our neighbor came out, remember?"

"A cute little girl, probably eight years old. Stephanie Hoskins. Yes, I remember," Mom said. "I gave up my tray so she could join us."

"And you guarded the bottom to make sure Stephanie didn't slide into the street. But Aunt Tina gave her running launches. And she cornered Stephanie's parents afterwards and discovered they played on a co-ed volleyball team."

"They got so excited when they found out Tina played in college," Mom said. "We stayed out in the cold talking until my lips cracked."

"And then Aunt Tina invited them to church with us. And they went."

Mom laughed. "Probably because she volunteered me to make homemade pizza afterwards." She sighed. "I never would have made friends with the Hoskins if it weren't for Tina."

"She had different priorities."

"Volleyball. The game consumed her." Mom's eyes narrowed. "And she taught you that mindset too. Planted all that foolishness in your life."

"It's true, I love volleyball more because of her." I met Mom's gaze. "But I would have still loved it without her. Because books, outlines, arguments, those are the things you understand. I'm not wired that way. Volleyball is my strength. And I use that strength to interact with the world, with other people."

I warmed up to the idea, feeling the truth of the words.

"Volleyball helped me connect with Gwen in a way I never could have without it."

"If volleyball is truly your mission field, then you can fulfill your purpose no matter what level you play," Mom said. "Be that Division One. Two. Three. Or recreational ball."

Her words sobered me. She was right.

"Well, anyway, it brings me joy, like the snowy hill did." I paused. "It brought Aunt Tina joy too."

"Those simple things she loved—a quick text with only emojis. A walk in the park. Even fuzzy holiday socks. They seemed so precious to her, and so frivolous to me." Mom shook her head, her lips twisting. "I bet she hated me."

Lord, help me know what to say.

"She didn't hate you." I put a hand on her knee. "When we were in the yard running drills or on her couch watching game footage, she talked about you all the time. She was proud of your accomplishments. She'd tell me how her courtroom sis with the Ivy League degree inspired her to work harder."

"She did?" Mom's lip quivered.

"She talked about your stuffed animal collection. Your tooth fairy episode. Your game nights. Your stupid retainer. You brought her so much joy, Mom. So much frivolous, meaningful joy."

Face splotchy, Mom squeezed her eyes shut. "As much joy as volleyball?"

"More. She may have showed it differently than you wanted or needed to see it, but Aunt Tina loved you."

"That night. That night she died." Mom choked, her voice lined with anguish. "She wanted to go home, rest up, take you out the next day for a special time. Just the two of you. But it was your birthday. I didn't want to do things on her terms. I wanted her there *that* night. So, I pushed her. I made her get behind the wheel of that car. I—" Sniffling, Mom ran her sleeve across her nose. "I killed her."

Leaning forward, I caught her gaze. "Mom, it's not your fault. Stop punishing yourself. You couldn't save her. And you can't protect me all the time either." I glanced back at Taylor and locked eyes with him. "You have to believe God is in control. And since He is, good will come from every situation."

Taylor bobbed his head, as if giving his support. Or maybe he was jamming to a song. Hard to tell.

"She loved me?" Mom whispered. She reached up and touched my hand. "Do you think she understood that I loved her too?"

"Aunt Tina was a volleyball player, Mom. She studied people, looked for predictable patterns," I said quietly. "She knew."

The rain started again, kissing the roof of the car.

Taylor's phone buzzed. He glanced at it, and then at me. At my nod, he slipped the headphones off and cleared his throat. "Sorry to interrupt, but my parents said they'd meet us at the hospital. Should I let them know we're on our way?"

Sniffling, Mom nodded. She gave my fingers one last squeeze before letting go, then started the car.

"Let's leave all this behind," she said.

I wasn't sure if she meant the park or her pain or her fear. Maybe all three.

CHAPTER THIRTY

NEWS

At the hospital, Mom rested her head in the palm of her hand and studied the couple sitting across from her. "Lorali says Taylor doesn't play sports anymore. He's into hardcore knitting? Is that right?"

Good-natured laughter erupted, followed by animated explanations from Taylor's parents. I could tell where he got his energy from.

I patted Mom's shoulder, then hobbled across the waiting room floor to where Taylor and his sister Terri sat. A nurse had cleaned and bandaged the cuts on my feet and treated my other wounds. My finger was jammed, nothing too serious.

Since my clothes were a wet mess, I'd changed back into my volleyball uniform, which was only mildly less disgusting.

"You look cold." Taylor shrugged out of the sweatshirt his parents had brought and handed it to me. "Here, this will help."

Static made his hair stick up at a funny angle. I resisted the urge to smooth it down. With a grateful sigh, I pulled the fuzzy softness over my head. The excess material dangled like moss from a tree.

As I settled into a chair next to him, Terri eyeballed me.

"You look awful," she said.

I lifted an icepack to my cheek. The cold pack bit my skin more than the bruise. "Well, I didn't have time to put on any makeup."

"Me neither." Taylor crossed his eyes.

Snorting, I pushed him.

He winced, cradling his chest with his good arm. Fearing a cracked rib, a doctor had ordered an X-ray of his chest. Until we had results, I needed to be more careful. "Sorry."

"It's okay." His lips twitched. "It only hurts when I smile."

"You're in for a painful time of it then." I shifted my attention to his sister. "Terri, we never really got a proper introduction. We met on the court, but at the time I thought you were Taylor's girlfriend."

Terri wrinkled her nose. "Gross!"

"Right? I like you a whole lot more as his sister."

"I liked you immediately," she said. "Volleyball player and churchgoer. A perfect girlfriend for my brother."

Heat shot up my neck. "Thanks."

For the next ten minutes, we talked game. Top contenders

in our conference. Playoff chances. Opposing players that annoyed us. That kind of thing.

Finally, Terri yawned. "Taylor, why are we still here? I'm ready for bed."

He shared a look with me. "We wanted to stay until we found out how Gwen was doing."

Slouching, Terri frowned. "That could take a while. Anyone hungry?"

"Yes," we said together.

Terri stood and stretched. "I'll check the vending machine. What do you want?"

Taylor arched a brow. "I'm a teenage boy. Haul the whole machine over."

"One of everything coming up." Humming to herself, Terri strolled off.

After she left, I scooted closer to Taylor. A cooking show played on TV, but I switched the channel to the news.

"You look good in that." Taylor motioned at his oversized sweatshirt.

"Thanks." I traced a finger on the edge of his chin. "I look better than you do with that cut on your lips. Will it scar?"

He shook his head. "The doctor didn't think so. I'm just glad I didn't end up with another concussion."

"Me too. You'll live to knit another day."

His eyes danced. "Knitting? It's baseball now, remember?"

"My bad. Blame it on the sweatshirt. I can't think straight." I snuggled the hood over my head. "All this luxurious softness distracts me."

Stretching out his arm, he pulled me closer, fuzz and all, and kissed the top of my hooded head. "I'm glad you're okay," he whispered.

Goosebumps raced up my arms.

The meteorologist came on. With the low volume competing with the underlying hospital background noise, I could barely make out his forecast. As his voice droned on, my eyes drooped. I snuggled against Taylor. "You make a good pillow."

"Hmmm," he murmured. Warm breath tickled my face. "I must be the good you're looking for. You know—the verse? You meant it for evil. God meant it for good."

Scoffing, I nestled further into his arms. "Didn't Joseph have to wait, like, twenty years before good came his way?"

Taylor laid his head on top of mine. "I guess so. By the way, Emily and Joel are headed here now. She texted the team too. They're coming."

"How many?"

"All of them."

My heart warmed. My team. Together. United.

His phone buzzed, and he checked it. "Emily sent a picture of her tonsils. I think she's screaming at the phone, maybe?"

Glancing over, I peeked at the shot. "That's a close up of her happy face. You're lucky she didn't focus on her nose. Her nostrils get really excited."

The news transitioned to sports. National football teams showed off their moves to lively commentary. Local high school teams battled it out on the field.

Terri returned with an armload of snacks. I nabbed a bag of M&Ms. Taylor snatched three bags of chips and a granola bar.

"Leave something for Terri." I turned my eyes on her, but her attention was on the television.

"Look! It's the trail!" She grabbed my arm. "You were just there!"

The screen showed a reporter interviewing a policeman. Behind him, flashing squad car lights colored the night.

My eyes widened. "Mom!" I yelled. "Come here! We're on TV. Hurry."

Chair legs scraped on the laminate floor. Mom and Taylor's parents scampered to our watch party.

"That's Officer Ty!" Taylor said.

Fully alert now, I groped for the remote and cranked up the volume. I caught Officer Ty mid-sentence.

"...suspect into custody until further investigation."

The reporter turned back to the camera. "Live from Echo Park, this is Maria Esparza reporting."

The news anchors picked up the story from there. "Police confirmed that they received a call from the residence three months ago about a domestic violence case, but no criminal charges were filed. Tonight's events unfolded while the girls were on their way home after their final game of their season at Williamson High School. One victim is in stable condition. Two other teens suffered minor injuries. We contacted the school district for more details, but they have no comment."

During this time, they looped a four-second video clip from a recent game. It showed Emily making a fantastic dive for a ball, then Gwen rocketing me a quick backset, which I pounded inside the ten-foot line. When the ball slammed home, our arms flew up in a silent cheer.

"Wow." Terri's jaw went slack. "I recognize that giant from West Side. You smoked her like a college player." Pouting her lip, she sized me up again. "Y'all have improved. A lot."

The television transitioned to an ad, so I muted it.

"We made the ten o'clock news," Taylor said. "Maybe tomorrow's news too."

Mom nodded. "They'll probably want to interview you, Taylor, since you're the real hero of the day."

His cheeks colored. "I just showed up at the right time."

"True," I said. "But you get extra points for executing a tackle only a star football player could pull off. Text Emily. Tell her what we saw on the news."

"Okay." Taylor's fingers flew across the screen. "But I bet she's the one who sent in the footage. Who else is always posting selfies and videos to social media?"

A nurse in pale purple scrubs pushed an empty wheelchair into the room. "Ms. Mathews?" she called.

After my mom waved at her, she approached us. "Excuse me, you asked to be notified when Gwen Rodriguez could see visitors. We're done with the blood tests, and she's alert."

I stood. "Let's go."

"They sent this wheelchair for you," the nurse said. "The doctor is worried about the swelling in your feet."

"I'm fine. I made it all the way across the room already. I can walk."

The nurse lifted her chin, a hard set to her eyes.

"Get in the chair," Taylor ordered. "It may be the only chance I get to push you around."

Making a face, I eased myself into the rolling seat.

Three sterile hallways later, we entered Gwen's room. Her mom, puffy-eyed from crying, sagged by her side.

"Lorali." A weak smile crept across Gwen's face. With the mud cleaned off her, color had returned to her cheeks. An IV dripping clear liquid snaked off her arm.

As we crowded around the bed, the nurse stepped out.

Gwen's mom stood to shake Mom's hand. "Hi. I'm Sophie Rodriguez. Nice to meet you."

"Likewise," Mom said. "I don't think I've seen you at the games."

The woman hunched her shoulders. "I work the late shift."

"That's tough." Mom gave a cursory frown. "But don't worry. I always cheer extra loud for Gwen. Lorali loves her sets."

Mrs. Rodriguez's gaze lingered on my face. "I'm sorry for your injuries. I don't understand why John—" Her voice quivered, and she paused to dab her nose with a tissue. "Well, anyway, how can I say thank you for helping Gwen?"

Taylor shrugged. "You just did. Although if you want to throw in a dozen cookies, I'm cool with that too."

A sputtered laugh escaped Mrs. Rodriguez's lips. Leave it to Taylor to put her at ease.

We spent the next twenty minutes retelling the events at the park and filling in gaps Gwen had in the story. As Taylor and I talked, Gwen cringed at all the appropriate places—her passing out, the confrontation between me and her uncle, and Taylor's home run swing with the stick.

Gwen stared at her fingers. "I'm sorry for what happened, Lorali."

I encased her hands with my own. "It's okay. I'm on your side. And I'm grateful."

Pulling back, Gwen blew out a derisive puff. "What for?"

"I'm grateful for surviving," I said. "For friends."

"For answered prayers," my mom added.

Gwen studied us through thick lashes. "My prayers haven't been answered yet."

The nurse knocked on the metal door, startling me. "Visiting time ends in five minutes," she announced.

"Understood," Mrs. Rodriguez called. She turned to me. "I'll text you updates on Gwen's progress."

"Sorry," I said. "My phone died. Literally. By gunshot."

"I'll send you my number." Mom rummaged in her purse for her phone.

Taylor's phone buzzed. "It's my sister. She says Emily is

here polishing off our snack stack, so hurry up if we want anything."

Another buzz. Taylor shook his head. "Now she says the rest of your team showed up too, so forget about the snacks, but still hurry up because Emily is telling everyone what happened." *Buzz*. "And apparently Godzilla makes a dramatic appearance in her version of the story."

"Yeesh! I'd better straighten things out." I locked eyes with Gwen. "Are you going to be okay when we leave?"

"I guess." She shrugged. "I just need a little rest. I'm tired."

"Tired?" Grunting, I cocked my head. "Oh, c'mon. My feet are all torn up, my face is bruised, it feels like a buffalo kicked my back, and you're *tired?*"

Mom gasped. "Lorali!"

Smiling, Gwen held my eyes. "It's okay, Ms. Mathews." Her voice came out slow and even. "It's an inside joke. Our own little secret."

As Taylor pushed me out the door, Gwen's mom said, "What was that all about?"

Gwen's response was quiet. "The truth is...well, Mom. I might need more than a little rest to recover. We need to talk."

Closing my eyes, I threw up one more prayer.

Dear God, please help Gwen express what's going on in her heart. And help her mom to listen, believe, and support her. And thanks. Her problems were too much for me to handle, I still believe that. But they never were and never will be too much for You.

CHAPTER THIRTY-ONE

GOOD

Emily waved her phone in front of me. "Read it! Out loud." She pointed. "Now."

Glancing up from her math homework, Gwen took another apple slice.

Michelle exhaled noisily, wiping her fingers on a napkin. "She has her own phone, Emily. And she probably already downloaded the article, printed it, and framed it."

"I don't care if she created a Godzilla-sized movie poster of it." Emily shook her head. "I want her to read *my* phone. Am I being unclear in any way?"

"No," I laughed. "Hand it over."

Giving me a sidelong look, Michelle coughed *coward* into her hand. Then she lifted her eyes. "Don't do it. You'll only encourage her."

"Ah, well." I shrugged, accepting the device. "Here we go. 6A Volleyball District All-Star teams." I paused. "Should I read the whole thing? The MVP for each position and the lists for first, second, and honorable mention teams?"

Emily blew a stray hair out of her eyes. "No, just the good part."

"Okay." I cleared my throat. "Second team, sophomore Lorali Mathews and—"

I glanced at Emily. She shook both fisted hands like baby rattlers. "And...!?!"

"Emily Cribbs."

"Yes!" Emily executed an awkward dance move. "This calls for a celebration treat. Be right back!"

The crunch from Gwen's apple said she'd taken another bite. "Well, don't stop there. It was just getting interesting."

I let coyness lead the way. "You mean, it's getting interesting because Emily left behind her cell phone and now we can snap a bunch of crazy selfies with it?"

Gwen snorted. It was almost playful. Almost. "Read the rest of the article."

Grinning, Michelle poked me. "You heard the girl."

I scrolled down. "Let's see. Honorable Mention for District Teams. Gwen Rodriguez."

"Hmmm." Gwen had a content smile on her lips. "Okay, now we can take selfies."

"Yes!" Scrambling to her side of the table, I squeezed between Michelle and Gwen. We took six or seven crazy shots before Emily came back with four bags of M&Ms.

With a finger flick, I exited the camera app, hiding the

evidence. All innocence, I held out her phone. Before she took it, it vibrated in my hand.

"Message," I said.

Emily touched the screen. "It's from Coach."

The color drained from her face, and she sank into her seat. "Guys? I'm glad you're sitting. Check your phones."

Worry flickered in Gwen's eyes. Michelle and I glanced at each other. Heart pounding, I read the message. "Emily? Do you know what this means?"

"It means I'd better not wash my lucky kneepads yet because—" Emily slapped the table. "We made *playoffs!*"

We squealed. Several students stopped to gape at us. Suddenly self-conscious, I touched the still tender spot on my cheek. It had started out an angry purple color, but two weeks later, had faded to a lovely shade of green.

Emily giggled. "First playoff invitation since 1983."

Imagine—we got what we wanted. Even Audrey, who would enjoy the preferential treatment she craved at a future pep rally.

"I bet we'll beat Weatherford this time," I said.

Michelle frowned. "The chances of us making it into the quarter finals or even the championship game are slim and none."

"I don't want to think that way," I said. "For me, simply getting this far counts as a win."

"I know." Gwen's voice came out quiet. "We made it."

Her words brought that night in the hospital to mind. Our present euphoria made that whole Echo Park thing seem surreal. Like it happened to someone else. Or never happened at all.

Except the aftermath. The arrest. The court date. The interviews. The phone calls. The tender feet and bruises.

And that four-second volleyball news clip that went viral.

It's funny how God used a traumatic event to give me and my friends exposure in the sporting arena. After our local broadcast reported the conflict at the park, the story got picked up at the national level. More interviews followed along with more of Emily's video clips of us in action.

College recruiters contacted Coach about all three of us. They had seen the news footage and were impressed enough with our performance to probe more.

Taylor and I had discussed this on the phone last night.

More than anyone else, he knew the challenges I faced earlier in the season. Team dynamics. Learning a new position. Gwen drama. He sounded as delighted as I felt when I told him the news about the All-Conference teams and the recruiters. "This must be your good," he'd said.

"Lorali! Stop daydreaming!" Emily snapped me out of my memory. "We need to take a picture. This is so totally mind-blowing. I'm posting a screenshot."

"It's been a crazy year." I looked at Gwen.

She nodded. "Crazy good and bad. I still have nightmares about the park."

Reaching out, I grabbed her hand and squeezed it. "I do too. But we'll get through this together. We're a team."

Gwen clenched her jaw. "Thanks."

"Now you have to come to youth group with us." Emily swatted her shoulder.

Wincing, Gwen pulled away. "Why?"

"Because. You need to smile more." Emily gave a toothy demonstration. "And it's so much fun. I mean youth group, not smiling. But smiling is fun too, so I guess both. Yay. And wait until you meet Hank. He's awesome. Plus, they serve snacks. But stay away from the cupcakes. Trust me on this."

Gwen's eyes met mine. A spark of distress colored them, and my heart broke for her. At least she had someone more qualified than me to help. She attended therapy twice a week to learn healthy mental and eating habits.

I tapped the table to grab Gwen's attention. "I get it. Emily talks too much. You can't digest it all. Excuse the joke. Just come with us sometime for the friendship." I touched my chest. "Come with us inside the ten-foot line." It was something Aunt Tina would probably say.

Swallowing, Gwen nodded. "I will if you stop saying dorky things like that."

Emily squealed, of course, and a strange idea lodged itself in my brain. My breath caught. "Y'all, excuse me. I've got to call Taylor."

Leaving the noisy buzz of the lunchroom behind me, I found a quiet spot in the hallway and called. Taylor picked up on the second ring.

The words tumbled out of me. "I found my good!"

"Uh, hello Lorali. Yes, I'm glad you found me." His voice got husky. "It's nice to know I'm the good you were looking for."

"No. I mean, yes, you are a good force in my life, but it's something else. We made playoffs and—"

"Wow!" he interrupted. "That *is* good. Congratulations."

"Thank you. Yes, it is good. But it's not *the* good. UGH!" I growled at my tongue getting all tangled up.

Letting out a hiss of air, I chose my words carefully. "I found my good. It wasn't what I thought it was before. I was missing something."

"Was it me? I miss you too."

"Yes, I miss you." I clucked my tongue. "But no, it wasn't

you I missed. I mean, I do miss you, but...Argh! There I go again!"

"Okay, slow down." I imagined him holding back a laugh. "I won't interrupt."

I closed my eyes, focusing on how to express the seed of understanding growing in my heart. "Remember how Joseph suffered even though he had big dreams? He must have believed God had forgotten him, but you said God put him in those situations because He had the big picture in mind."

"I did say something like that," Taylor said. "I'm very wise that way."

I ignored him. "I prayed all season for one thing. *God, please help me discover what I need to do to be successful.* Taylor, I measured my success by the number of wins. By whether recruiters knocked on my door. By the percentages of my kill stats. I thought all those accomplishments were what I needed to be successful. But they weren't."

"I'm confused."

Sighing, I leaned against the wall. "Joseph dreamed of his family bowing down to him. His path involved slavery and imprisonment and humiliation. Eventually, he stood second only to Pharaoh and ruled a nation. When that happened, he must have told himself that God had fulfilled his dream. But God's view of success looks different from ours. Don't you see? All that glory wasn't the good God had in store for him. At the end of the story, what stood out?"

The line went silent. I waited, holding my breath. My chest tightened. *Come on, Taylor? Can you see it too?*

"He forgave his brothers." Taylor's voice came out breathless. "God healed a broken relationship, and that reunion changed the course of history."

A tear leaked out of my eyes. He got it. My hand shook

as I swiped it away with my sleeve. "That's what I needed to be successful. A healed relationship. It's our team, coming together. It's my mom, forgiving herself. It's Gwen, bonding with me. That's my good. My better. My best. God answered my prayer, and it had everything and nothing to do with volleyball."

A sense of marvel filled me, wide and wonderful, soaring above the court and into the infinite sky.

"You're a remarkable girl, Lorali Mathews." Taylor's voice was low. "I'm glad you're on my side of the court. Pun intended."

I grinned. "Me too."

The lunch bell sounded. "I'll catch you later, my knitting knight." I paused. "After all, I can't resist a guy who always keeps me in stitches."

I hung up before he could shoot back another quip. Sometimes it's nice to get the last laugh.

Dreaming about what tomorrow might bring, I headed toward the cafeteria, where my teammates and friends waited for me.

My mom once said, "Trust the Lord to direct your path."

My aunt said, "If you allow it to, hardship will push you to be the very best you can be."

Both were right. So, I'd do both.

I'd trust the Lord while I pushed myself, inside and outside the ten-foot line.

ACKNOWLEDGMENTS

"Write what you know," they said.

I know volleyball. So that's what I wrote. And now that this book is set, I want to pass on some thanks to the team that helped me serve it up.

To Christ, who is always faithful, always loving, and always full of surprises. I didn't see this one coming. It was like an off-speed spike except in hug form.

To the Serious Writer team and the unstoppable Victoria Duerstock, who branched out from there. Thanks for all your patience, training, and support. The wisdom you offered sure came in handy. (I avoided pitching a story idea in the bathroom at that last conference. Yay!)

To J.A.M's Critique Group—Julie Marx, Marie Sontag, Gayle Veitenheimer, Marcia McIntosh, Jennifer Ashcraft, Heather Chock, and Paul Thrower—who sat through multiple revisions of this adventure and gave outstanding feedback. Plus you threw in a few ribbon dances and a game night.

Hard to beat that. Unless you're each interested in buying 5,000 copies of my next novel. (We'll talk later.)

To my sisters, Sandy, Linda, and Joy, who never complain when I borrow and mash up their family names when I need a new character. Thank goodness none of you married a Flizbisket or Humperdink.

To Marianne Hering, who is just pure awesome sauce. You make me laugh, keep me accountable, and inspire me to do my best. Maybe one day we can puzzle out answers the sphinxlike questions that still plague us: exactly what is WordPress, and what happens when I click this green button?

To Julian, who forces me to watch Godzilla movies and hides weird gifts like Mandalorian posters and fuzzy socks all over my house and then waits for my reaction when I find them. If you keep being so nice, I might let you borrow my Batman cape someday. You know—the one you bought me and hid on the toilet seat.

To Michael and Meghan, the two best kids in the world. You both bring me so much joy and inspire me with your own creative ideas. How did I ever get to be so lucky? You mean the world to me. (Maybe I should get out more often.) (Kidding. I love you.)

To Mom and Dad, who always pick up the phone when I call, even though they know it might lead to an hour of book talks and lame jokes. You never stopped believing in me, even when I didn't believe in myself. Thank you for a rich and wonderful childhood. And, of course, for playing volleyball with me.

ABOUT THE AUTHOR

Former Wheaton College volleyball player Lori Z. Scott knows a thing or two about writing. Besides her **10-title best-selling chapter book series** (known by some as "the Christian version of Junie B. Jones" because of its heart and humor), she has contributed to 13 books and published over 175 short stories, devotions, articles, poems, and essays. Some of these won awards, including Pockets Magazine's fiction writing contest. She currently teaches second grade and writes articles for Story Embers, a growing website geared for Christian writers.

DON'T MISS THE NEXT SPORTS
NOVEL BY LORI Z. SCOTT

OFFSIDES

COMING FALL 2023!

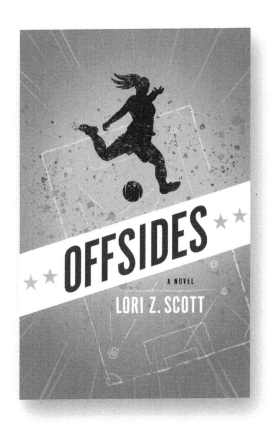